Royals

ROYALS

EMMA FORREST

BLOOMSBURY CIRCUS
LONDON · OXFORD · NEW YORK · NEW DELHI · SYDNEY

BLOOMSBURY CIRCUS
Bloomsbury Publishing Plc
50 Bedford Square, London, WC1B 3DP, UK

BLOOMSBURY, BLOOMSBURY CIRCUS and the Bloomsbury Circus logo
are trademarks of Bloomsbury Publishing Plc

First published in Great Britain 2019

A catalogue record for this book is available from the British Library

ISBN: HB: 978-1-4088-9521-4; TPB: 978-1-4088-9541-2;
eBook: 978-1-4088-9520-7

2 4 6 8 10 9 7 5 3

Typeset by Integra Software Services Pvt. Ltd.
Printed and bound in Great Britain by CPI Group (UK) Ltd,
Croydon CR0 4YY

To find out more about our authors and books visit www.bloomsbury.com
and sign up for our newsletters

For Shana Feste,
Audrey Millstein
and Andrea Remanda,
without whom...

'Nothing is a mistake. There's no win and no fail. There's only make.'

— Sister Corita Kent

CHAPTER 1

Mum had black hair and red nails with half-moons, and the glamour of her extremities was highlighted by the fact that she rarely wore anything other than a tracksuit. She was decades ahead of the velour craze. She had me do her nails that morning because she was too nervous to do it herself and the moon (the part at the base of the nail where there is negative space) was both difficult to get right and highly important to her. If the moon was wrong, her day went wrong, like it dictated the pull of her tides. Right after I'd finished, I had to re-do them because she'd anxiously touched her hair, leaving slender trails of red on black, and pattern in the polish of her fingers where there should be only shine.

I found it difficult, the way my mother was vibrating with excitement, as if we were witnessing the greatest love story of all time, when the poor bride was obviously marrying him because she didn't have anywhere else to be.

Mum had been baking a massive wedding cake for them, in parts, over the week, going through pans and tracksuits as her efforts intensified. It was like tuning in to one of her beloved mini-series, the way she spaced out the cliffhanger moments in the life of the wedding cake. When she asked me to help her, I gratefully did, ready to be made a fuss of again after so much focus on the bride-to-be. I designed the iced rosettes, alternating lilac between deep red roses. Mum looked at it and said, 'You are so brilliant.' She was also proud of my illustrations, my skill with the sewing machine, my skill with taking out the rubbish, the luxuriance of my hair, my gentleness with animals, my bread-toasting abilities, my ability to name Elizabeth Taylor's husbands in the correct order and the temperature at which I drew baths.

Now we stood before the cake, like five-year-olds admiring a tinsel tree. Even my two brothers were in the spirit, accidentally telling me it looked great, when usually all they ever said to me was: 'Are you a sissy?' or, if they wanted to be more inclusive, 'Typical women.' They got shoved at school for being yids and they shoved me for being a sissy and Mum for being a typical woman, rolling their eyes at her, exasperated at all she did for them, resentful when it took too long for her to do it. You don't have to guess who they learned it from.

But she was happy that day, as if she herself were the one getting married, re-married, maybe, since she had the vibrancy of a woman getting a fresh start. With all the excitement about the wedding, we never spoke out loud about her own marriage. Her sense of hope lasted not just for the ceremony, but through all the weeks of party preparation.

'Go and get ready, darling,' she said, ruffling my hair. ('Your crowning glory!')

I remember every song in the Top 40 Countdown playing in my bedroom as I got dressed in a suit the shade of Indian ink – sartorially, I was trying to be the fun one at the wedding, while also respecting the occasion. Obviously, I'd made it myself, because I could only find suits in navy blue. Life is very disappointing when nothing gets close to the specific colours you have in your head. That's why I started making clothes in the first place. To be less disappointed. My mum said I was far dourer than she'd imagined a gay son to be. Touched that she'd imagined having a gay son, I tried to smile more, but I was never very good at it. It falls outside my skill set.

I've played back that day so many times, I've cut and spliced my memories so you start at the top and work down.

It was no big surprise that Number 1 was Shakin' Stevens singing 'Green Door'. I was fascinated and appalled at a Welshman channelling Elvis, someone pretending to be someone else from another country and era, and people rewarding them for it. That happens in fashion, like when the 1970s channelled the 1930s, the trickle-down effect of the costumes for *Bonnie and Clyde*. Girls were still wearing the odd beret and long, A-line skirt around our estate.

Number 2 was 'Happy Birthday' by Stevie Wonder. I loved how Stevie moved his head as he played, his brain visibly connected to his fingers, the multi-coloured beads dancing in his hair like drunk guests at a wedding. Hearing people arriving in the street outside, I tried to decide if there was a pattern to Stevie's hair beads, or if they were randomly placed.

'You look beautiful!' I heard my mum say, in a tone she used when someone looked hideous.

'So do you!'

It was Mrs Leansky from next door. That Jewish voice; I don't know how I knew it was Jewish, I just did. Like knowing that Superman is Clark Kent even though he behaves differently. Our neighbourhood was sprinkled with Yiddish accents bestowed through generations, increasingly faint, maybe only noticeable to the owner, like a T-shirt that used to be red and had become pink.

Number 3 in that week's charts was 'Hooked on Classics'. Fuck that.

Number 4 was 'Chant No. 1' by Spandau Ballet. Fuck that: number two.

As the guests gathered, I listened carefully for his voice. He'd often make his entrance by saying, 'Oh, let me get that chair for you!' Or, 'After you, ladies.' The more effusive he was with gentlemanly manners aimed at acquaintances or neighbours, the worse it tended to turn when they were gone. But he'd been lovely the whole week she'd been baking. He'd dip a cheeky finger in the batter or have a cheeky pinch of her bottom as she bent to get the dishwashing liquid. Cheeky. Not like someone of whom anyone should be afraid. There seemed to be an unsaid agreement that he'd behave himself that day, because it was such a special day. But how many of us have at some point rued that something challenging should happen 'today of all days'? And the universe says: 'Yes. Today's the day.' You cannot plead. It will not reschedule. It is the universe.

Number 5 was 'Ghost Town' by The Specials. Yes! I laid on my bed looking at the two-tone sky, wondering if they'd let me in their gang, feeling pretty sure they wouldn't.

Kate Bush was Number 19, and I was very, very scared of her. If I saw her, I would walk backwards, like you're meant to do if menaced by a shark, but Siouxsie Sioux was Number 23 and she was even scarier to the teenage me. I secretly adored them both and believed they wouldn't like me back.

Kate was a teenager, like I was. Looking back, I'm aware just how strongly teenagers avoided me, but I pictured her dancing towards my room, her arms swooping in forwards/backwards circles, a swimmer in the sky. My dad made lewd comments about her leotards in front of my mum, I thought to put her down, perhaps like, why wasn't she, at forty-three, wearing a leotard as she served us our bananas and custard each evening? He said Siouxsie Sioux was a waste of a good-looking woman; he might give her the time of day without the witch make-up. As if she were waiting for him, a Whitechapel cab driver, to decide whether or not to give her the time of day.

I only narrated my reaction to the chart countdown with my inside voice, which is to say: the voice inside my head. It's where I practised anger, hoping I might one day be permitted to project it outwardly. I wanted to breathe fire but instead I cut fabric quite angrily and probably sewed it a little faster than was sensible. I wanted to scream, but it came out as phlegm.

Mum treated Dad like he was in the Top 40, and so did my brothers. It bothered him that I didn't. Even if he hadn't been how he was, even if he could have controlled himself, I could never imagine worshipping him, because he didn't glitter. He absorbed light, like a black hole. His hair was dyed black, like Mum's, but his eyes really were black. In old photos they read as brown. But, by the weekend of the wedding, the iris was near indistinguishable from the pupil.

I imagine that's how they'd been together so long: Mum glittered and he didn't. Not that she knew it. Might have known it once, for a summer, as a teen, but now the memory was long gone, the Yiddish accent that had finally washed out. So she stayed with him and felt grateful. I'd decided that when I made it, I'd buy her a ring with diamonds all along the inside, so she'd know what I thought of her. Jewellery, like clothes, like accessories, like all fashion, is an expression of a feeling that you're having a hard time putting into words.

Even today, the feeling I have most often is what I call a funk. Funks have bedevilled me my entire life, so much so that I made an acronym: 'Feeling Unsure, Not Knowing'. It's the hardest feeling. The teenage me, sequestered in my room that summer, said: 'People probably don't like me. But some might. But I don't know if they're the ones I want to like me. I kind of hate myself. But I also think I'm amazing. I'm so lovable but I don't think anyone will ever love me but I don't know that I want to get that close, anyway. I just want to run and keep on running and never look back. But I want to take my mum with me. My body is disgusting to me. But just touching my body, I feel turned on. Feeling it is amazing. Seeing it is repulsive. Someone's getting married when they shouldn't but they don't have a better plan. The wedding is about to begin and I am in a funk.'

I remember I went downstairs trying to prep myself for the amount of people who'd have gathered. The cake was the centrepiece, of course, and the guests were suitably impressed. Fourteen of them looked hideous and three of them looked amazing. That's generally the quota in really any situation of hideous to amazing, whether you were in the library, the Tube, the cinema. I've always found it accurate and still do.

There were scones and sausage rolls to feed eighty, everyone from our street and the streets around us.

I remember my mum was not wearing a tracksuit. Instead she had on a jumpsuit. I was a bit affronted at having to see quite so much of her, and jumpsuits are disingenuous beasts; they pretend they're covering you when they actually reveal just about everything, like someone who says, 'I don't like to gossip!' But her body looked great, younger than I'd known it to, and her hair looked older than it ever had; usually it was set like the queen's but today it was more Queen Mother. It was a *look*. 'You look lovely, Mum. Really lovely.' And that was important. But second to the bride.

Everybody squeezed their hands in anticipation, these neighbours, some of whom I knew well, some of whom I'd wave to most days, some I'd never spoken to before. They were squeezing my hand and pinching themselves and trying to hold it together. Some hadn't cried in years, maybe decades, certainly not in public, in front of their neighbours, and here they were, welling up and she hadn't even come out yet.

When she came out, I gasped, so did Mum. I mean: that look she gives. You know the one. It's a cousin of The Look that Lauren Bacall became famous for because she was discovered at nineteen and trembling so hard she couldn't look at the camera straight on, had to look up at it, her chin pressed down. Well, here was our girl, also nineteen, and she was looking down too, then up through her lashes.

8

Walking up the aisle, I wanted her to see me smile, to let her know I could see how shy she was, but that I believed in her. I wanted to reach out and steady her. But the TV screen was between us.

My mother held her breath. I could smell the cake in the kitchen, pungent with spice from her mother's mother's old-world recipe. I could see each step and with each step my heart skipped a beat.

Nobody cared what he looked like, but he looked all right. I mean. You could tell they weren't attracted to each other and I say that as someone who gets crushes of such intensity I can't get to sleep when they descend on me, and they do feel that way, like a descent. I hate having crushes because my designs fall apart, lose their intensity and focus. But I'd also never had sex. I had a horrible, horrible feeling she hadn't, tiptoeing up that long aisle. I tried to unthink it. It took reaching middle age to say, with shock, 'Nineteen? She was nineteen when they made her do that? No wonder she got so fucked up.'

But on that day, as it unfolded with the precision of an accordion-pleated skirt, I leaned into my mother, who kissed the side of my head, overjoyed, like every other immigrant mama with false memories of Little England.

Chapter 2

Afterwards there was a huge party in the street. A lot of our neighbours were sitting down on folding chairs because they were too excited or too old or, in one case, too fat to stand up. Seated good cheer has always been a challenge for me. It's why I reacted so poorly to the Sooty and Sweep show my parents paid good money for me to see, then, not learning their lesson, taking me to see Rod Hull and Emu. The puppets filled me with ennui. Being trapped in my seat doubled the sorrow. I can fake the funk better if I'm standing up.

I don't like roller coasters or fashion shows. I'd already decided that, when I got my own atelier, I'd have my models going about their lives – walking the dog, shopping for Babybel cheese, in line at the cinema – and journalists could just catch up with them. It would be a kind of treasure hunt. And it would mean the critics couldn't gather together and make a group decision. I followed their writing as closely as I followed designers' work. Sometimes I found it superior to the clothes themselves. But, even as a teen, I didn't want to be on the wrong side of it.

Marsha, the older auntie, was adorable, and looked like a walking mushroom: her shape, her skin, her earthiness. Edna, her younger sister, had thick glasses that made her look like a creature that covets mushrooms and, indeed, she clung to her sister like her shadow, matching her footsteps around the party. They had thick Yiddish accents, but Edna's glasses seemed to make her accent thicker, too, as if the glass had refracted her vowels.

'What did you think of the frock?' she asked me.

'Well...'

'I knew you'd have a strong opinion.'

'I noticed that—'

'So what's your professional response?'

'I'm not a professional...'

'Yet,' said Mum.

'...But I'd personally have done a cleaner line. What's so lovely about Diana's face is those round eyes and her Roman nose. The circle of blonde hair with the long neck. But since they didn't do clean shapes, I'd have gone even further with the ruffles.'

The Jews I knew don't listen; they wait, trying to get their turn to talk, and their turn was never soon enough.

'You'd have done a better job, I suppose?'

'I'd have done a different job,' I said evenly, though, obviously, my version would have been better.

I pulled out my notebook and showed them some alternative dress designs I'd sketched during the ceremony.

'He's really very good,' Marsha said to my mum.

'I know,' she beamed. 'I told you.'

And she had; she'd told everyone. When they saw us walking together, I sometimes noted they'd cross the street, I thought so they wouldn't have to hear my mum say how wonderful I was.

I wasn't sure that I wanted all these middle-aged Jewish ladies to love my work. But then I looked at the ones who'd made it: the Emanuels. Calvin Klein. Ralph Lauren. Zandra Rhodes. They'd all come from backgrounds like mine. But none of them talked about it. They just changed their names and got to work.

My mum liked the Emanuels the most because she was hung up on the romance of a couple designing together. It made no sense to me. She liked pink-haired Zandra (my favourite) like she was a fascinating new girl at school she was too afraid to talk to but watched constantly from afar. She'd never wear her clothes, but she loved looking at photos of people wearing them.

'I thought her hair was perfect,' said Marsha, and my mum agreed.

'I'd have done it shorter or longer.'

They looked at me like I'd said something really shocking and both moved away from me.

Union Jacks were hung from one end of the street to the other. We had plates and mugs and we were serving lemonade from them because it was too warm for tea, but we wanted to use them. That moment when Diana's enamel face, blushing hot with tea, was near yours.

Edna came back to me. 'You're not one of those anti-royalists are you?'

'No! Of course not! All I said was, I'd have done her hair differently.'

She whistled through her dentures. 'Don't rock the boat. You're lucky enough to be in a country that accepts us.' And then she ate a sausage roll, as if to press home her point.

It made sense to me, when I heard them talk like that, that the corset business was where my family had made what little money we had. What I mean is: bones, pressing against flesh, so when you said it felt like your heart was in your throat, you meant it. The business had been in Bethnal Green since the late 1880s, my dad's side. That it existed, still, in the same place, was quite amazing. My mother was forever pushing me to go visit Edna and Marsha there. She thought I might even be able to work there since I was... not pursuing girlfriends. I avoided, like the plague, every offer to visit the corset shop. You might as well have asked me if I wanted to visit a *shtetl*.

By now it was a full-blown street party, and the neighbours were doing unfathomable things like dancing around the maypole. The bunting I'd made out of coloured glitter was sparkling under the sky, and Mum's sausage rolls were reheating under the long stretch of sun. 'It means they're meant to be together! God is smiling on them!'

13

Well, first, she was wrong. And second, I wanted very much to believe in G-d, but not one who is so intimately involved in your love life as to announce himself through meat pastries. I find it invasive. I know you're not meant to say things like that out loud and that's why I was quiet much of my teenage life. I wrestled, endlessly, with the idea that my inner life was abnormal. But nothing ever felt inappropriate when I put it into a design. The most Jewish I feel is when it's a massive relief any time a serial killer turns out not to be Jewish. But I imagine that's the same for all minority religions and ethnicities. In that we are united.

Mrs Patel was wearing an incredible saffron-coloured sari and I saw my mum covet it as much for the fabric as for the way her belly was permitted to hang out. My mum was always on a diet and she was always covered up. I saw her in a swimsuit one or two times at the local baths, and when we stopped going, I couldn't figure out if it was because I was being teased by the other kids in the pool, and she felt helpless, or if she didn't like her body anymore. And worse than strangers was the people she knew to wave to. It's easy to reveal yourself in front of people you'll never see again; that's why none of us minded when we were half-naked on the beach in Brighton or Kent or any of the rubbish places I hated to visit, until I grew up and understood they were actually lovely.

Your childhood holidays are, naturally, infected by the memory of your childhood pain. It's incredible to go back years later and find not only does it not hurt, but that you can relax there. Mum always took her stitchwork, that's what I see beyond the pebbly beaches, grey sky and sick seagulls.

Mum did beautiful stitchwork. If you've wondered why that's been a theme for me, it came from her. Tiny rosettes, red against gold, royal colours in a domestic setting: teapots, cats around flowerpots. This rose-tinted vision of Britain that is actually true, a real, partial truth. Our roses, our flowerpots, our cats, our china – they are lovely enough to withstand the ugly underbelly of England, these beautiful, delicate things standing tall in the face of ugliness: motorway flyovers, drunks pissing on sleeping tramps, Pakis out. And the Pakis they want out love the tea and china, too.

Mum told me her own mother had sewn all her jewellery into their clothes before they escaped the Warsaw ghetto. They didn't get far. She thinks the Nazis never found the hidden jewellery. I always assumed they did. I assumed they ripped the clothes apart before setting them to work.

It's like Americana, cowboy hats, cowboy boots, lassos, Sam Shepard plays, all these things are sturdier and more useful, but in their usefulness, now that I've travelled the globe, I see the appeal of theirs, but I love our cornucopia more. Because the things we have are just as good at being alone as a cowboy on a never-ending plain. A pink-rinse old lady drinking from a cup of never-ending tea. She knows as much as the cowboy. She's just more frail. We're just more frail. The stiff upper lip is the last bastion against completely and utterly floundering from the lava crust and into hell. The terrible, terrible stories from the generation before covered in the lace you could only see through at certain angles to what lay beneath. To what was holding it all together. It's weird to imagine that trauma can hold you together rather than be the thing that destroys you. But that's how I saw my mother. The nails and the hair were the nod to polite society; the tracksuit was for the moment polite society falls apart and you need to run. In case it happened again.

So, she was admiring Mrs Patel's sari and I was admiring the way the light bounced off my Union Jack glitter bunting, the sausage rolls were ageing rapidly, becoming visibly rife with despair. Edna and Marsha were saying, 'You must come and visit us at the shop,' and I was saying, 'Yes, I should. That would be lovely,' when every fibre of my being wanted to shout, 'Get fucked.'

Perhaps my latent bad manners drew him back. Because that's when my dad came home from his shift. 'Oh.' He looked surprised. He looked how someone is supposed to look when they feel the emotion of surprise. 'Did you start without me?'

'We had to start when the wedding started,' Mum said.

'But you didn't wait?'

There was no use repeating it. One of my brothers kicked a soccer ball to him and he caught it with his foot, and did not kick it back, just rolled it back and forth with his toes like it was a lie he was burnishing.

'Look how beautiful Mum's cake is.'

I said it too loud, like a tour guide at a world heritage site: 'Look here, the pyramids! Look here, the painting by the pharaoh's tomb!'

He looked at it, which once I thought about it I didn't really want him to do. I should have known it would just upset him.

'Steven helped. He was brilliant.'

Mum must have known she shouldn't have said that. It took her a beat, like a live show on time delay to catch rude words, but then it hit her. That was a mistake. The bunting glittered.

Somehow, even Charles and Diana's wedding was supposed to be about him. But he was drunk and I saw him as the court jester. His shift had ended an hour earlier and he'd stopped by the Crow and Eagle. He was jealous of me and Mum. It upset him that I made her happy. He wanted her to be happy, but he didn't know how to do it himself. He bought her perfume on her birthday and he hit her. He got her kitchen remodelled, and he hit her. He gave her three wonderful sons. And he hit her. He cheated on her. And he hit her. He told her she was beautiful and he hit her. He told her she was a wonderful mother and he hit her. He told her she was a terrible mother and he hit her.

17

I was too little to help. And then, one day, I was big enough to help. And the anger was redirected at me. I was just grateful he wasn't hitting my mum any more. She was my world. Now my world was safe; I was just an inhabitant of my world. This was more bearable. It was a terrible time. But it was worse when it happened to her, the person I loved most.

There was a football game going on, but I sat among the old ladies, trying to blend in with them, hoping they would protect me from him. Edna and Marsha said 'Hellooo' and then went right back to talking to each other. Perhaps it's what had drawn them so close, their disinterest in their brother; they had to be fascinated by each other, or there wouldn't have been much left to talk to except the wallpaper.

'Darling,' Mum said, fumbling for the right words, like they were keys at the bottom of her handbag, 'We're just so happy you made it.'

'Not too happy to wait.'

The neighbours shuffled. They knew. Edna and Marsha picked up their purses, barely nodding at him on their way out. Suddenly I wanted to say, 'Yes! I want to see your corset shop!' but they were almost out of sight, as if they'd shape-shifted rather than shuffled. Even an elderly human mushroom could pick up the pace when they sensed a family argument brewing.

The Indian family left. I memorised the gold thread against the mustard yellow, how it tricked the eye. I love it when fashion does that. There were Jamaicans who'd made a flag with Hailie Selassie standing next to Charles and Diana.

In the news analysis still going on from the television commentators, no one much noticed Charles, as if he wasn't even at his own wedding.

Dad took a slice of the cake. 'This is too spicy. We're not in the old country now.'

'Oh. Everyone else likes it.'

'I don't give a shit about everybody else.' He looked at the blaring TV. 'Why don't we let the blessed couple decide? Let's give them a taste.'

He smeared the cake across the television screen over Diana's face. 'I can't eat, it's my wedding, I have to fit into my frock!' He pretended to do her voice. Mum was trying not to cry. Then he turned to her: 'Go get your wedding dress!'

'Why?'

'Yours is better than hers. Go put it on.'

'No, darling. We're having a party.'

'Your guests don't look like they're having much fun.'

'We are!' someone offered.

'Go get your dress. It was pricey. Don't you know where it is?'

'I know where it is.'

'Don't put it on, Mum.'

'Was I talking to you?'

I shrunk deeper into the old ladies, as if I could cover myself with their pink and blue hair. Even in my anxiety about what he'd do next, I noticed Mrs

19

Misher's hair was apricot this time around and the colour danced in front of my eyes even as my heart sank.

I got up and went to the kitchen to get a cloth to clean the telly. He followed me.

'Shame you'll never have one.'

'A telly?'

'A wedding.'

I looked deep into the cake as if it were my security detail. But it wasn't helpful, my lack of courage always made him angrier.

He picked up my sketchbook and flicked through, laughing.

'Those are precious to me,' I began.

I could see my mum in the distance, begin to stand up, very nervous now. I didn't want her further involved so I tried to move back outside to the protection of other people, hoping he'd forgotten about the wedding dress.

'You frighten us when you're like this, Dad. Just lie down. Go to bed. Take a rest and then come back to the party.'

'Don't treat me like I'm a monster. You gang up together, and you make sure not to let me in. You started this without me so it could just be you and her.'

'Everyone's here. The whole street is watching.'

'Oh and judging? Is that what you're saying?'

'I'm saying they can see us. So let's be polite.'

'Don't tell me what to do, you little shit. I am polite.'

He walked back outside, right up to her. 'Did you get your wedding dress?'

She looked at her feet, the half-moons of her pedicure pulling her in place, a Revlon undertow.

'Well, did you? I don't see it anywhere.' He mimed looking around. Guests continued to scatter.

'I'll get it,' she said, from within the waves.

'You don't have to, Mum.'

'*What*?!'

'Calm down,' said Mrs Misher. 'You're making a terrible flapdoodle.'

The word 'flapdoodle' seemed to tip him over the edge.

'I don't have to be driving a cab. I could be a doctor or a lawyer like the fancy Jews. They're still not really English, you know. None of this makes you really English. Your sausage rolls. Your wedding mugs. Your fucking bunting.'

He ripped it down. I remember that glitter spilled from a Union Jack and was sprinkled across his angry face. It made me smile.

'Don't you dare fucking smirk at me.' It might have been 'fucking dare smirk'. There's a difference, like a seam at the side versus a seam at the back.

And the glitter kept dancing. And it made me laugh.

Before I could move, he landed the first punch. I stumbled out, crashing through a stall of Pimms. Strawberries rolled across the pavement. A ginger cat looked at me with disdain, his fur clashing with Mrs Misher's hair as she bent down to me. Where were all these ladies' husbands? I felt in that moment – or maybe, in all moments – like Dad was the only man present.

My mother was on her knees. My father was already gone, saying 'He's fine' over his shoulder, as he headed upstairs.

Mum was afraid of a great many things, but they weren't ever the right things. It's as if every weather report she ever read gave a notice about 'extreme weather' but she'd be too in a tizzy to hear the rest. She'd just start stocking up with canned goods to see us through the inevitable floods. And all they'd been alerting the viewer to was that the weather would be 'extremely nice. Unusually pleasant.' She had no portion control with her fears, especially when it came to my well-being. And yet she'd seen my father hit me several times now and, each time, she'd tearfully patched me up, but as it was going on, she was a stone statue.

You could hate her for it. You could. But I've come across several children of Holocaust survivors who've ended up in abusive marriages. Parameters of what is acceptable have been irretrievably damaged. She kept telling herself, 'This is nothing compared to that.' But I knew when she saw me that day that she knew it was something. She knew, I believe she knew, time was running out for us to stay with him; the ghetto was about to be sealed. She kept cooking, she kept cleaning. But she was ready to be awakened, the rapid eye movement when someone is on the surface of sleep, between worlds almost. Some key part of her was ready to be told: time to wake up, now.

Likely she knew, before I did, that I was not like her other boys. Likely she knew, before I did, that I would one day find my way and that I would not leave her behind. I thought, as I was lying there, that she was licking my blood from my hair, but it was one of the neighbourhood cats. It didn't even seem that odd that my mother was licking away my blood. It seemed like something she'd be prepared to do for me.

'Shoo!' shouted a neighbour, and her husband said, 'Don't shout, it might be the last thing he hears, you don't want it to be your shrieking voice.' Using our terrible family breakdown to have a miniature marital dispute.

Someone tutted, 'It's not right, on such a lovely day,' as if there could be better-suited days for such behaviour.

Somebody called an ambulance. My mum was sobbing and clinging to me. As I waited, I thought 'Plum blossom with jade would be a good colour combination.' As I waited, I could see Diana on the Union Jack bunting as they carted me away, see her blonde through my blood. I hoped it wasn't bad luck for their marriage.

CHAPTER 3

I woke up on the paediatric ward of Guy's Hospital. There was a vase of extraordinary flowers on the windowsill and I let my eyes adjust to them: roses with snapdragons, honeysuckle and pansies, as if someone had taken the most British things and decided they could be passionate, too. I hadn't thought of that until I saw those particular flowers.

I looked around and saw other teenagers of various races and shapes and in various positions, some prone, others propped, a few walking. There was a dull throb in my left arm. I tried to sit myself up but I was in pain. The lower rib. The same one he'd cracked before. I don't think he especially aimed there. It was just his height and my height. It's because I was too big for this.

'Your mum was here with you. Lovely lady. She just left for her shift.'

The nurse didn't judge Mum for letting this happen and neither did I. Her tag said 'Edith' and Edith helped me sit. She turned away a moment and returned with a cup of Angel Delight, a cheese sandwich and an orange juice.

'Do you think you could manage some of this?'

They all looked great and I scoffed them down.

'Good lad. Oh. She left you your pens and paper. Are you a writer?'

I shook my head gently so as not to further twist the rib. 'Clothes.'

'Oh, I wish you'd redesign this uniform. But I hope you won't be here long enough to do it. I think you'll have a couple of nights here, then you'll be home.'

She didn't ask where home was and I didn't say, 'I don't want to go home.' I was on a hospital ward and it felt like the dream I'd fostered from Enid Blyton books of how boarding school might be. They would feed me and keep me safe but I could be alone. Alone, left entirely to my own devices, but with back-up protection if anything went wrong or got scary. This was the first time he'd landed me here. I'd been to the emergency room before, but they'd treated me there, clicking my nose back in place as stars spun.

I tested myself by swinging my legs over the side of the bed. Bad idea. The nerves in my chest were tweaking out as I tried to straighten my back. Sometimes a teacher would shout at the boys in my class, 'You're getting on my last nerve!' I understood, as I winced with the kind of pain that makes people want to die, that nerves might, in fact, be finite.

I was so contorted in agony, it took me a moment to realise there were some very sick kids on the other side of the room. One was badly burned. But the parents turned to and looked very sorry for me.

At eighteen, I thought I was just on the cusp and, even though I had no friends my own age, I was relieved not to have been sent up to the adult wing. Jasmine, on the other hand, was furious about being sent to the juvenile ward.

'I'm nineteen years old!' she said. 'I had my nineteenth birthday last month at Annabel's.' It was the first thing I ever heard her say.

I thought she was one of the most frightening things I'd ever seen. She looked like a witch from a fable, an illustration from the Oscar Wilde children's book I sometimes read when I was trying to block out the sounds of the house.

She was bone white, cuts on her arms, holes all the way up her ears, piercing the cartilage like a nightmare, black charcoal staining her chin where they'd induced the vomiting. I'd no idea there was a great society beauty on the bed across from me. She looked around – saw the burns kid being tended to by their parents, the comatose boy, the painfully thin girl being pushed in a wheelchair – and decided I was the one worth talking to. It was night-time, of course. That makes it easier to meet anyone. Even on a hospital ward.

'Can you hand me my cosmetics bag?' she asked, and though it was a query it had the cadence of a demand. 'It's in my handbag, over there.'

Like moving towards the vampire to drain it of the power to scare you, I let myself take one step,

26

and then another. She just watched me and said, 'Cor, you're in a lot of pain.'

Her vowels were rounded and she said 'cor' like someone who'd repeatedly watched *Oliver!* on a summer beach vacation. She let me move towards her in my wincing, mincing agony.

I gave her the handbag, noting, 'That's Bottega Veneta.'

She raised an eyebrow. 'Did you peek at the label?'

'I know by the stitching. Only Bottega does that latticework. Is it real?'

She reached her hand to her mouth, smudging black across her jaw, which I could see was small and pointed, like Elizabeth Taylor's, only covered in grime.

'One of my dad's girlfriends left it behind and I snatched it. I'm sure he got a new one.'

'Girlfriend?'

'Handbag, Funny Face.'

'You can talk.'

And that was how we started flirting. Although I was not that way inclined, considering myself thoroughly asexual, I knew, though it had never happened to me before, that I was flirting, or being flirted with.

She opened her Bottega and pulled out the make-up bag, rolling mascara, lipstick, pot of crème blush and a few eyeliners onto the tray by her jelly.

'Are you any good at make-up?'

'Why would you ask me?'

'You are a homosexual, right?'

I looked nervously around the room. Nobody was listening, mainly because the others were unconscious or demented.

'I haven't decided yet.'

'Yeah, right. I bet that's why you have the black eyes. You were cottaging on Hampstead Heath?'

'My dad beat me up.' I took no pride at all in saying it, but her response was ecstatic.

'Of course! So you are a gay! How marvellous. I mean, sad for you that your dad doesn't accept you, but my good luck that you're here with me. Can you imagine if I was all alone with them?'

She nodded to the vegetative patient and the burns victim. She tested a kohl on the back of her hand, as if it were new to her.

'I like that eyeshadow,' I said.

Her face lit up. 'Have it. No really, please! I want you to!'

I realised, almost immediately, that if you admired something of Jasmine's out loud, she would give it to you. If you were in a shop and you said you liked something, she would buy it for you. You either had to keep your admiration of beautiful knick-knacks to yourself – which is a constricting way to live – or you had to spend a lot of time at museums, where at least if you admired something she couldn't get it for you.

28

I accepted the eyeshadow to shut her up. She started to curl her lashes with the little metal spoon that had accompanied her jelly.

'I learn all my best make-up tricks from the Golden Age of Hollywood.'

I twinged with excitement. 'Warren Beatty used to arrive early on the set of *Splendor in the Grass* so he could look in the mirror and separate each individual eyelash with a pin.'

She nodded: 'That's genius. I think he collected such incredible women because he was jealous of them. He wanted to keep Julie Christie and Natalie Wood and Joan Collins close because he was worried they might be more beautiful than him.'

My body started to tremble. I wanted to cry hosannah, but instead I quietly replied, 'I collect vintage fan magazines from the forties and fifties.'

'Me too!' She was so loud that patients who weren't meant to move their necks tried to turn their heads.

'Really?'

'We have to compare them when we get out.'

My brothers swapped football cards with their friends. I never imagined I'd have someone with whom to perform the equivalent. I felt my way towards the idea of a kindred spirit and, even though one was right there in the room, mentally my arm still wasn't long enough to touch her and I imagined groping towards her with an outstretched stick.

'This is a trick Rita Hayworth used to do, when she wasn't being fucked by her father.'

I didn't laugh, and she looked at me, anxious.

'He doesn't fuck you, does he?'

'No. Just the punching.'

'Oh, phew. I hate to put my foot in it with a brand-new friend.'

The horrible nerve pain began to subside as my heart swelled with the possibility that this was real and not a morphine-drip hallucination. That I had somebody I wanted to talk to. Right now, and I knew it was happening, like a lucid dream. It took me a moment to find my voice. When it came out, I could hear my own accent for the first time, as if I'd moved outside my body.

'Why are you here?'

'I took an overdose,' she said cheerfully, her newly curved eyelashes nearly reaching to her eyebrows.

I got back in my bed. 'I'm sorry.'

'It's my fourth. They're never successful but this was the first one I really *meant*. The housekeeper found me in time.'

There followed a lull in conversation, after which she brightly offered, 'Would you like to see my note?'

I demurred, which seemed to surprise her.

'People usually want to see it, then?'

'Of course! I mean, I assume so. I've never offered before now. The nurses had a peek.'

'What did they say?'

'They said I had beautiful handwriting. They were just being kind. It slopes rather leftward, a sign of psychopathy, you know.'

'Are you a psychopath?'

'Well, if I was, I wouldn't tell you, would I? I'd adapt to the situation so you wouldn't know. I'm probably a borderline.'

'What's that?'

'Well, politely put, it means I'm a troublemaker.'

I quite liked the sound of that and I got back off my bed and leaned in closer.

'Do you want me to help you clean your face?' I asked.

She looked at herself in a hand mirror.

'This is rather Adam Ant. But, yes, I'm done.'

I wiped her down. Underneath, her face was lovely. Wide-set green eyes, black upper lashes and the bottom lashes were a double row. I looked at her numerous eyeliners and handed her a grey one.

'Use this colour. You've got some golden flecks in your iris within the green. The grey will make them pop.'

She seemed impressed and said, 'You know, Marilyn used this. It looks like black liquid liner she had on in photos, but it's grey, always grey.'

'So she used the same tricks.'

'Well, yes. But she used this actual eyeliner,' and she pointed it at me.

31

She may as well have been wielding the sword in the stone. But I knew she was telling the truth.

'My father bought me it from Sotheby's. It's hers. I'm not lying to you. There's no real stars any more. Who do you think has replaced them?'

'The royals, I guess.'

'I don't think so. Because they don't really want to be there. They don't want the golden contract; they all want the hell out.'

'Diana married in.'

'Diana looked like she was being frogmarched up the aisle. That's why her dress was so big. Someone was under it, forcing her to keep walking.'

'No,' I frowned. 'She's happy.' I needed to think she'd end up happy.

'I think Siouxsie Sioux has immaculate bone structure, don't you?'

'So does Adam Ant.'

Jasmine was only asking the question so she could tell me the right answer. 'He does, and so does Debbie Harry. Why would you be born with bones like that if you weren't meant to be a star? I was right down the front at Siouxsie's last gig and the light was bouncing off her browbones as if it was a shot set up for Marlene Dietrich. Have you seen her play?'

'No. I've heard there's a lot of spit.' I didn't even like seeing my own saliva, and I changed the subject: 'What does your dad do?'

'Nothing at all.'

It was very intimate and strange to watch a girl put on make-up for no one except me, on a hospital ward late at night when the world was sleeping (and some, vegetative). It was more intoxicating than any drug experience I would ever have.

She patted the bed beside her and I found myself sitting down, closer to any woman than I'd ever been before, except my mum.

'If your dad does nothing, then why is he so rich?'

'Hello? Have you ever been to Great Britain before? It's a class system rooted in antiquated notions of land ownership.'

She took a spoon of rice pudding, the texture of which is seared in my mind. One day, looking at a cream blazer bearing a lapel scattered with intricately shattered lumps, I realised that I had, for years, been attempting to commemorate that rice pudding in my collections. She was using the same spoon she'd used to curl her eyelashes.

'He's rich because his parents were rich, and his grandfather and his great-grandfather were rich. It's completely absurd. But that's how I ended up with Marilyn Monroe's liquid eyeliner.'

She handed it over for me to admire.

'Where's your mum?' I asked, as I examined the liquid liner, marking the inside of my wrist.

'Oh, she left us some time ago.'

'I'm sorry. That's tough' I said, and tried to give her back the liner.

'Please take it,' she insisted, 'I'm sure Marilyn would have wanted you to have it.'

I fell asleep that night, clutching it as lightly as I could without dropping it, trying to keep it safe, but knowing I was holding something very rare and fragile.

CHAPTER 4

The best week of my life up to meeting Jasmine had happened the previous year, when 'Mirror in the Bathroom' reached Number 4 in the charts. Now I had met her, I hoped I wouldn't be checked out too soon. The nurse had said it should only be a couple of nights and, if I'd seen it as an appealing respite before meeting Jasmine, now it was a necessity. I couldn't go home when I'd finally made a friend. I tried to make myself look as beat-up as possible, which, of course I was, but in truth this was less of a beating than I'd endured before. It just landed on such a special occasion that a lot of people happened to be watching.

I was relieved to see Jasmine emerge from the bathroom. As she did, she handed a waiting nurse a razor.

'Thank you,' she said sweetly, and then less sweetly, 'See. Shaved my legs and I didn't try to top myself.'

I was thinking of a way to get over to her bed, but instead, she stopped at mine. She was wearing a dressing gown.

'That's lovely,' I said.

'Thanks, my dad picked it up for me in Tokyo, from an artisan kimono maker who'd learned the craft from his grandfather.' It looked just like a hospital dressing gown. I tried not to blink. She waited a blink and then laughed in my face. It's difficult to explain how the tricks and teases that would have seemed cruel if they'd come from one of the kids at school were friendly in her hands.

'Can I get in bed with you?' she asked.

'Jasmine!' warned the nurse with the razor.

'*What*? He's a homosexual.'

'He hasn't decided yet,' said the nurse, and I nodded, grateful to her but wanting her to fuck off. 'And anyway, I don't want you lounging about all day. Neither of you. You need to be moving about, get your blood flowing. It will help you heal, circulate oxygen to your lovely young brains.'

'Shall we take a post-prandial perambulation around the grounds?' Jasmine asked.

'Yes,' I said, not knowing what it was I'd agreed to, only that it would be with her.

She slipped her arm through mine as we walked, adjusting my elbow height to her specifications. It was a rubbishy garden, heavy on patio.

'Do you go to college?' I asked her, the concrete surroundings drawing from me a pedestrian question.

'Well, yes,' she said, 'of course.'

'Where?'

'I mean, "Yes, of course, I thought about it." If I had gone, I'd have studied history of art or classics, probably both.'

'So why didn't you?'

'Well...' She thought about it. 'It did seem like quite a lot of work. I like knowledge as much as the next person. But I prefer it on my schedule. One doesn't like to feel like one is being pushed to the ground and having education kicked in one's face.'

I nodded and she clasped my good arm.

'They really need some peacocks here. Wouldn't that brighten things up?'

'It would be nice for the patients but it might be sad for the birds?'

'Oh, you're terribly thoughtful! And I notice you often end a sentence with a question mark, even when you aren't asking a question.'

'Maybe it's a Jewish thing.'

'Does that run in your family?'

'Judaism does, yes.'

'No, the self-doubt in speech patterns?'

'I don't know. I think it's just me.'

'Oh, you're lovely. I'm so glad we've met. Do you feel blood oxygenating your brain?'

'I feel in pain.'

'Well, darling, that's the human condition. I mean, just look at us. We're like a Neapolitan ice cream of pain, sandwiched together in our different flavours of suffering.'

I thought for a moment. 'If we're a Neapolitan ice cream, don't we need a third flavour?'

'No. I don't think so. I like it just us. The world can be the vanilla against which we lean.'

I smiled. My ribs hurt so much but I couldn't remember the last time I felt this happy.

'Have you ever been to Naples?'

'I don't think so.' I racked my brain, even though I knew full well my brain contained only a slide show of pebbly beaches in Brighton and Portsmouth, pebbles of different sizes like different troubles.

'Oh, well, you must go. You must.'

'Okay.' I didn't ask her how. It would not have occurred to her as a question.

'I usually stop there after Paris. It's easy, you know?'

'I've never been to Paris.'

'What?'

She reared back, startled.

'But how can that be?' She put a hand on my chest. I curved my spine backwards so as to feel her palm less without having to ask that she remove it. I didn't know what I wanted then, and I still have times I crave touch but my brain denies me it.

'I just... I guess our people travelled through enough countries way back in the day. Now they've found somewhere we're accepted, we just stay. We don't move. I mean, ending up in this hospital is quite a long way for me, geographically speaking.'

'It's not right. I mean, look at you. You have "Paris" written on you from head to toe.'

I scanned myself, seeing only poor posture and skin the colour of mayonnaise. The one piece of writing I knew of was on the band of my Y-fronts, which said

'Marks & Spencer'. My mother hysterically maintained their freshness and whiteness in case I ever ended up in hospital. And that had worked out, at least in that sense. At least none of the blood had reached them.

'They're on their honeymoon now,' I noted.

'Who?'

'Them. Charles and Diana.'

'Oh, them.'

'How do you think it's going?'

'Oh, horrid, I'm sure. When I get married, I'm going to do it in a favourite hotel, Claridge's probably...'

'Claridge's is good.'

'...Have one beautiful night of blissful passion with my brand-new husband...'

'Obviously.'

'...and then each of us should go our separate ways for ten days, the appointed honeymoon period, and just revel in what it is to be alone, so when we reconnect we know how to be alone, together, how to reach for each other, as loners.'

'I think that's what you'd have, like, a bachelorette weekend for. I think that's the point of those.'

'Yes, I know, but I don't have any friends.'

'Why not?'

'I mean, of course I have friends, just nobody I really like. Only people I enjoy saying bad things about. I've really been waiting for a friend I could say good things about. But then, I hadn't met you. So I might rethink it all now. Maybe I will have a honeymoon, but bring you along.'

'I don't think he'd like that.' I was getting really stressed out about her imaginary husband and how pissed off he'd be to see me there in their private plane, or in a cabin across the hall on the *Orient Express*.

She must have felt me tense up because she said, 'We can talk about it nearer the time.'

'So you want to get married?'

'Why not?'

I told her about my mother and my father and how rotten it was to grow up watching their toxic love simmer on the hob next to the porridge. And how I feared they'd stayed together because of the kids.

'No. She probably just really loves him. It's an addiction, you know, with women like that. Goes across the classes. I know society lasses who are patrons of charities for battered women. It's happening to them at home, too. They're just not allowed to talk about it, so they raise dosh for working-class women who can.'

'Did your dad ever hit your mum?'

'Gosh, no. My dad is the best. It's my mum who was trouble.'

'He doesn't hit my mum any more, not really.'

'He's moved on to you instead,' She sniffed the patio's one rose. 'I'll kill him if he ever harms you ever again. I'll fucking kill him. So, just know that.'

I didn't know how to process such a threat from an heiress I'd known for one night, so I changed the subject.

'What do you think of Diana? Do you really think she was marched up the aisle?'

'I've met her; she's very naïve.'

'You've met her?'

'Yes, at a very dull wedding in Surrey.'

'What did you say to her?'

'I told her I liked the bows on her shoes. I didn't; they were foul.'

'You lied to Princess Diana?'

'Firstly, she wasn't a royal yet. Second, you'd rather I'd told her the truth? We must live by the harmless untruths that make us healthy and happy. Kurt Vonnegut wrote that, as you know.'

I didn't know, and she may as well have said, 'Starfruit tastes like a cross between apples and grapefruits, as you know.' She'd seen and read and eaten so much more than me. It felt like she must have been seeing some other level of this shit patio garden as we walked it, one full of medieval art and exotic Caribbean fruit.

I stammered, 'You're wrong about the bows. I know those shoes she wears and they conjure the French court.'

She sat us down on a bench. My arse was killing me.

'You're very into it. Frocks and all that.'

'Frocks and shoes, yes. I want to design.'

41

'Can I see some of them?'

'I don't have anything with me.'

'Draw me something now.'

I did, while she whipped out a bottle and painted her nails. By the time they were drying, I'd done her a sketch.

'Oh, so you do design.'

'I said that.'

'No, you didn't. You said you wanted to design. But this is a design and it's very good.'

'Thank you.' I couldn't tell if she was teasing me. 'I never know when I'm being made fun of.'

'That's a strange Achilles heel. Or should I say, Achilles kitten heel.'

'Oh no, I hate kitten heels. I'll never put a woman in them. They're degrading. Life is hard enough to navigate as it is. If you're going to challenge a women's balance it's a crime not to lengthen their leg.'

'I agree with you!' Her mouth and eyes were round like planets seen at a distance. 'I heard that high heels are meant to mimic the foot at the moment of orgasm, stretched out with delight.'

I blushed a crimson Diana would have been proud of. 'I've read that, too.'

Seeing my scarlet cheeks, she used the paper to fan me.

'Don't do play on words with me again.' I said. 'Like Achilles kitten heel. I feel close to you. I don't want us to have words that distance us.'

42

She said nothing, but kissed me on the lips. Our mouths were closed but soft, and she brushed her lips up and down mine. I wanted to open them but I was scared. She smelled of red roses and peppercorns, the scent saturating the downy hair on her upper lip. I was hard, but I was thinking of Shakin' Stevens, who I hate. It was a very confusing time.

She stopped and sat upright like a uniformed nanny. 'I love this sketch. Can I have it?'

'Sure.' I folded the paper and pressed it into her dressing-gown pocket.

'No, I mean, will you make it for me?'

I must have looked alarmed because she added, 'I'll pay you for it, of course.'

I saw some beautiful pale white flowers, rows on a stem, hanging downwards.

'I always think Lily of the Valley look like a corps de ballet...' She misread my expression and added, 'Like dancers.'

'I know what a corps de ballet is. But I don't think that's what they look like. To me, they look like tears.'

'Yes. That's why another name is "Our Lady's Tears".'

I went to pick them.

'Don't!' she said.

'They won't notice.'

'It's not that. Lily of the Valley is poisonous, the whole plant, not just the flower.'

'How do you know?' I asked, doubtful. She seemed like a person who could spin glorious lies to pass the time.

'I used to help my mother with her garden. She'd never pick them without wearing gloves.'

I gazed into her eyes, green against green, flecks of mint and emerald interlocked: here is the church and here is the steeple.

'If you don't go to college, what do you do all day?'

'Oh, darling, I have a job!'

'You do?'

'Yes! You must come and visit me there one day.'

The sky was dimming a notch, winding down for a bath, tea and bed.

'Oh God,' she shrieked, 'I have to charge my crystals!'

'What?'

She had the urgency of someone who'd left the house with the kettle on.

'It's a new moon tonight!'

She clutched her robe around her and hurried me back towards the ward.

'Are you a witch?'

She cocked her eyebrow at me.

'You can fight the patriarchy in many ways.' Then she added, what seemed to be from nowhere, 'I hope Diana's honeymoon is picking up.'

I stopped her in her tracks.

44

'Have you cast a spell on Prince Charles?'

She glided around my pause, shrugged her shoulders.

'I've done a lot of things.'

Now I was following behind her.

'Aren't you meant to do it on a full moon?'

The nurses waved at us as we came back inside.

'Yes, that's true if you're doing a receiving spell. But if you're doing a spell to try and clear something, you do it on a new moon.'

The burns victim's family were here, as ever, and they looked at us pityingly. I wondered how many times people in bad situations had looked at me with pity in order to assuage their own sadness.

'What are you trying to clear?' I was whispering because it felt like something you should probably whisper about. We weren't talking about drugs or sex, but the occult seemed to deserve the same public parameters.

'I'm clearing this fucking overdose out of my system!'

I nodded.

'And the patriarchy from this government. Thatcher's made it up there as a woman, but she's got an all-male cabinet. She's using her feminine wiles on them, I'm telling you. She's been using witchcraft, I guarantee it.'

'Maybe. Or maybe she's just an arsehole.'

'It doesn't matter. I have to fight back.'

She fished past the make-up bag and pulled the crystals out of her handbag.

'I need a bowl, some warm purified water and some sea salt.'

I put on the face I wear when I help my mother with her baking.

'I don't have any sea salt.'

'Go ask the nurses.'

Even as I resented being bossed around by a posh girl, I found myself hobbling to the nurses and they found me a bag of Epsom. They didn't even look at us curiously. Perhaps they'd seen many an odd-couple friendship flourish under the auspices of illness.

'Wonderful!'

Jasmine put Epsom in the bowl, then the water, then popped in the crystals. She turned her back, as if I was trying to copy her homework, and did a blessing with her hands, moving them up and down like a hula dancer. I tried hard to overhear but failed. I still have occasional dreams where I'm able to hear of her secret incantation. Sometimes it's my mother's shopping list for dinner. Other times it's been the Kaddish, the Jewish prayer for the dead. Sometimes she's reciting the Top 40 countdown.

She finished and turned towards me with the bowl.

'Put these on the windowsill, please.'

As I opened the window, the pigeons looked at me like I was mad.

'There's no moon out there.'

'That's the point,' she smiled. 'You can't see a new moon. You have to trust it's there, watching out for you.'

'Do you think the moon's watching out for you?'

'Of course.'

The scars on her wrists varied in colour and texture from pink to greyish-white, keloid to flat, some ancient history, beneficent grandparents of the youngest scars.

'Well it's not doing a very good job.'

She looked hurt for a microsecond, but she recovered.

'That's not true. There must be a perfectly good reason I've landed here, at this moment in time.' She studied me, checking if I might be the reason.

'It's not me,' I said, pre-empting her. I didn't want it to be me. I'd been sent to this hospital to think, to be alone with my chattering brain, try and calm it down and figure out what to do with my life. She'd distracted me. She'd intoxicated me. I needed to focus inward. But, look: out there! A friend!

She was chattering and I tried to block her out, but she was very beautiful and I found I kept looking. Like when there's a baby in the room. Even if you don't really like babies, you watch them the whole time. It's impossible not to.

'When I have a daughter, I'm going to call her Luna. That's where the term "loony" comes from, how we are influenced by the phases of the moon.'

'Well, you're not going to have a daughter if you keep on trying to top yourself.'

'Now, I object; the other times were cries for help – this was the only real attempt.'

'So the cries for help didn't work?'

She lay back on her bed, pulling from her bag a pale blue shawl of thinnest cashmere.

'My dad gave me some beautiful history of art books to cheer me up. That did work for a while. Here, let's call him, I should let him know what's happened and where I am.'

'He probably knows where you are by now.'

'He's very busy. Nurse? Has my father called?'

The nurse shook her head. When the nurses left the floor to get their dinner, Jasmine lit a cigarette, curling the cashmere around her body, the smoke twisting around the cashmere, the burns victim across the aisle unmoved. She slipped into a funk for a few hours and I went back to my bed and tried to draw. But I kept looking over at her until I fell asleep.

When I woke up, she was back to her old self, chatting and opining as if her life depended upon it. Even when the nurse brought my food, Jasmine stuck her nose in, wanting to know what I was eating, Oh, chicken? Had I ever tried the chicken at Le Cirque in New York?

Then she put on my nemesis, Kate Bush, which I could hear tinnily through her headphones and when I made a face like she was bothering me, she offered to share the headphones so I could listen too. Her radar was always up to help you, but it was never quite right. My mother used to say, 'If you can't help, don't hinder,' but Jasmine would do both at once; that was kind of her specialty.

We were standing at the window, painting a watercolour from her bag of make-up, when a doctor we'd never seen approached her.

'I'm Dr Thomason.'

'Hi,' she said, without looking up.

'We want to run some tests,' said the doctor.

Now she looked at him. 'Who are you?'

'Dr Levin is on holiday for a week…'

'How nice for him.'

'…And, looking at your files, I think your proteins are low, which isn't surprising given what your body's been through. But it's worth investigating. So I'd like to get some blood from you today.'

'You want to get more money, you mean.'

I looked around.

'But this is all free. You're in an NHS hospital.'

'You wouldn't understand.'

I walked back to my bed. She followed me, a tad anxious.

'It used to happen to my mother all the time. People were always after her money.'

'You'd have to be pretty nefarious to train for four years so you can become a doctor in a paediatric emergency ward so you can divest wealthy teenagers of their parents' cash.'

'You're not going to let me get away with anything, are you?'

She agreed to have the test run, looking out of the window at the moving clouds as her blood filled first one vessel and then another. She winked at me: 'I've done this before.'

The nurse marked Jasmine's name on the tubes, designer labels.

'I won't let you get away with it, either.'

'With what?' I asked.

'I haven't decided yet. But you won't get away with it.'

My mum came to see me that night. Jasmine was in therapy and I was glad because I definitely did not want them to meet. With everything else Mum was dealing with, she should not be subjected to the philosophical ramblings of a half-demented posh girl.

Mum was wearing a blouse I'd made her and I could tell she'd been trying, because she'd worn more make-up than usual to try and cover the bruising up. She read me to sleep from the Oscar Wilde book. When I woke up, it was the next day and she was gone.

So was Jasmine. I knew she was gone and not just in therapy because her belongings were absent and her sheets were neatly folded. Her perfume left a crime-scene sketch on the bed where she'd been lying.

'Where's the girl?' I asked the nurse on duty, trying not to sound frantic.

'The damaged princess? She discharged herself. She said she had to get back to her shop.'

'Do you know what it's called?'

The nurse shook her head and I shook with anger at her, wanted to tear apart her machine-stitched uniform and string it together to make an escape rope. Instead I just said, 'Thank you, anyway,' accepted a fruit bowl and went to my bed.

After sitting, numb, in my bed for an hour, I set about tracing any remnants. There were eye-pencil shavings under her hospital bed. I held them under the light, identifying the kohl as black with jade streaks.

The bigger find were her crystals, which remained on the windowsill where she'd placed them. I was hoisting them back in, when I heard my name called in that handwashed Yiddish accent, colour still vivid. I turned to see my aunties waddling towards me on their sausage-dog legs, torsos so close to the ground they'd get soaked if it rained.

'What happened?' Edna cried, dragging her sister behind her like a toy caterpillar on a string.

'I don't really want to talk about it. You didn't have to come all this way. I'm really okay.'

'But you're family. Of course we show up.'

'He's family, too,' I said sharply, my voice a bitter herb on their comforting dinner offering.

'He's a horrible man,' Marsha said, looking up at me as she stretched to take my hand in hers (I wondered if her sister had to reach her toothbrush for her from the bathroom shelf).

'But,' interjected Edna, 'but it's his spirit.'

'What does that even mean?' I snapped. 'Look,' I said, lifting my shirt, showing my bruises.

'*Ach du lieber Gott*,' said Marsha, and I knew they had to face the gravity of what their brother was. Then she continued, 'What a marvellous body you have.'

'No I don't!' I snapped, lowering my top.

'The girls must be lining up to get to you. You're such a catch!' agreed Edna, before adding, 'Not facially, of course.'

I sighed and sat back on my bed.

'We brought you something to cheer you up.' And Marsha pulled a fat envelope from her handbag. It appeared to contain a diploma. When I looked closer I saw that it was a membership to the Monster Munch Club.

'The Monster Munch Munchers!' said Marsha. 'With a pen and a storybook. Because we know they're your favourite food.'

I took it, sadly. 'I loved them when I was a kid. I don't think I've eaten a packet of Monster Munch in years.'

'Oh,' said Marsha, downcast. Then she brightened. 'Well, here's your chance.' And she handed me a packet of crisps. On the front was the orange monster, the flavour described beneath his face as 'Giant Prawn'.

'You can't taste a size,' I sighed, uselessly. But she opened them and handed me one, which I was too depressed not to eat. Edna took one from the crinkly bag.

'Isn't shellfish *verboten* for you ladies?'

'Oh, Steven, it's just a baked corn snack with some flavouring. You're so literal-minded.'

I looked again at the orange monster with its flavour descriptor.

'Prawn and orange is a terrible colour combination.'

But they sat, smiling and watching and patting my arms until I finished the bag.

'We love you,' they said. 'Get your strength back and come and see us at the shop.'

After they finally left, I put the crystals in the empty bag of Monster Munch and held it to my heart. As I was staring at the ceiling, trying to feel the energetic waves, the nurse tapped me on the shoulder. 'I meant to tell you: this was on her pillow for you.'

It was a pale blue envelope so thick it felt heavy in my hand. Scented with red roses and peppercorn, inside was a folded note that said: 'If you need to fit me for my dress you can reach me at 01 988 7651. I meant what I said about your dad.'

If I hadn't have searched so diligently for some sign of her, would the nurse, overworked and under-slept, have remembered to pass on the letter? As I thought then and say today: refusing to let go (of a person or a dream) can occasionally pay dividends.

I decided my sides no longer hurt. I put on my clothes, called my mum and pleaded to go home.

CHAPTER 5

I called Jasmine as soon as I got back, but the phone just rang, no answerphone and I was afraid she'd written down the wrong number, by accident or on purpose.

It was difficult at home. My dad couldn't look me in the eye while I was still hobbling or had bruises, so he stayed out. It was always this way. My brothers played loud football outside our window, chanting, 'Go on, my son!' and other sentences that culminated in exclamation points. My mother sat on a stool in the corner of my room and did her embroidery. The in and out of the needle was rhythmic, as comforting as the imperceptible movement of water in a lake.

I was so anxious from not being able to contact Jasmine, I had to talk about her to someone and there was only one someone in my life, at least outside my daydreams. I remember thinking that referring to 'daydreams' was better and safer than saying, 'Inside my head,' which always indicated the possibility of mental instability.

'Mum. I met someone.'

She looked up, her eyes glowing with hope and confusion. We hadn't had the conversation, but she knew I was gay, even though I hadn't decided yet.

'I met a girl.'

'Where?'

'When I was in the hospital.'

'Which one was she?'

I was protective of a relationship I didn't have yet. If you're meant to hold those you care about lightly, I was squeezing my 'future' like a toddler holding Play-Doh. You have so little, then, that's actually yours, what you imagine is yours you're constantly breaking with the ecstasy of ownership.

'You didn't meet her. But she's out now, too.'

'Was she very unwell?'

I thought about this for a moment.

'No. Not really.' I mean, they'd wanted her to stay so they could run more tests, but that was a legal precaution. We all saw she'd bounced back like a Victoria's Secret Model after a birth. Her suicide attempts were her children and they gave her renewed purpose. I was too young to dwell on how sick that was. That, yes, she was quite unwell.

'She's fine. I want to go and see her.'

'Oh, of course. Do you want your dad to drive you?'

I looked at her like she was insane and she seemed to remember, just then, that I had recently been released from hospital and what for and by whom.

'I can come with you?'

'I'm all right by myself.'

And I really had been, all right by myself. I'd got by. But there was this secret little flame, this ember in my heart of wanting someone to talk to, someone I chose and who chose me back, someone who wasn't family, who wasn't tied to me by blood and duty. I'd kept it small for years but now it was spreading around my body. I felt it in my tummy and my brain like an arsonist had been on a street-to-street spree. This could not be contained. Not without a fight. And I was too injured to fight.

I tried her number every fifteen minutes.

'Well! I've been waiting for you to call! I thought you didn't like me.'

'I like you. I called you a few times.'

'I was at my shop. Are you coming over then, or should I come to your atelier?'

I looked around the room. My brothers' wet soccer kit was hanging off the radiator, the newspaper open to page three, there was a half-eaten cheese sandwich on the sideboard that had given up on any sort of an ending and was just lying there, disconsolate.

'I'll come to you.'

It was pissing with rain as I waited at the bus stop and then, by the time the bus arrived, the sun was out. One of those London weather days when you just want to throw up your hands and say, 'What do you want from me? What are your needs? My needs are:

I don't want to carry three cardigans, a cagoule and a pair of fucking shorts every time I leave the house.'

I did carry a load of fabrics on the bus, tipped at angles as I tried not to bother my fellow passengers with them or, even worse, encourage conversation. I desperately wanted a friend, but not one on a bus. I know that sounds snotty from someone who'd just made a friend in a hospital, but still. Transport befriending is a rancid idea. Thankfully, they were a sullen bunch. I got some dirty looks and some interest and that's how it's continued for the rest of my life, if I'm honest. That thirty-eight-minute bus ride was every response I'd ever elicit, encapsulated within one double-decker.

I rode at the top, moving forwards when a seat became available to fantasise that I was 'driving' the bus. This was a happy memory I had with my mum from childhood, driving the bus, her as my co-pilot. But when I fact-checked it, I found it was actually my father who'd been sitting beside me.

I got off where Jasmine had told me, right after a bookshop but before the laundromat. The laundromat threw me, that they had one in her neighbourhood at all. I peered in, and it looked like a regular laundromat with people no different from my mum, looking at their clothes and wishing they were less dirty, like their lives. But it was surrounded on all sides by things that weren't part of our neighbourhood: fancy wine shops, rare-book shops, boutique clothing stores, florists with bouquets that looked like jewellery, jewellers with diamonds clustered on chokers like flowers.

I turned left at the appointed red letterbox, picturing myself sitting on top of it, like Peter Cook in *Bedazzled*, which I'd watched with my mum but, when I fact-checked again, it was my dad roaring with laughter beside me on the settee. Mum was looking in from the kitchen as she made bananas and custard, smiling at us.

I checked the address and knocked on the door. I waited and waited and grew anxious, more anxious than I already was, so anxious that when I fact-checked again, my memory of watching *Bedazzled* with my parents was this:

Dad guffawed at the leaping nuns. Mum brought us our bananas and custard and Dad took one bite of his, said it was disgusting, pushed back the coffee table and stormed out of the house. As he left, she said, 'What's wrong with it?' and he said, 'It's lumpy. If you're going to make it, do it properly, don't be so bloody lazy.' Then we watched the rest of the film in silence while she silently cried and I kissed her shoulder. He didn't reappear until morning. I was upset she was upset, but pleased I got to sleep in her bed with her.

Finally, I heard footsteps in the distance, snapping me out of the ugly memory and back to the lovely street on which I was standing, wisteria creeping from windows and Neighbourhood Watch signs on gates.

A middle-aged dog was in the arms of a middle-aged woman and they were both dressed in small fluffy jackets. It would have been the idiom about people and their dogs looking alike, but their faces were very different and I wasn't sure if I felt impressed or depressed that she'd tried so hard. I saw a young nanny leading her charges while wearing a pair of kitten heels and she didn't look off kilter at all and I started to badly doubt myself on everything. When it comes to clothes, being a true believer can elevate your confidence, but it can also really fuck up your day. Thank G-d, the door finally opened.

By this point, I'd decided it would be a butler, an intimidating butler like the one in *Sunset Boulevard* who turns out to be her ex-husband. But it was just Jasmine, all alone with five floors to herself. There was no trace whatsoever of her hospital ordeal. Her dark hair was up in a bun and, with it sitting high like that, I could see traces of copper at the temples, like someone who'd been playing a lot of tennis in the sun. Her arms were covered by the sleeves of a billowing kaftan, white with gold and blue embroidery round the square neck. Everyone who knows me knows how I feel about blue and gold and they know, obviously, how I feel about square necklines. I almost fainted with pleasure but it might just have been the weight of the fabrics I was carrying.

'Hi!' she cooed. 'You made it! I was just upstairs making Spanish eggs. Do you want some?'

She pulled me up the stairs. I remember it as physical pulling, but truth was she had more of a gravitational pull.

'Go on, let me feed you. Oh, good, you brought your fabrics. Oh, wow, this is going to be fun.'

And then she tried to put them down in the remnants of her egg murder, but I intervened. The dish itself looked tasty, scrambled with tomato and spinach and served on a porcelain plate. She'd just raised a forkful of it to my mouth, when she said, 'Do you want to see the house?'

I took the biggest bite I could and followed her up the next flight, leaving behind the chef's kitchen with a big enough centre block to stage a burlesque performance on, knives, colanders and exotic equipment hanging down from overhead like gallery spectators.

There seemed to be a living room on every level and each floor smelled of something new. This floor of patchouli, the next of Fracas perfume, the third of incense, the last of candles and then cannabis at the very top. The windows were almost floor to ceiling and they hugged the curves of the wall like drunks. In the centre of each was a built-in bench covered in cushions on which a real-life drunk could lie back and let the grand view spin.

Every now and then, a cat would appear and at first I thought it was the same one moving really fast, but then I noticed each had a slightly different placement of dots on its ears, like how a child's flipo-gram booklet works to make a still image seem like it's moving.

Notting Hill was a conundrum. Here we were, in a listed mansion, yet I could see real people outside the window, shopping bags splitting, families splitting.

We reached her bedroom, which was painted pista-chio with dusky rose trim. There was crown moulding on the ceilings, which were so high that you could let go of a helium balloon and have time to kiss before it reached the top. I know because she told me. She told me everything, like I imagined an American would.

How many lovers she'd had. Who had been the best. When the best time was for a woman to have sex. She had a lot of opinions, mainly about me, and she wanted to be involved. It's like she'd taken out a flag and stuck it in my chest. It's really hard to say 'no' to someone who has a brass claw-foot bathtub in the middle of their bedroom.

'I'll bathe you and then I'll feed you properly.'

I watched in silence as she poured various tinctures into the tub. Who takes a bath in the daytime? People with time on their hands and depressives, I can tell you, with a life of experience behind me now. But I was a teenager. I didn't know anything. She was so peppy, she could have poured herself under the running tap and been the bubble bath. I didn't know that people who are always happy are the ones you have to watch.

'You didn't get enough to eat. Does your mum make you matzo brei?'

'She doesn't really make Jewish food. We don't talk about Jewish things or even go to Temple unless somebody dies.'

'Oh really, who was the last person?'

'My grandfather. Who was your last person?'

She started to strip off her clothes, undoing the sash on her kaftan and lifting it above her head. Her body, in its white cotton underwear, was sensational. White cotton knickers don't sound chic, but hers were the thinnest pointelle, like you'd expect a Cuban baby to wear as a onesie on hot nights. Lots of little tiny perforations letting her tan skin breathe. Coco Chanel popularised tans to show that one had leisure time and was therefore upper class. It remained instantly effective on a drizzly day in London.

'The last funeral I went to? My mother.'

'Oh, my God, I'm so sorry.'

'But she was a wonderful mother.'

I didn't know what to say. So I said, 'Poor Diana doesn't get on with her mum at all. You know that, right?'

'It's probably better that way. That way, when they pop their clogs, it doesn't leave you so gutted.'

'How old were you?'

'Mmm, fifteen. Yes. I remember because my father had moved out of home the year before.'

'Moved out of home?'

'Left us.'

'Shit.'

She pulled down her knickers and got into the steaming bath.

'Darling, it was so shit. But… life goes on and here we are!'

She sounded like my mother, who wouldn't tell any of the bad stories from our history. And there were so many of them. All of them were sealed off, though some wormed their way to the surface, like whack-a-mole. She'd slam down and that was it, not to be discussed. But something would always pop up, somewhere.

I wanted to know, just like I wanted to know how it was her mother had died. I waited for her to tell me, but when she didn't I had to let it go. This was before the internet. You couldn't sleuth out someone's background. They were allowed to keep secrets until they felt like sharing.

'Are you getting in, then?' she asked.

'No,' I said, immediately. She looked at me.

'I'll wait until you're done.'

'I'm looking at you askance.'

'I don't care. I'm not having a bath with you. We just met.' The last person I'd had a bath with was one of my brothers. I was probably five and he'd shoved a peeling rubber duck between my buttocks. He already knew. The memory rising to the surface, I turned around, took off my clothes, took a big breath, faced her, and got in.

I don't think I've ever since done anything so strange and so glamorous as having a bath, in a bedroom, with a girl, in the middle of the day, oak trees beyond the window, and beyond the oak trees, people going about their business. It wasn't that time stood still, it's that we seemed to be in a parallel universe.

Whatever it was she'd added to the running water, my muscles, still warped from the beating, started to unwind. My mind, tight from eighteen years in Bow, started to soften and expand. I could see it before me, a miniature sponge thrown in a tub that slowly unfurls to become a star or butterfly.

She said she'd bathe me and she did, scrubbing my back and flicking a washcloth behind my ears. While my mind expanded, my penis shrunk into the form of a sleeping cat, curled up, content and semi-lifeless. I was relieved.

She looked at me and smiled. 'I'm so glad you came over!'

It occurred to me later that she may have wanted me to wash her too. I just wasn't there yet. We dried ourselves in huge towels that she told me her dad had brought back from a Turkish hammam. After she'd moisturised with an oil that smelled of tuberose regret and which stained the towel like a scratch-and-sniff Turin shroud, she put on her pyjamas – right there, in the middle of the day!

'I got these pyjamas from the Paris flea market. Nineteen forties' dead stock. When I take you there, we're going to have to allocate a day to the flea market, make a battle plan before we get there of which stalls we're going to hit first, and then stay really focused. Otherwise, you get overwhelmed by the choice and come home with a Dior suit that's too small, three wicker chairs and a porcelain dildo. Okay?'

'Okay.'

She had a cigarette and then she wanted to work on her dress.

She was short, not like a model at all, but it only made her body more amazing. All the lengths were just right. Out of the bath, I got to look properly.

'Do I turn you on?' she asked.

'Does everything have to be about sex?'

'Everything is about sex. Take you and me, for example. We see that the other is very attractive, but we aren't going to fuck because we're of different sexual orientations. So what do we do with that undeniably sexual excess energy? We make art! Or, rather, you make art. I just inspire it. Do you want to see my bum?'

She turned around. I blinked, because I don't think I'd been asked that since I'd ridden the bus with my toddler cousin ten years ago. I said what I said to him: 'No!' but I felt what I felt with him: 'Yes. I do. I didn't know until you asked me but now, yes.'

He showed it to me on the bus and that's one of the first times my dad walloped me. I'd inspired the behaviour, you see. I'd been a muse, in my way, as Jasmine hoped to be to me. But now we were free.

There was no one here to chastise me. There was no way I could get hurt.

She pulled down her pyjama bottoms. 'There.' Then she lifted off her top. 'Bonus tit!' She put the top back on, what the Americans call a wife-beater, a term, for obvious reasons, I could never warm to. 'I think, with design, you need to have something concealed to really make clear what you're revealing elsewhere. That's my bum. How should we dress it?'

I felt like I was in a life-drawing class. I tried to take it seriously and not giggle. 'I'd like an A-line skirt in gold…'

'Unconvinced.'

I picked up one of my fabric rolls and wound it around her.

'In pleats of very light chiffon.'

'Convinced!'

She sucked in her stomach and turned forty-five degrees towards the full-length mirror, whose glass was framed by Baroque angels.

'Well, you're easily won over.'

I pulled a cord of golden rope around her waist then removed it because it was too Wonder Woman and, if I ever invoke a superhero through my designs, I prefer it be via their human alter ego.

'I trust you. Do you think I invite anyone into my home, let alone my bath? Just anyone that I strip off for?'

In truth, that's exactly what I thought. I could see a ghost chorus of near strangers she'd invited in, traipsing up all those flights of stairs, lying across the kitchen table on their backs, blind drunk, pulling the chain on the loo, passing out beside her. But I was happy to be wrong, and I kept it to myself.

'Do you think your shop might be a good venue for my clothes?' I asked, and she shook her head so quickly I immediately added, 'One day... when I'm more established?'

'No,' she said firmly, 'it's not the aesthetic at all.' She ruffled my hair, an absurd gesture from a teen a year older than me. 'Really. Come by one day. You'll see. You wouldn't feel right there.'

I was hurt because, it was her shop, her aesthetic. Was our taste so different, and if so, why had she asked me to make her a dress?

When the sky turned the shaky streaked red of a cheap cocktail, my hurt dissipated. We lay on velvet sofas in the upstairs living room and turned on the TV. Trevor MacDonald told us, in his sonorous baritone, that Charles and Diana continued their honeymoon, moving on to the Greek island of Hydra.

Jasmine mixed a drink and lit a spliff.

'Do you worry about Diana?' I asked.

'In what way?'

There were actual gold flakes in the drink she made me, which was served in a shot glass with 'Las Vegas, Nevada' printed on the side.

'That she is so much younger than him? He's her first love. Have you been to Las Vegas?'

'My dad has.' She drank her shot. 'I don't think she loves him at all.'

'Why do you say that?'

'Look at him. Would you?'

'Maybe. Why not? I think he's elegant. He likes gardening.'

My mum would be putting dinner on.

'And that's your big sell on a partner. They like gardening?'

'What's wrong with it?'

'Do you garden with them? No. They do it alone.'

'That's okay. Maybe it's like a therapy session where you don't just feel better for talking, you see a literal outcome. Every day. You manifest beauty.'

I thought about my mum bent over her embroidery after one of Dad's bad patches.

Jasmine was unconvinced. 'A devotion to gardening means he'll always be able to get away from her. Have his private time to think all alone.'

'That seems like a good thing.'

'No. We're meant to be around other humans. We shouldn't be alone.'

The ghost chorus yawned from the billiard table, their past midnight wins ricocheting across green felt. There is no game I am good at. Not even solitaire.

'That isn't what you said before. You said even honeymoons should be taken separately.'

'I said no such thing!'

I didn't fight her, even though she had. 'Okay, I guess I just don't know enough of them I want to be around,' I said.

'You should get out more.'

'But I like being by myself.'

'You're here with me.'

'Yes, but I feel like we're alone, together.'

'Well, that's certainly not why I asked you to hang out.'

The shot had made me feel funny, my chest so relaxed it felt too relaxed, an unzipped tote bag on the Tube. I might never see her again (I mean really, a girl from the hospital ward, it was amazing we'd met up this once). So I asked her, 'You have your own ideas about clothes. And about art. And architecture and... so many things. Everything you say is interesting. But you can't really do anything with your ideas if you don't ever want to be alone.'

'Well, we're yin and yang like that. You stay stuffed up in your bedroom; I go out too much. What are you gonna do?' she asked, raising her arms. Jewish slang from an upper-class goyish mouth is as confusing as porcelain fruit in the middle of the dinner table. My mum would have laid the place mats by now. My brothers would be hiding in the TV room so they wouldn't have to help. Maybe I would see her again.

I tried to press a little more.

'Don't you want something for yourself? Something to keep that's just yours and that you can only get done alone?'

'No. That sounds horrid.'

I understood, much later, that, of course, for some-one like her, when you're by yourself, the bad feelings come, and with them, if not interrupted, the bad thoughts come. And that if you don't get interrupted, you can end up acting on them.

She would often read books during our time together, but she'd always have to keep reading passages out loud. She used her boom box, like Debbie Harry in the music video for 'Rapture'. She needed to know you knew the words, too, that you had the same song in your brain, looping from her mind to yours in a figure of eight.

'Face to face. Sadly solitude,' she sang from her sofa.

'Twenty-four-hour shopping in Rapture,' I called back, from mine.

Debbie Harry was the polar opposite blonde to our royal blonde: fiercely independent, confident, too old, too experienced, really, for the pop game she was in. I wondered if Diana had the tune stuck in her head like the rest of us, if she knew the words off by heart even if she didn't know what the words meant. Maybe someone spun it at the after-party for her wedding.

'Maybe Fab Five Freddie played their wedding recep-tion and the papers just didn't get that salient detail,' she said, 'because they didn't know how important he was. And even if the marriage is a sham – which, my love, it is – she got to dance to that at her party.'

'Maybe under the poofy dress,' I continued for her, 'like, he whipped it off, Bucks Fizz-style, and underneath was a very sleek forties-style bodysuit. So she could really dance and let loose.'

Jasmine's face was flush with enthusiasm for my vision. 'Afterwards her hair would hang down instead of the winged updo, fall like Debbie's around her cheekbones.'

'Yeah. In her bedroom, afterwards.'

'But Charles would be waiting in the bedroom,' she said, darkly.

'I don't want to know!' I cried.

'I bet she didn't want to know, but it's true. And then...'

Jasmine crept towards me. She started humping me from behind. No one had done that to me before, not ever, and though she was the wrong gender, I instantly got an erection. I had to tuck it away and waddle off and thus, the action replay of Charles and Diana's wedding night led to our first truly awkward silence. She looked politely away while I rearranged myself.

But she was never able to be polite for very long. 'Well. Now that's happened, you may as well stay the night.'

I called my mum, who sounded almost as excited as on the day of the royal wedding. I was relieved not to eat her lonely broccoli tonight. Part of me thought how well her half-moon nails would go with all the

71

emerald velvet in this house and wished she was here with me. Part of me felt ecstatic she was not.

'Debbie Harry is so beautiful,' Jasmine whispered as she started to get sleepy, 'that if I ever saw her walk into a room, I would need to stand up and applaud.'

Then her eyes closed and I looked around the room at all the other beautiful things: the flowers, the vases. The clothes that hung outside the wardrobe instead of inside so she could fall asleep looking at them. The pastel satin hangers themselves. The dress I made her would become part of this parade of well-wishers. The only ugly things that were treasured in the house were gifts her dad picked up at duty free.

All around her, beauty was cheering her on. Keeping beautiful things alive was keeping her alive: the flowers were all well tended and had bloomed at the right time. The herbs were healthy specimens. The roses in the Wedgwood vase were the half-moon fingernails my mum looked at three times a day when she did the washing up. The pursuit of beauty can be vapid but it isn't meaningless.

The only place I'd seen this done before was in working-class homes – my aunties'– where the lack of storage space meant the most precious things were on permanent display. But at their house, you looked at impeccable porcelain plates while eating from cracked plastic ones. Here, every good thing was always in rotation.

The toothpaste, I noticed, was the colour and flavour of Parma violets. I could not imagine it quelling decay, but the tube was silver with cherubs on it and a label from an Italian pharmacy.

I napped on the sofa on the third floor. I felt quite distant from her, after having shared the bath hours earlier. But she'd covered me with a down quilt of such luxuriance you'd offer it to a child prince. One floor up, Jasmine slept in a bed with the boxed urns of two dead cats, plus two live cats, and a book I examined when I went to up to see her an hour or so later.

'If it's wrong to go to sleep each night with the remains of your dead cats and a copy of *Cold Comfort Farm*, I don't want to be right.' She yawned. 'You can borrow that, by the way.'

Uncomfortable, I picked up the urn. She started to laugh. 'The book, not the cat!'

'Oh. Good. Thank you.'

I put it in my bag.

'Are you leaving?'

I thought about the long bus ride back, balancing the fabrics, hoping to incite neither abuse nor conversation. But clubs would be locking up, the drunks would be getting on about now and the 'driver's' seat at the top would be taken by a couple whose furious snogging would remain immune to the glares of six old people and one teenage boy.

'No. Not unless you want me to. I suppose I should be going?' I was checking. I wasn't really confident of anything, except my talent, which I also suspected might be a mistake.

'Come lie down with me. I won't bite.'

She put the novel in her mouth and pretended to gnash it.

I lay down, telling her, 'I'm not sure why I feel so shy after I've seen you naked, got an awkward erection, bathed together and had you scrub me down.'

She yawned. 'Because sleep is so private, you can have just had sex with someone, been inside them or had them inside you, and then you separate and, even if you don't roll to the other side of the bed, even if you're spooning, you still go to your own world and leave them behind.'

Because I hadn't had sex, I said, 'There's a ceremony to break the Sabbath, the idea being it's really hard to leave the world of the spiritual for the challenge of being earthbound. It's meant to ease you between those worlds and I always think of it when I'm waking up.'

I lay over the cover as she lay under it, staring straight up at the ceiling, whose crown moulding was grape vines dipped in lavender. I'd been wide awake and nervous but now, staring into the lavender grapes, I felt sleepy again.

'This is cosy.'

'Yes, linen sheets for summer, brushed wool for winter. My mother taught me that.'

74

I turned to her, propping myself on one elbow. 'Not satin?'

Now she propped herself on an elbow, facing me like a mirror far more beautiful than the object it's reflecting. 'Oh how horrid! No, never satin, it doesn't feel good, neither does silk. That Hugh Hefner nonsense is a poor person's idea of how rich people live.'

I bristled. 'That's me, I guess.'

'Yes, since I've met you I thought how much you remind me of Hef.' She could be dry as a cat's tongue. 'And when you do get rich, trust me, you must have linen on every bed in each room of your house.'

'I'll only need two rooms. One for me and one for my mum.'

She got out of bed and took off her pyjama top.

'And you'll have a lover and they might be a nuisance, so give them their own room.'

'Okay.'

The word 'lover' made me feel embarrassed. But I felt embarrassed a lot. I waited for her to replace her pyjama top with something else – I could see in my peripheral vision a lovely mohair cardigan – but she remained topless.

'And you'll likely want a work space in your home, even just for noodling around.'

'Okay. So that's three sets of linen.'

'Have a daybed in your studio because some of the best ideas come lying down. But that could just be some velvet fainting-couch situation.'

I stayed on the bed, the better to focus on my fantasy future. 'I'd like it to be teal.'

'Yes,' she pondered. 'Or maybe duck-egg blue. So how's it going to happen, then? Have you made a plan?'

'No.'

'What, you just sit in your parents' house and the women of Paris flock to your living room while you're all watching *Match of the Day*?'

'I don't watch *Match of the Day*. That's when I go to the library.'

'So they'll all find you in the library and whisper, so as not to raise the ire of the librarian, "May we have our gowns please? You can fit us behind this bookcase..."'

'Yeah yeah, and here's a million pounds.'

'A million pounds is not very much. You can't live on a million for very long. I think you should be aiming higher. Are you going to be like Vivienne, you come out of a movement?'

'I suppose so?'

'There's no movement left to come out of. You need to go to art school.'

All of this was in her bed and I rolled further from her as I confessed the truth, until I was practically hanging off the edge. 'The best one, I reckon, is Saint Martin's.'

'Well, obviously, darling, where had you been planning, the London College of Toilets? There's nowhere

76

for you to go but Saint Martin's. May I read your application letter? I know that sounds pushy but I'm a Capricorn, I'm going to have to get quite involved.'

'I don't have one.'

'Right, well, we can do that tomorrow. I believe you'll need to submit sketches and several pieces. So you'll finish making mine and you'll have to do one or two more. When's the deadline?'

She was making it all sound very real and I was starting to feel myself sweat against the linen. I'd like a ranking of fashion designers, according to who sweats the most as they work and who the least and then compare to the fabrics they lean into. I'll bet you the most prodigious sweater leans heavily into silk with their designs.

'Is the deadline coming up?' she asked, as my mind continued to accelerate. I went to the bathroom and ran my hands under the tap. The taps were gold. The sink was marble. My face was still bruised. The poor people were still visible beyond the oak trees. What was I doing here?

As if sensing I might be considering making my excuses, she appeared in the doorway.

'Don't go home.' She could tell. 'Not yet. You can have your own bedroom. I don't know why you slept on the sofa. Stay. There's so much more fun to be had.'

There's always more fun to be had. She said it with the edge of a hard worker, someone who would power through the difficult uphill part of their jog to get back onto flat land and pretty views.

'Don't you have to go to work?' I asked.

'I don't have to,' she said. 'I can take a day off.'

But the people beyond the oak trees had sealed it. I missed my mum. I really did want to go home.

'I won't ask about Saint Martin's again today. I can see it made you nervous.'

'No, it didn't, no worries,' I said, wrapping up my fabric rolls. 'I just think my mum will really be worrying.'

She seemed so thrown by the memory of matriarchal anxiety, as if it were a country she'd definitely visited because the stamp was in her passport, but she had no memories of it. In a bit of a tizzy, Jasmine started pulling things out of drawers.

'Wait! Do you want to see a picture of a female lion?'

I paused, confused. 'Okay.' She showed me the picture. It was a shoot from Paris *Vogue*. The lion was wearing beautiful gold chains with lions on them.

'I don't think the lion much likes that.'

Jasmine looked genuinely crestfallen, as if she'd automatically assumed that the lion, like a reasonable human, would love to wear solid gold chains depicting herself.

I tried to backpedal. 'Animals don't like being dressed up for the camera. How sad chimps always look on TV sitcoms. But maybe she does.'

'I hadn't thought of that. Chimps on TV sitcoms look sad because sitcoms are sad. Why do you have to think of the sad things?'

'I think, maybe, I'm naturally quite a sad person. I agree with you about sitcoms. But that's not how everybody else sees them. So maybe you're as sad as me.'

'Well, that's nonsense. Nobody has to be that way. I'm a happy person. You're just not trying hard enough to be happy.'

But she knew. Because she was one. Because she tried twenty-four hours a day. Only sleep gave respite from trying to fill every corner of her heart and mind with *joie de vivre*. I looked at her and thought, if I still know you ten years from now, you're going to look older than me, because you're wearing yourself ragged with your *joie de vivre*.

The sadness had made Jasmine very sleepy and she was out within minutes. As soon as she fell asleep, I took the opportunity to snoop, something I did even in my own home. But this house had five floors to explore. The best room was the library. There was a section about classical Arabic music, histories of Polynesian peoples, a big shelf just for travel writing. The editions of Debrett's seemed silly in this context, but maybe you can care about both: the history of Polynesian tribes and your place in the social strata. Maybe it was the same thing.

I lay on my stomach, looking at atlases, my happy place, alone, but with someone within shouting distance. She just needed a rest. In the morning, she'd wake up brave again. And if she didn't, would I like her less? I feared the answer might be 'yes', that I was coward enough for one person.

I could see, quite clearly, why Victorian gothic centres around grand homes. You could go mad here.

The huge rug on which I lay was embroidered with flowers, like my mum liked to do, but these were exotic blooms, woven, I suppose, by exotic peoples a long, long time ago. Before we ended up under the grey skies of the East End, watching *Match of the Day* in the TV room, my family was an exotic tribe from a faraway land.

I'd been so busy climbing the rolling library ladder, it was only when lying on the floor and rolling onto my side that I noticed there was a whole section, at a lower level, of children's books. They were first editions, mainly, and had notes to Jasmine from her mum. Doting, heartfelt notes. Why did she not talk about her? How present she seemed to have been for such a good period. They went all the way up until 1975. Then, abruptly, they stopped. I thought of how my father's record collection stopped the year the first child was born. Like he'd switched over all his attention to his kids. Too much attention.

I took a book and went back to my room, which was her room, she having taken over her father's four-poster.

In the morning she was standing over me with a cup of tea and smiling. It wasn't a fixed smile. She was happy again. It made me happy, too. I sat up against the pillows and took the mug, but she only permitted me a few sips, and then she couldn't help herself. 'Let's get out of our fug. Let's go and buy something.'

'What?'

'Anything! What do you want? Or we could just go and look; we don't even have to spend money. But let's go into the world now.'

I allowed myself another big slug of tea. 'I could do with some interesting buttons, for your dress.'

She leapt straight on the spot, like she was front row at The Clash.

I called my mum. She sounded less excited now, and more curious, an edge of anxiety creeping in. I listened for the sound of Dad raging, but I could only hear my brothers and him chatting normally about the game.

It seemed a big deal, to go out into the world when we had, so far, only spent time together indoors, beginning with the hospital. I wondered if the natural light might blow out my features in such a way that she might suddenly think herself silly for pursuing my friendship.

I felt my anxiety and excitement grow with each flight of stairs. The world would see me with her, this beautiful creature (and she really was: she'd done up her eyes so she looked like a raccoon who was the life

81

and soul of the woodland forest party). If we went into the world, I would have an eye out to protect her from it, as I always did with my mum. In our home, I knew I had no powers to keep Mum safe, but on the street, I steered her by her elbow, far taller than her now. If I saw a street drunk I tried to give them a fearsome look, even though I was trembling inside as we passed every pub.

The worst would be if my dad was visible in the window or doorway of one of the pubs. When I was not inside the walls of our house, I didn't know how to act around him. Neither, to be fair, did he. In a different context, both of us seemed confused about our roles, and he'd come out and smile. Once or twice he even asked Mum and me if we wanted to come in, but we made our excuses and left, and at home that night, it was not mentioned.

As we approached the front door, Jasmine took a coat from the hooks, a denim jacket that she held up against my chest and then slung over my shoulders. Then she rummaged deeper into the layers hanging from those brass hooks and pulled out a peach capelet that she tied around her neck. We looked at ourselves in the mirror and it could not be denied that we looked ideal together.

'Do you use the mirror by your front door to check your outfit before you go out, or are you more interested in using it to see how you look on your return?' Jasmine asked. 'How the weather and the world has diminished or enhanced what you left the house with? I think the world can be divided into two sets of people. Those who really study themselves closely in that glass both before and after are mostly psychopaths and only really fit to govern. However, having dressed in tandem with another gives you, I believe, a pass to look at yourself both times.'

I threaded my arm through hers, as happy as I'd felt in a very long time, and we were about to open the door when we heard footsteps approaching.

Jasmine cocked her head like a dog waiting for the sound of its owner to return from work. Then her face broke into a smile as a key was heard in the front door.

'Who's that?' I asked, nervous, alert to the possibility of being murdered.

The door pushed inwards and before us stood a tall, slim middle-aged man with Jasmine's same piercing blue eyes and black double row of bottom lashes.

'Daddy!'

CHAPTER 6

'I came as soon as I heard!'

Unless he'd come from somewhere inaccessible to planes or trains, he hadn't. He took her face in his hands, which were exceptionally large, something I noticed and then despised myself for feeling instinctively a-flutter for.

He was wearing a Savile Row suit with a pair of busted Green Flash tennis sneakers and a white T-shirt whose torn neckline showed off his old man chest. From the neck up he radiated youthfulness, with thick hair more chestnut than grey and freckles outnumbering the crow's feet around his intense eyes, the light blue centre surrounded by a stark navy ring. The outer rings seemed designed to hold in the overflow of periwinkle. I've learned, since, that eyes that intense, that full of complexity, often betray an emptiness behind them. There was a heavy gold ID bracelet on his wrist, its impressiveness undercut by him carrying a bag that said 'Duty Free'.

'You been at it again, baby girl?'

She collapsed into his arms. 'Where were you?'

'I'm here now,' he said, 'and I'm going to squeeze you and squeeze you until you haven't a breath left in you.'

It was an unfortunate thing to say to a suicidee.

It didn't seem like we were going out any more. Still. As much as I'd wanted to make my exit the night before, now he was here, I didn't offer to leave. Even though she didn't introduce me. He reached into his duty-free bag and pulled out one of those retractable perfume cases they only have at airports.

'I told you: I always come back. Even when I'm away for a month. Even when I'm away for more than that, I always come back.'

They held each other for a while and, seeing myself in that mirror by the door, I cleared my throat. They both turned around as if startled to find me there. Jasmine remained attached to her dad, but took my hand in hers.

'This is my dear friend Steven. He was so good to me in the hospital and really nursed me through my recovery.'

None of this was true. Plus, she'd discharged herself within forty-eight hours.

'He's Jewish. And he's a homosexual.'

'That's wonderful,' her father said. His teeth were a white I've only ever seen on Americans. That her father was rarely without a cigarette or cup of coffee just went to show, as we are reminded in myriad ways each hour of every day, that life is not fair.

I didn't really know what to say in front of him. Jasmine sat with her retractable make-up case and put on more batwing liner that went out to her temples and then painted a constellation of stars on her cheek-

85

bones. He didn't say, 'Why are you wearing so much make-up? You can't leave the house like that!' like any normal parent would have said. I didn't know if I admired or disliked him for it.

Now and then he'd stop holding her, but then he'd think better of it and go back to playing with her hair. He'd lifted her onto his shoulders – as if she were still seven – when the phone rang. He answered it with her still balancing there.

'Daddy!' she squealed, wobbling, and he steadied her with one arm, speaking into the receiver: 'No. She can't talk right now. She'll call you back,' and he hung up.

He bounced her round the room on his shoulders and she asked, 'Who was that?'

'The hospital.'

'You should call them back,' I said and they both looked at me.

'Yeah, yeah, let her hang out with her old man for a bit. I haven't seen her in for ever.' He said it as if some terrible force had conspired to keep them apart. From the way she let him squash and squeeze and clutch her, I felt she was complicit in his narrative. It was distasteful. But not so distasteful that I would leave.

She made coffee, again, while her dad showered. He had left the duty-free bag on the table and I saw it also contained long multipacks of cigarettes. When he came back into the kitchen, wearing a towel around his waist, he was smoking one and had another tucked behind his ear, where it rode his chestnut hair obscenely. I'd never seen an adult smoke without an open window before. Even my dad sat on the patio to smoke and my mum made a big huff and drama about it, picking his least offensive trait to take a brave stand against. As if by saying the smoking was not okay with her, she'd inoculate herself against having to ever deal with the rest of it.

Her dad hopped around the kitchen, quite manic, one minute hugging her, then making marmalade on toast, the spread going over the countertop and being left there. Then the toast had been put aside and he was sitting on the kitchen counter reading aloud from Keats. I needed to do a wee, but it didn't seem like you were allowed to go to the toilet until he had finished reading.

Then he turned his attention to me, as if reciting poetry had given him the ability to notice other humans for the first time.

'Where have you appeared from, young man?'

'He lives in Bow!' said Jasmine, feeding her dad. 'Isn't that fantastic?'

Her father nodded sagely and, on finishing his mouthful asked me, 'You know who came from the East End?'

'I don't know if I'd be thinking of the same person.'

I'm just going to say it now, and then later, maybe more than once, I'm going to say it again: her dad was a handsome man. My dad, beyond being shit, was also just a dad, there was no recognisable human form beyond his place in and effect on our family. This man was a man, first and foremost. I suppose maintaining that delineation with his frequent world travels was his intention and, unfortunately for her, it worked.

I've come to believe you can be attracted to an entire family: the sister, the brother, the mum and dad, even the grandparents.

I wanted to fill the silence and stop looking at his chest, so I said, in a voice far higher than I'd intended, 'Angela Lansbury was from Poplar.'

He frowned. 'I wasn't thinking of Angela Lansbury.' He paused. 'Harold Pinter! From Hackney!' He shouted Pinter's name like he was in a Pinter play. 'He's a Jew! Like you!'

'Samesies,' I answered, absurd, because I didn't know what to say, and Jasmine was staring at me in a way that was meant to be encouraging but was having the opposite effect, like when you make eye contact with an beggar on the Underground to show sympathy. 'Sandie Shaw, too.'

'You do like ladies,' chuckled her father, though a chuckle run through a cigarette is more of a bark.

'Yes,' I said. 'I do.' Then I racked my brain. 'Vidal Sassoon.' I was aware that naming a famous hair-dresser did not make me sound more masculine.

Now her father smiled. 'I've been at some of his parties. He's a dour sort. Of course he lives in Bel Air now.'

'Probably the weather has lifted his mood.' I said, awkwardly, and Jasmine wasn't helping even a little, now taken in by the retractable duty-free make-up box, as if it contained all of life's secrets.

'Well, Daddy, we were just on our way out to look for some buttons. He's making me a dress.'

'Ohhhh,' said her father, and tapped his nose, as if the word 'buttons' explained everything about me he could ever want to know.

'Do you want to come with us?' she asked.

'I'm absolutely knackered from the travel. I think I need a kip.'

The recovery time needed to get over holidays is a consistent issue of the ultra-wealthy.

'But, I really want to hang out with my girl. So let me get my clothes on and we'll go.'

She waited on the pavement in her cape, twirling a parasol, beaming with happiness. When he materialised on the doorstep she said, 'Daddy!' again, as if each reappearance to her stage warranted a celebration, like how American audiences clap when a movie star enters or exits a Broadway play.

We walked down Westbourne Grove to Portobello Market. I know because she said, 'This is Westbourne Grove,' as if giving me a tour of a museum. The museum of her childhood. 'I used to skip here. I did my chalk drawings on this street.'

She had a wealth of happy childhood memories for someone who'd repeatedly tried to kill herself.

They held hands as if she were a little girl, and sometimes he leaned on her shoulder and other times she leaned on his. They helped each other pick out jewellery and then they pinned a war medal on me, which they thought was hilarious. 'For services to flattering bias cuts.'

'Don't you think that's kind of disrespectful to war heroes?'

Jasmine's dad leaned on her and started singing 'R.E.S.P.E.C.T' to her, while she sang the backing vocals. They were in perfect sync.

I realised that I was, left to my own devices, a curmudgeonly sort. Like Vidal Sassoon. I found their *joie de vivre* rather repulsive. But I was also jealous of it. I'm barely different from my teenage self in that sense but, thankfully, as you age, there's less requirement to ride roller coasters or attend New Year's Eve parties. They say being young at heart keeps you looking great. Whereas, being prematurely curmudgeonly aged me early enough that now, as an older man, I barely look any different.

We all went to the button stand, where she decided she wanted nineteenth-century French military buttons, but I explained to her that they'd be too heavy on the silk. Her father concurred and I was both flattered and irritated by his involving himself in my vision for her dress. I guided her to little white ceramic ones with tiny Russian folk-art flowers painted on them and he was very interested in them and then, all of a sudden, not.

At the vinyl stand, her dad bought a few records for her (*Damn the Torpedoes* by Tom Petty and the Heartbreakers and *Kind of Blue* by Miles Davis), which I found to be tonally incompatible but I kept that to myself.

She plucked out a copy of Adam and the Ants' *Kings of the Wild Frontier* labelled 'Gently Used' and asked the stallholder to play it, 'just to check it isn't scratched'. As soon as the staccato drumming and howls of 'Dog Eat Dog' began, her father began to dance, doing a Cherokee war cry and beckoning us both to join in. Jasmine took his hand as I pressed myself as deep as I could into the stall, seeking camouflage between a copy of *Bridge Over Troubled Water* and Peggy Lee's *Greatest Hits*.

But she pointed at me and called to her dad, 'He loves Adam Ant! He admires his cheekbones!'

I blushed as her dad held his hand out to me, proclaiming, 'He's right to,' as he pulled me into their dance. It was fascinating to me that upper-class men could openly admire the beauty of other men without having their straightness queried. I've learned since that so long as they're 80 per cent with women and only 20 per cent with men, that counts as completely heterosexual to them.

I shuffled my feet uselessly like a prehistoric creature trapped in tar about to be eaten by something larger. When he sang the line asking what's a warrior without his pride, her dad beat his chest like a great ape. A really great one. People were clapping and cheering, and I tried to pick up my feet a little to the beat, but it was so complex, I had the sense I was now doing an Irish jig. I still don't know how to dance to New Wave. I don't know if my jig tipped him over the edge, but the stallholder turned off the music and said, 'Are you buying it or not?'

'Not,' said her dad, and returned the album cover to its place, adding, as he did, 'Though they've quite brilliantly brought the Burundi beat to popular music.'

'What's the Burundi beat?'

He turned his bright gaze to me. 'The signature tribal drumming of Burundi. It's the Central African nation that borders Rwanda. Jasmine's been there with me.'

'No I haven't.'

'You didn't come along on that trip?'

Then he walked ahead with all the swagger and camp of the Dandy Highwayman. She bit into any anger she felt and from it oozed a soft centre of admiration.

'See? Dad knows everything about music!'

I nodded and tried, then failed, to bite my tongue as I motored forwards to call to him, 'I'm surprised you bought *Damn the Torpedoes*. Tom Petty's sort of a bit hard to avoid. I couldn't wait for "American Girl" to leave the Top Forty.'

I don't think I understood, necessarily, that this was an attempt to flirt, but it was.

He turned to face me. 'Well you're wrong, because he's a genius! You can write him off as a lightweight of the American singer-songwriter canon when compared to Dylan and Cohen and Paul Simon – all your people – but it's that lightness that makes him such a relief and a release. He's a brilliant, brilliant artist.' I thought he lingered rather too long on the word 'release'. But it might have just seemed that way, because his lashes were so long; I might have got his lashes confused with his phrasing.

Jasmine was listening keenly to this discussion of the virtues of keeping things upbeat.

He moved purposefully up Portobello, stopping to buy us all corn on the cob doused in butter and lime. He fed her a bite and I thought it was a disgusting sight. I am, in many ways, the most puritanical Jew I know. Watching him feed her also made me jealous. I just couldn't identify which one of them I was jealous towards.

Then he turned to me and tried to feed me and I was disturbed and turned on, and in trying to take a step back from him, trod on an old lady's toe. He made a great show of tending to the lady, who scowled at me as she accepted his kindness, which was as demonstrative and loud an act as any of the street performers strolling the market.

And then he drifted off.

Jasmine realised, with panic, that he was missing, and I could see her give him what she considered an appropriate amount of time to return, having us wait where we were. She clearly had experience with this. It made me think of being separated from my mother in the supermarket. Walking those aisles by myself, knowing she'd be worried but still feeling excited about being on my own. Like I'd felt in the hospital. When the voice came over the supermarket tannoy saying my name, I was suddenly sick with fright. It felt like police and fire trucks might come and perhaps, also, a rapture, plucking us from the aisles, taking us both to heaven, but different heavens, and we'd watch each other vanish upwards, she from household cleaning, me above the sugary children's cereals I'd been stalking. When moments later, we were reunited, I sobbed into Mum's chest with gratitude and stayed glued there, pretty much for the next ten years.

Jasmine's mood was downcast when she realised he wasn't coming back. Unable to fake her customary *élan*, she suggested we go to the pub. It wasn't like the pub in my neighbourhood, the ones Mum and I avoided because we knew Dad was likely there, with pickled eggs on the bar in a jar and old men playing darts.

Jasmine leaned us against the bar stools (upholstered in deco palm trees). The room was full of people who looked like her, but not as young and not as beautiful. They all knew her and smiled at me as if they knew me too, because I was by her side. Even though she was clearly feeling low, she helped me up onto my stool.

'He's a designer,' she said to her public-school pub acquaintances.

'Amazing,' they answered as one, with slight variations for jaw setting.

It seemed that getting a positive reaction to her support of my talent was easing the unease at her father's vanishing.

'He's the real deal,' she said. 'I discovered him in a hospital, of all places. He's a brilliant but troubled young artist.'

I didn't know what she was talking about, because I didn't know at all that I was the real deal. But nothing she said about me felt phoney or like I oughtn't to trust her. I didn't think of myself as troubled, but I had to admit I was surrounded by trouble. They looked at me expectantly, as if I might get down off the bar stool, slide down onto the floor and design something. I looked back at them.

'I should call my mum.'

'Oh my God, you and your mum, it's pathological.' This coming from someone who was having a near meltdown after her father wandered off at Portobello market.

I went to the payphone in the back and tried to be heard over the din. I tried to decipher whether or not Mum had been crying but I couldn't make it out over the music. 'I'll be home, soon, Mum!' Then my brother came on – I couldn't tell which one and I couldn't tell what he was saying. But everyone sounded okay.

I looked across the room at Jasmine, who was laughing and pouring champagne – who drinks champagne? At a bar? – and I decided I'd rather be there, with her, than go home.

I did my best to put home out of my head, because I wanted to stay here, with Jasmine, whose huge empty house – for better or worse – left her alone to be herself, just as my tiny one was filled with family crushing in on me.

We had a few drinks with the public-school pub patrons, who were perfectly nice. Problem was, a lot of posh accents together all at once is a truly horrible thing, whereas one alone is charming. I steered her back on to Portobello and we bought a bunch of gladioli, which she asked them to thread with irises. They didn't want to, but they did it, accommodating her as a regular, like a familiar face in a restaurant who asks for something not on the menu.

We were considering seeing a film at the Coronet when we found her dad, taking cash out of the cashpoint by the World's End. He was smoking and the woman queuing behind him huffed, then smiled and blushed when he turned around.

'I think I need my lie-down now,' he said, as if we'd been walking alongside him the entire time with no interruption. Maybe he thought we had.

'Steven. I bought these for you,' he said, and handed me a blue plastic bag. Inside was Adam Ant stationery, sealed in cellophane, his image at the top where the letterhead would be. Many packets of it.

'I wandered into Woolworths to get some jumbo matches. You know, the kind you can use to light a votive if you've a day off in a Catholic country? I saw these on the shelf between a beach ball and buckets and spades, which is quite weird because you're not going to write a letter to Adam Ant on the beach, with all that sand.'

Jasmine took them out of my hand to examine them.

'You're not going to write a letter to Adam Ant with his face on it. You'd send it to anyone but him.'

Her dad took them from her and handed them back to me.

'I wouldn't mind. Anyway. I got you them all. Fourteen packets. That was all they had left.'

Unencumbered by the bag, he wrapped his arm around Jasmine's shoulder and I noted, and have never forgotten, what a difference there is between someone putting their arm on your shoulder to comfort you versus using you to balance themselves. I don't think she even knew how much of his weight she was shoring up.

Jasmine was so happy to see him she made no attempt to convince him to stay out with us. In fact, she seemed quite relieved to drop him off at home, staying until she'd seen him get into the bed and fall asleep with her own eyes. She gently took the cigarette from his hand, took a drag, then stubbed it out. You'd think he'd burn to death if that's how he fell asleep every day of his life. But then I imagine there was a woman in every room he ever slept in, ready to put out his lit cigarette as he slumbered.

We had an afternoon pastry and a cup of tea and took catnaps ourselves on the sofas of the third floor, and I fell asleep pondering the meaning of the fourteen packets of Adam Ant stationery. I woke up before her and started work on her dress; just the pattern-making. When she got up, she didn't change out of her silk pyjamas, just added make-up and heels and we went out again, her dad still snoring.

'How does he know about Burundi tribal drumming?'

'And Arabic classical music. And Appalachian folk. He was left to his own devices by his parents.'

'Where were they?'

'They were just huge narcissists. They'd go out to parties and leave slices of ham on the edge of his cot in case he woke up hungry while they were out. By the time he was ten, he'd just spend all his free time listening to music and reading. I think he's read every book in our library. None of them are for show.'

She brushed my eyebrows with a tiny comb on a stick, explaining as she did, 'It's why he got married and had a kid so young. To build a real family.'

'But…'

She looked at me. I couldn't believe I had to relay to her what he'd made of his family.

'But what?' she asked. So I didn't.

I tried to get the image of ham on a cot out of my head as we ate Thai food in what was, apparently, a Thai restaurant, but also seemed to be somebody's front living room. As the noodles were set before us, an old lady walked down the stairs in curlers and turned off the TV. 'I'm trying to sleep.' And she went back upstairs. 'Mothers,' said the waitress.

The waitress hovering behind me, I called my mum again, just to let her know I wouldn't be coming home. I think I woke her. But I could hear her clearly, now.

'Have you been drinking?' Mum asked.

I detected a note of hopefulness. That I might have friends. Even with Dad and his drinking, the signifier of sociability, of social success, remained alcohol. Despite the myriad ways class made its peculiarities known between Jasmine and me, we had this in common.

'I haven't, Mum. Sorry to disappoint you.'

'You've never disappointed me. Just stay safe.'

That's different from telling someone to be happy. I didn't feel safe. But I did feel joy.

Jasmine, who'd paid the bill while I'd been on the phone, threw her arms around me and took me back into the night. As we left, I saw the mother come back down the stairs, still in her slippers, now holding a pair of green ballet slippers that she threw at the waitress. It struck me that not only might we not have been in a restaurant, but maybe the 'waitress' had never invited people in before. Had we been invited? Or had Jasmine just walked into someone's house and asked for dinner? I started to laugh and couldn't stop. Then I started to drink and kept going, far longer than I ever had before.

I've sipped wine before and thought not too much of it. But the bubbles of the champagne she kept conjuring, and the glasses it came in and then eventually no glass at all (we sat by the Thames swigging straight from the bottle), that was worth drinking for.

'You'd keep your mother there with you?'

'I couldn't leave her there with him.'

'You have to take your mother with you, when you leave home?'

'I just said that. I said I'd not leave her there.'

'Well, you really shouldn't, it would be so wrong.'

'She's coming with me.'

Jasmine looked uncomfortable and held her tongue a moment before speaking. 'But she can't really live with us. It changes the dynamic. When you make it, you have a home atelier so, rather than a home, you probably need a castle.'

'Okaaay.'

'I'll start scouting for castles next to each other that can be joined by a footbridge or a moat.'

'Are there lots of castles near each other? Is that a thing?'

'I honestly don't know. But I'll find out. *And* maybe we find one in Portugal and we replace the moat with a swimming pool.'

'I think we should stay Britain-based.'

'Would Ireland be okay with you?'

'I suppose Ireland would be fine.'

I got so carried away in her daydreams that it took me a while to notice she was the only friend I've had who conjured daydreams on my behalf. She whiled away hours, losing herself to the fantasy of what my life could become. You'll hardly meet anyone in my business, or any business, who thinks that way. Maybe managers – and maybe she could have been a manager – guided some actor she truly believed in to an incredible career. But her heart was too big. And she was rubbish at maths. Her brain wasn't linear, and it wasn't lateral; it seemed to jump backwards and forwards in time like jazz, with a portal here and there to another dimension. But it was a fucking great brain. I think it's why she had such a lovely high forehead; her brain was always working away.

The quietest I'd seen her was when she was doing her make-up and I reckon that's why she reapplied it four or five times a day, not because she was insecure about her looks (she knew quite well she was beautiful), but so she could make her mind stop racing. Everyone has a mirror face, usually pouting or arching their brows or both. But when she was looking in the glass, applying her slap, her face would go slack like the look a kitten gets when it's being carried around in the jaws of its mother. She was relaxed.

'We could have two homes.'

They say that money can't buy you love, and that's true, but it can buy you a great view. That's what the very rich have that we don't. They have weeping willows. They have palm trees swaying in the breeze. Cherry-blossom trees in Kyoto or on the Washington Mall, for that matter, a gift of friendship. I thought of twin towns as I wrapped my time up with Jasmine's. This has been gifted to this random, shitty city from this ineffably exotic and beautiful town on the other side of the globe. Why. Why were they connected?

Beaches – white sand like you've never seen! Pink sand like you've never seen! There's different textures right there; that can keep you going for a long time. This patch of ocean is a different temperature from that patch. That'll keep you alert to life. This area of California is so different from this one that you need a place in each, your Los Feliz Spanish revival and your all-glass Malibu beach house, sunlight streaming in. And they're not wrong.

Great views and new places can keep you going for a very long time. I can't imagine how much earlier she'd have made her first suicide attempt if she'd grown up where I had. If her people had travelled from country to country to make it to England, but then she herself had never left London. And life can be very sad when you're poor, but that's not necessarily the case, not by a long shot, usually because you have your family. But the richer you get, the sadder you get, that's for sure. There's no way to get above a certain point and not be riven with existential doubt and melancholy. There's a reason all those billionaires have yachts of their own. They have to be able to get away at a moment's notice. Get to a new textured beach, different kind of tree, seasonal cuisine, better party, but most importantly, at a moment's notice, be able to get away from themselves.

'I've thought about buying a place in Paris, but I think it might take the magic away to have roots. We can look, when we get there, if you want.'

'Where are we?' I asked, leaning into her as the water glittered, shards of glass bobbing along the buoys.

'It's the Thames.'

'But the Thames goes all through London. Which part is this?'

'How long were we walking for before we got here?'

'About an hour.'

'Then we're probably in Hammersmith.'

She looked into the river, its filthy waters varnished by the night, and smiled. 'I once had sex in Ravenscourt Park. In a greenhouse at night, among the most beautiful flowers. It was summer and the glass had heated the room, so we moved so easily. Then, as we were recovering, it started to rain. We lay on our backs and looked up at the trees as the branches shook. It was one of the most beautiful nights of my life.'

'It sounds so romantic. Who was he?'

'I don't know. I don't remember. But I know it was one Tube stop from Hammersmith.'

She seemed neither sad nor troubled that her partner for this great event was anonymous to her. I buried the thought that I might not matter to her enough to be remembered, that she might one day search the recesses of her mind for the name of the boy from the hospital whom she sat on the banks of the River Thames with.

We tired of reflecting on our reflections in the water and took a cab back into town. There were no mobile phones then, no group texts or e-vites, so how she sniffed out the place to be, the room that had spontaneously become a fantastic party, missing only her, I don't know. The truly great stars, the real 'It Girls', not only have 'It' but also a nose for the best, most invigorating rooms. They never end up queuing for dud events (they never queue) and, like a figure skater skating the thin ice of their own life, they get out before it all goes wrong. They're so good at getting away from a party, premiere or playdate before it does go wrong, they tend to leave their own lives before it turns ugly. Think about Edie Sedgwick. Jasmine was one of the few who got away with it, that final suicide attempt failing to take.

We needed to talk about that.

We needed to have a real conversation.

But not tonight. Wasn't this closeness real? Wasn't the intimacy she made me feel we were sharing really a way of talking about the hard things without actually having to? Idolising someone is the opposite of intimacy, but I didn't know that then. Breathing her name calmed me down. Breathing her name meant I wasn't alone with myself.

We ended up on someone's rooftop garden, gorgeous, secret, looking onto a private garden square filled with revellers, looking down on all the people who thought they were moving secretly, not knowing of our bird's-eye view. Strange to be looking at a garden from a garden.

'Can you smell the honeysuckle?' She took a few buds and held them in front of my nose.

'Are you taking those for one of your witchy moon potions?'

'No. I just like stealing.'

We drank more and did the dance from Bucks Fizz, and she really let me whip off her skirt and then she didn't want it back and walked down Ledbury Road in her underwear. It was around there I noticed my pain was gone. It made me want to lie back on her bed and look up at the ceiling and feel my body with its newfound silence.

'Are we going home?' I asked.

'Not yet,' she said, knocking on a red door doused in black graffiti. A slot opened and a man's eyes appeared. 'Wah g'won?'

She answered him in perfect patois: 'Bombaclod!'

This being the password, the red door opened and we got let into a Jamaican after-hours club, descending a narrow staircase to a narrow room that reeked of weed and alternative narratives. Men who'd been policemen in Kingston working as dealers in Notting Hill; women who'd been married to abusive priests, leaving the marriage and the religion for London, taking all the kids and the responsibility. But someone else was watching the children tonight, as their mothers weaved the dance floor.

Needless to say, Jasmine was as well known here as she had been at the pub full of trust-fund kids. She sang along to Barrington Levy and leaned back into my chest as I imagine she had in Ravenscourt Park after the rain. It still felt like home – not the home with the needlepoint flowers, but the home I deserved, where night flowers bloomed on rooftop gardens. Hadn't my mother given me everything? Yes. Almost everything. Just not this.

She took a drag of a tiny spliff. 'That spliff is the size of a bumblebee,' I said.

She blew out the smoke and corrected me: 'It's the size of a bee's dick!' We collapsed with laughter.

'That spliff is so tiny, Prince could use it as a hair clip.'

'That doesn't make any sense!' she laughed, but it made sense to me, especially after I'd had a drag.

'You don't have…' – she fumbled a moment with a new wrap but was also rolling up her words – 'way-back cash?'

'We have a family business in Whitechapel. We don't have much money, but the business does go back to the 1880s, I think. It's run by my aunties. The money goes to my dad, too, except no money's been coming through lately. The neighbourhood's changed so much.'

'That's where Jack the Ripper stalked.'

'Yes, exactly. Now we know it was maybe the royal doctor but at the time, there was a Jewish community and they were just so terrified Jack would turn out to be Jewish. That was what the anti-Semites were putting about.'

'Everyone was an anti-Semite then.'

'Feels like everyone is now.'

'I'm sorry you feel that way. Do you really feel that way? I love England so much, I can't bear to believe it's true.'

'Well, you're proper English.'

'So are you.'

'No. I remember reading the most beautiful book of Oscar Wilde children's stories. It just set me free and I knew that he would have loved me, that he'd have seen my talent and felt my heart.'

'And you'd have been lovers?'

'No. But he'd have taken me away.'

'He didn't have anywhere really to go himself, poor Oscar.'

'I just knew he'd understand me. Then I turned the page and within this beautiful story was this description of the nightingale flying over the ugly, old haggling Jews as they argued over money.' I can still feel how my heart just closed in on itself. That the person who would take me away from the ugliness might see me as the ugliness to be taken away from.

'It was just the times,' she said, swatting at the air, not wanting me to harsh her high. 'Everything's different now.'

I nodded, but I still felt sad when I thought about it. I didn't know why I was in a Jamaican after-hours club talking the pros and cons of Oscar Wilde. That seems really an ideal situation for someone who cares about the fabric of our country. But I was tired and didn't care just then. I wanted to go to bed.

She asked what the aunties who ran the shop were like and I said they were a pain in the bum. 'I avoid them because they keep kosher. My dad looks down on them because they're religious.'

'And you look down on your dad because he's a violent drunk. He believes in getting blotto. They believe in religious reverie. I know which one I'd rather be around.'

'You make them sound like Sufi mystics; they're just East End Jews. I don't want to be around any of them. You know that.'

'I think you're a snob.'

'You think I'm a snob?'

I looked around us. The smoke was hurting my eyes.

'Yes. I do.'

She seemed to really believe it and she seemed also not to hold it against me. I did not believe it and I would have held it against myself. But she had me turned all inside out with my zipper flipped and my label showing. It's like, she did that and then said, 'Yeah, so what, that's your look.' When you think you might be gay but you haven't decided yet, your look is very, very important. It's both a protective stance and an invitation to conversation. I'd wanted to have someone my age to talk to for so long, and now I did, I couldn't get a word in edgeways.

When we got home, her father was up.

'Where have you been? I missed you so much!' And he sat on her lap. She didn't say he was hurting her, though I could see he was.

Finally, she bounced him side to side. 'Get off my lap, you fat old junkie!'

And they laughed as, muscles rippling, he cut out a line of coke and she shoved him out of the way to get to it. They both sort of offered me some, but without turning themselves from the powder or each other. It was easy to say no. I've never really been a happy person, but I did, basically, always know who I was and what I needed. Even then.

They played records for each other as I fell asleep. I remember seeing Tom Petty going onto the turntable, the visual of them carefully handling the vinyl, despite the fact they were both wasted, and that out-of-nowhere verse with the lines about memory and desperate longing. That it's never mentioned again, swept under the New Wave rug to be crushed by the powerful dancing feet of the broken-hearted... it always gets me. I was listening and watching and teary, and then into sleep as one sinks into a hot bath after a crying jag.

When I woke up, both father and daughter were passed out, he on the sofa opposite mine, and she in the four-poster bed he'd been sleeping in. He had one foot touching the floor and a hand on his heart, like a painting of a Romantic poet cradled by a painless death.

They liked all the same music. She liked the music she thought would make him like her more, that if they shared the same interests he would be interested. Those same things he'd interested himself in because his parents weren't interested in him.

After checking they were both well and truly out, I bent and brushed her lips with mine, so soft she might have dreamed a butterfly had landed on her. Then I wondered if I dare do the same to her dad. His breath was so heavy and it stank of nicotine, like the priciest, most highly concentrated cologne. But his skin, like hers, was lit from within, votive, not ashy. As I moved closer to him, I saw that the trousers he had fallen asleep in were raised rigid at the groin, as aggressively hard as the smell of his breath.

I stood there, transfixed, not daring to take another step. Then I thought of him alone in his childhood library, reading Melville and listening to classical Arabic music. And I took a step forwards.

I very gently bent and kissed him, as delicately as I had his daughter.

His hand moved upwards from his chest, circled my wrist and squeezed. Then, just as quickly, he let go, his hand falling to his side. I couldn't breathe, and because I wasn't breathing, I was able to hear that he really, truly, was still asleep.

Astonished by her father's subconscious touch, I went to his bathroom to feel closer to him, leaning against the wall, trying to calm my breathing. I was almost too terrified to urinate. I had to talk myself down. 'They're just people. Ordinary humans, just like you.'

'His' bathroom had a painted de Gournay silk wallpaper showing cranes pecking the water beside a lake and I was standing in front of it, tapping away the last drops, when she approached. 'There you are. I was worried you'd gone.'

I tucked my penis back into my trousers.

'It's beautiful,' she said.

'These trousers were handed down from my grand-father.'

111

'The trousers are all right. I meant your penis. Though I imagine that was handed down from him, too.'

'I'll have to be getting along.' Could she see, could she sense what I'd done?

'I understand. I'll walk you out.'

I put my backpack on.

Of course, with that many flights it takes a long time to get walked out, especially with her pausing to explain the provenance of things. The house was a mish-mash of places he'd been without her. There, on the second-floor patio, was a painted porcelain tortoise he'd had sent back from the Florida Keys.

'Which Key was he in?'

'Oh, all of them!' She said it proudly, when I imagined he'd have just taken longer to get home to her.

'After your mum passed away, he didn't come back?'

'Oh heavens, no! That's when he really got going! He was quite devastated inside, I think.'

'But you were, too, I bet.'

It was a stupid thing to suggest 'betting' over, even as a figure of speech. It felt a difficult conversation to be having while wearing a backpack. There are certain conversations ill-suited to ergonomic travel accessories.

'Yes, but I didn't have any guilt attached to it, that's what really powered him. He had screwed her over massively, of course, and that was all a bit much for him. I understood.'

'I don't.'

'You do understand, you're just being judgmental. That's a dreadful quality.'

'One of my many. People should be judged on their behaviour, don't you think? You must have been heartbroken. I'm so so sorry. You were just a kid. All kids need their mum.'

Her lip trembled for a second, but then it stopped, like a gymnast sticking a landing.

'Hand-painted fans?' she said.

'Excuse me?' We'd made it to the kitchen. The front door was in sight.

'I think it's something we could make and market.'

'Okay. I don't know what made you think of that…'

With time, I discovered that her schemes emerged when there was a topic she preferred not to discuss. I think it's why she had so many schemes. Because there was so much to hold inside.

She pressed close to me. 'Do you paint them when they're open or closed?'

She didn't want to talk about her mum and for that, honestly, I was relieved. I waved and walked to the bus stop, my backpack weighing on me like a conscience.

CHAPTER 7

'So?' said my mother. 'Did you have a nice time?'

I concentrated on painting her nails, getting the moon shape sharper than ever before, as an act of penance for having been gone so long.

'We thought you'd run away with the circus!'

I looked up. Had she actually had a conversation with my dad? About me? Had he initiated a conversation about my safety and happiness or simply put up with one? Or, most probably, was she lying?

'It was a bit like the circus. Incredible. And then it's time to go home.'

She smiled. I'd never noticed before the thin white strips on her two front teeth, like cirrus clouds against the yellowing enamel. Imagine how much of her I'd notice if I went away every weekend.

'I missed you,' I said. 'I wished you'd been there.'

I was starting to miss Jasmine, as I'd known I would. Wondered if her father was awake and if they were talking about me.

'Where? Where did you two go?'

'Just around where she lives in Notting Hill.'

'It's very dangerous there.'

'It isn't, Mum. You're being racist. Because that's what you actually mean. You're channelling Dad.'

She looked around to make sure he couldn't hear.

'Come on, he doesn't care. He knows he's racist.'

'How can we possibly be racists? We're a minority.'

'But we stick to ourselves, don't we?'

'That doesn't make me racist! I just don't know anybody else to hang about with except us!'

'Well, wouldn't you like to?'

'I've never really thought about it.'

But she had. I know she had. I know she'd thought up a lot of inner lives, from the meticulousness with which she maintained her black hair and half-moon nails. No one ever creates a solid look – no matter the look – if they don't harbour fantasies of escape. That's the whole point of signature style. To take you away from it all when you have to spend a lot of your time standing still. You can look at your fingers as they stir the pot. Or look down at your cowboy boots at the bus stop in Finchley.

I'd been home a night, waking up to the same pigeons outside my window – if not the same ones, then they deliberately dressed all alike and moved in the same manner, like early forerunners of the Blue Man Group who, like pigeons, are also rubbish. A designer should be able to find beauty in the mundane and very often I do. But there are limits. Sometimes depressing is just depressing.

'We're going to take a trip to Paris for a weekend.'

'When?'

'We're just figuring it out.'

'You'll give me the hotel number and your room number, too?'

'Yes, Mum, we're just figuring it out.'

I was itching to call her. It was starting to make me feel off balance, like people who have that disease that gives them the sensation that parasites are moving under their skin. How long could I wait before I excused myself and picked up the phone?

I dialled her number with trembling hands, placing my finger in the holes of the rotary phone, as anxiously and as awkwardly as I would a vagina. I had started to feel relieved that she wasn't answering. And then, as I was hanging up, the phone was lifted from its receiver at the other end, the sound of a cigarette being inhaled before the smoker deigned to say: 'Hello?'

'Hello?'

'Yes?' said her father.

Hearing his voice, I felt ill, as if he had definitely felt my kiss and had pretended to be asleep to spare my humiliation. 'It's Steven.'

'Yes?'

'Steven your daughter's friend who just stayed at your house? Is she there?'

I tried to avoid my mum's glances, mortified.

'My God,' he answered, 'I have a thumping head-ache… I've drunk a gallon of coffee and I still feel like something the cat dragged in and then took a piss on.'

Was this hangover from our night or was this a new one? Or was this just him in his natural, waking state?

'Um,' I stammered, 'maybe you're dehydrated?'

'Yes,' he agreed, 'perhaps that's it.' And then he hung up. Imagining, I suppose, that the call had been a check in from the universe to see how it might serve him.

I sat down in front of the TV, concerned that my mother must now assume I'd fantasised an entire friend. I shame-watched *Match of the Day* because I was too embarrassed to move.

Mum had just placed a bowl of bananas and custard in front of me when the phone rang.

'Oh. Yes. Hello, dear. I've heard so much about you. How nice to "meet" you.' She made air quotations around 'meet' even though she was on the phone and could not be seen. She was bending and performing as if Jasmine were in the room, her accent becoming less Jewish and working class, or at least what she thought was less Jewish and working class. I thought she sounded like Sybil Fawlty.

'I'll just get him.'

I sat up straight, like only a bent boy can. I was about to leap out of my chair but Mum stretched the cord, delivering the receiver to me like a final course. It was thoughtful. But it was also a way to make me have the conversation in front of her.

Jasmine failed to say hello, launching straight in with: 'Hand-painted leather. What do you think? We could paint handbags with scenes from history.'

'Dead animals. Already an affront to be dead. I don't want to paint on them.'

Mum was doing the dishes, but in the terrified manner of one who's bathing someone else's newborn baby, her interpretive 'upper-class' posture restricting her movements.

'We could have a whole staff, like Andy Warhol's Factory.'

'I like being alone. My dream is to make a lot of money so I can be alone and have enough there that I don't have to leave. And an intercom where I can communicate with the other people in the house. My mum would be there.'

I said that part loud, so she could hear. I wanted her to relax. She dried the dishes, giving away nothing. I cleared my throat. 'I called but you weren't there. Your dad answered.'

'I was at work, darling.'

I heard my father's key in the door. I always knew it was him because it took him three or four goes to fit the key in the lock and he pressed his whole body against the door as he turned. My mum's ears pricked up on that second try, that third try, she stayed rooted to the spot, looking into the soapy dishes.

I wanted to stay and help Mum. I looked at my dad. If he was surprised to see me back, he didn't show it. I nodded slightly at him, phone at my ear.

'I always dreamed I'd have children who'd come running into my arms as I arrived home from work,' said Dad.

'Hello, darling,' replied Mum, and kissed him, and he clutched at her waist and kissed her back, hard.

I wanted to stay and help her. But what could I do?

'Steven? Are you there?'

'I'm here.' The walls of the room breathed heavy, like drunks, all four of them leaning against each other to stay upright.

'Who's he talking to?'

'I can hear him,' said Jasmine. 'You should come over.' She added. 'My dad's gone.'

And maybe a part of her did want to protect me from my shitty home life. But mainly she did not want to be alone. The woman who did not want to be left by herself was easier to try and save than the woman who had trapped herself for ever with people she did not want to be around.

'Yes,' I said, 'he was having a really bad headache.' And I could hear from my tone that I was trying to give her inside information on her own dad. That I was trying to inveigle my way in with both of them.

If I were older, or if Jasmine been younger when she'd met me, I could have helped more. If I was younger when I'd got sent to the hospital, I wonder if the damage would have been so easily overcome, both physically and emotionally. If we'd met in some other way, in a night club, would we have been drawn

119

together? It doesn't matter. I wouldn't have been at a night club. I spent all my nights in my bedroom, sketching. If Dad hadn't fucked me up the way he did, I wouldn't have Jasmine. And she's the best. I'm not saying I'm thankful for what he did. But I am saying things happen for a reason. I know people don't like to accept that. Once you open the door to coincidence, you start seeing it everywhere. It can be overwhelming.

'Come over,' she said again.

My parents had drawn apart from their kiss and were watching me, or rather my mother was watching my father watch me. She was trying to pick up from his gaze and weight against her, and the weight with which he was standing, and his angle, whether or not tonight would be a bad night or pass without incident.

'Okay,' I said. 'I'll be there soon.'

CHAPTER 8

Jasmine was in emerald silk pyjamas with a mandarin collar and embroidered hot-air balloons. When she opened the door she greeted me by asking, 'How are you going to mark out your label from everyone else?'

She stared at me and I took a shuffle forwards, hoping the entire conversation would not happen on the doorstep, as I was quite cold and tired. Thankfully, she ushered me to the fainting couch in the parlour. I lay back and she removed my shoes and began massaging my feet.

'It will be ongoing, always evolving, but the core is the woman who takes no bullshit.' I waited a beat before adding, 'I'm sorry your dad has gone.'

She pushed my feet aside and I immediately missed the touch. When would somebody touch me? Actually run their hands across my quivering limbs as I sighed with pleasure and they'd whisper, 'My darling,' and not vomit, laugh or wet themselves at the sight of my naked body?

'No, I mean, the actual label, inside the clothes. How will that be different?'

'I hadn't thought of that.'

I hunched up into a ball and stroked my own feet. 'When did he leave? Do you know when he'll be back?'

She fluttered at the air with her hand, a butterfly flapping its wings against a rainstorm, acting like everything was fine because how can you be in distress when you're so beautiful?

'Well, it's the first thing I would think of. Don't all of us spend our days at school not listening to the teacher because we're practising our autographs?'

That's exactly how I spent my school time. I'd gravitated, with age, from a neat, right-sloping italic to a left-leaning scrawl intended to conjure a poet trying to write after an absinthe bender. Not that I'd ever tasted absinthe. I don't really approve of alcohol, for obvious reasons, but if I did drink, I'd like to think it would be a green spirit from the seventeenth century.

'Here's what I've been thinking and it's really why I telephoned you: you could skip your name altogether and just have the label identifiable by fabric.'

'But I like my name.'

In the lifelong battle between overconfidence and self-loathing, it was one of the things about myself I really did like.

'Do you? That's bold. Okay, so your name, but maybe in relief, like your name is cut out from the label.'

'You're suggesting things that would be of great interest if I'm catering exclusively to the blind community, which is a niche avenue I hadn't planned on.'

'You think you're better than them?'

She looked like she might have been crying, but then I looked again and saw she just had a row of fake lashes that were bothering her eyes.

'No. Stop twisting my words.'

She sat and kissed my cheek. 'But it's really fun.'

'Not for me. I don't like being made fun of.'

'Why not? Come on! It's just joshing.'

'Because I get enough of that at school. And at home.'

The parlour fire was burning through logs like an old lady at an all-you-can-eat buffet.

'Oh. I'm sorry. Darling. That was insensitive. I suppose they call you yid and kike and Fiddles.'

'They don't call me Fiddles.'

'"Faggy Yid", I thought it might have emerged from there. But I am sorry. I like being teased because it means someone's paying attention.'

She handed me a silver-backed hairbrush and instructed me, with a wave of her hand, to brush her hair. I took great pleasure in it.

'What would they tease you about?'

'Oh my dad teases me about the suicide and the cutting.'

'Jesus. What else does he think is funny? That's mad.'

'He looks at me and says, "That's insane! Will I have to send you to the loony bin?"'

She smiled, but none of her teeth showed.

'Have you been to the mental hospital?'

'Yes, I mean, a few times. It's nice to get the rest. Better than rehab.'

She opened the lid of a Georgian writing desk and pulled out a small plastic vial of cocaine, which she tipped into her palm and sniffed.

'Do you have a drug problem?'

'Everyone at my school had a drug problem when they were fifteen. No, darling, I'm an intermittent user when it's around. I noticed someone left this here and I thought I might as well put it to good use. Might have been that party I had last month. Might have been my dad saving it for the next visit.'

I made a shocked face.

'Oh, don't be such a puritan, it doesn't suit you.'

But, actually, I knew it suited me quite well. She kept babbling, her father's visit having stirred a great unrest. She was, to herself, a new acquaintance at a cocktail party, to whom she thought it rude to delve too deep.

'You should put a snake in your label. I saw a Victorian snake ring at Portobello and it stuck with me.'

'They scare me. Snakes. Not Victorians.'

'You don't always have to explain yourself so thoroughly. I do understand you, you know. But I think it's a good idea for you and what you're trying to project. The average snake sheds its skin two to four times a year.'

'Shedding your skin doesn't connote anything good. Where I come from, it means you're an imposter. I hate snakeskin, it's the ugliest thing, belts, shoes, print on dresses. It really disgusts me.'

'Right, leopard print is hot, though?'

'Of course. It's like "Rarrr, Raquel Welch!"' I didn't sound enthused as I said it. It was the least emotion ever put into a reading of Raquel Welch's name.

'Snakes' skin doesn't grow with them, right? But do you know why they shed it?'

I shook my head. It felt good to say no, and I've always liked the sense of my hair as it whips in and out of my peripheral vision.

'It's a great reason: to get rid of parasites that might have attached to them.'

I hoped she'd offer me some pyjamas; soon I hoped they'd be her father's. I loathed him – apart from or as well as feeling attracted to him – and I wondered where he'd gone now, and on what terms they'd parted. But I didn't want to mention him for fear of making her sad. Selfish. I wanted her cheerful tonight. It better suited my needs. There were moments when I was just as bad as everyone else around her. Just because you love and care about someone, doesn't mean you're not a parasite, too.

'Jasmine. Don't you think it's… not normal to take drugs with your father?'

'In what way?'

'Shouldn't he be stopping you from taking drugs?'

'He should be stopping me from taking bad drugs, dangerous ones cut with baking powder and who knows what. He's very careful about that; he makes certain it's only ever absolutely highest quality, really safe. He's very caring. He always says I'm his everything.'

I looked at the floor. She seemed flummoxed for a moment, a record player stuck on a scratch in the vinyl. When she spoke again, it was halting.

'We could… source… little bits of shed snakeskin and put them in a pocket in every label.'

I laughed. 'That's disgusting.'

She turned serious, relieved to turn the questioning back on me: 'Who are you designing for? Don't you want to disgust people? Just a little? The killer ingredient in really fine perfume is oud. It smells like shit on its own. But it elevates a rose to dizzying heights. That's what I see in your work. That's why I asked you to make me a dress. Because you've got roses and shit. And you should be proud of that. A beautiful gay boy in a hospital, beaten up by his dad; that's the definition of roses and shit.'

I didn't correct her and tell her I hadn't decided yet. I just asked, 'Do you think I'm beautiful?'

'Yes!' She hugged me and I felt warm and loved, and then she added, 'You're beautiful-ugly.'

'Oh.' It was how I imagined it must feel to have her father come and go.

She saw my expression and continued, 'But you're stunning. You take all the light in the room. You eat it up.'

'You give all the light in the room.'

She kissed my head. 'I do hear that a lot.'

She went into the kitchen and heated up some chicken soup. That was Jasmine: chicken soup and cocaine, wind you up and try to soothe you at the same time. She reached onto the windowsill and plucked a leaf of bay that she added.

'My mother taught me that. She approached cooking in the same way she did gardening, as a time to be quiet, to be alone with yourself.'

That was gone. It had been gone a long time. She looked very pale and very young.

'Does it work for you, still, as a way to get calm?'

'Mostly. But even when it doesn't work, the food still tastes good.'

But here she was, growing herbs in an empty house too big for one small girl, adding them to her mother's dishes but eating them alone.

'Do you ever cook for other people?'

'I'm cooking for you.'

'I don't count myself.'

'Why on earth not?'

I thought about it.

'Jews, historically, don't get to stay any one place for too long. They always get kicked out in the end.'

'I'm not kicking you out! I'm keeping you! Even though you're *so* insecure!'

'How many times have you been to hospital?' I asked.

'For what, for suicide?'

'For anything, I guess.'

'It's not polite to ask a lady their age or how many times they've tried to kill themselves. It runs in the family. My mum. Her mum. My grandmother.'

'Did any of them succeed?'

She ladled the soup into two Japanese bowls.

'All of them.'

'Your mum… ?' I trailed off, like an endless train on a dress, put there to keep anyone from getting too close.

Had she let me think it was a natural death because she didn't want to talk about it, or had she done nothing of the sort? Had I just gone ahead and made an assumption so I wouldn't have to go deeper with her?

'That's absolutely terrible. I'm so, so sorry. I had no idea. Do you want to talk about it?'

She studied me. 'Do you want me to be more sentimental about it or brave? Which version?'

'Whichever version is real.'

It didn't seem like 'sentimental' was the right word.

She slurped her soup. 'We have stiff upper lips. The women more than the men. That's why we do it. They'd like to do it, too. But they haven't the courage.'

She didn't want to talk about her mum, or, rather, the only way she could talk about her was through herself. I tried to follow her lead, unpicking a tangled necklace of gold thread in the half-light.

'Why don't you get it right?'

But she couldn't go there. She put her bowl of soup to her lips, slurped it until it was finished. When she re-emerged, she suggested a scheme to do with reselling flowers from the market as dried arrangements, as if we'd never been speaking of anything else.

But I knew: she didn't get it right because she still wanted to be alive. Some part of her. Enough of her. Stay alive enough to keep getting it wrong. I saw, for the first time, there was a picture of her mother in every room in the house. All of them were small and tucked into a corner. All of them were there. Her bad stories were very, very quiet, diaphanous secrets hinting at the shape of the body underneath.

Whereas all my pain was noise. I wondered what passed through my mum's mind when she was picking up after one of his rages. Whether she daydreamed more of killing herself or of killing him? Or whether neither occurred to her, that she kept herself preoccupied with her embroidery, going deep into each pattern instead of deep into the dark thoughts. And every decade or so, there was a royal wedding to think about. None of us would get bored of projecting our desires onto Diana.

Jasmine and I lay on our individual second-floor sofas like an old, married couple, at peace with a silence broken only by the sound of the television. That night, BBC News reported the latest on Diana's honeymoon (we called it 'Diana's honeymoon' as if Charles had not even been present).

'Fourteen days yachting around the Greek Islands,' yawned Jasmine. 'That's too many days. And there's no way to get away from all the staff attending them. Nobody goes to a beautiful remote isle because they want to chat to a lot of people. You can't relax on a remote isle when, everywhere you look, people are standing to attention.'

'Maybe you can.'

'No. My father and I went to a remote island with Mick Jagger and Jerry Hall and it was extremely difficult.'

I found that so strange, this image of the super-couple with Jasmine and her dad as the supporting pair, and stranger still that she didn't think it strange. For all his faults, I never imagined her dad was sexually attracted to her, that never crossed my mind. But the adoration girls feel for their fathers was compounded by her longing for him through his extended absences and celebrated reappearances. Adding Mick and Jerry into the mix – a model and rock star, *the* model and rock star, designed to be adored – was unbearable.

After the chicken soup was finished, Jasmine brought out champagne and chocolates for dessert. She took a bite of each one, like a five-year-old would.

But there was nobody to send her to her room and if there had been, which room would she have gone to? It was all hers. And there were such wonderful things in every room. How could being shut in solitary ever be a punishment when you could stare into the birds of the de Gournay silkscreened wallpaper? How could you hope to grow up safe, how could you grow up to not attempt suicide? I pulled her into my arms and she lay beside me like a silver spoon.

She pressed her back into me, as if my limp penis were a friendly woodland creature and she Snow White. 'If I went on honeymoon I'd like to go somewhere that they say will eventually vanish.'

I stroked her hair. 'What sort of school did you go to? The one where everybody had a drug problem?'

She sighed, annoyed at the rising memory, like her still water had turned out to be carbonated. 'It was a rural boarding school where the philosophy was that the students made the rules themselves.'

'How did you know the drugs were a problem if there were no rules there?'

'Well, I knew they were illegal. But mainly, I just felt really bad about myself. I was too young, too little, much slimmer than I am now. It just wrecked my system.'

'You have to have rules so you have something to break.'

'I agree with you. I'd have benefited tremendously from boundaries. It was probably my parents biggest mistake.' She smiled and pulled herself up like a soldier. 'Well, too late now!'

I decided that that was a good way I could help her. I would tell her to go to bed on time and stop eating crappy food and drinking late and sleeping in to odd hours and managing on no sleep and sleeping around and giving her love too freely. Well, I meant to. I meant to do all that for her. It just didn't happen that way. I was having too good a time to set boundaries for her, and I think everyone felt that in her presence, even her dad. She made the rules. It might have been why he ran away. To get away from her setting the pace.

We fell asleep together on the sofa. It was the nicest sleep I ever had. We woke up occasionally to hold each other tighter; I'd wrap an arm around her or she'd roll her leg across my waist. And then we'd go back to dreamland. I felt strong, that night, in my body, in my head. I felt like I had some power – not too much, like hers, that rattled around her body and kept her unable to focus. But just enough power to start opening up my life, to finally figure out how to get the fucking top off the marmalade jar without asking my mum to do it.

At 3.12 a.m. I woke up just enough to whisper, 'Tomorrow, I want to go to Saint Martin's and pick up the application form.'

'Yes,' she said, 'I'd already planned that.'

CHAPTER 9

She insisted her shop could manage without her, that this was too important to not accompany me. I thought she'd dress up for our visit, but she dressed down, a simple uniform of black jeans, white T-shirt and ballet shoes. She was the first person I'd ever seen wear black jeans, and she'd dyed them herself in the bathtub. I didn't see anyone in black jeans again for five years, like they'd noticed her around town looking splendid and it had taken them all that time to pluck up the courage to give it a go. Her hair was pinned up so her lovely neck was showing and she didn't have on any of her crazy make-up. She looked like someone sensible and hard working, but still striking.

In years to come, St Martin's would count among its alumni everyone from Alexander McQueen to Jarvis Cocker. Stella McCartney. Hussein Chalayan. If you had serious aspirations to make art your profession, that's where you went. In the years I'd fantasised about attending, my favourite former students were probably Antony Gormley and John Hurt, neither of whom went into fashion but both of whose work informs my own.

As we walked to the Tube, I checked my notebook. 'We get out at Tottenham Court Road, then walk down Charing Cross Road.'

Jasmine looked at me askance. 'I'm not taking the Tube to one of the most important days of your life.'

Leaving aside the fact that you can't take a Tube station into an actual day (though I accepted that was how things seemed in her own life), I felt uncomfortable showing up in a taxi.

'Today isn't the biggest day of my life. It's not a big day unless I get in. We're only going there to pick up the application form. Let's just take the Tube.'

'No. I'm tired.'

For someone on a single-minded mission, she was moving like all her bones had fallen out of her body. Worried she was going to ask me to carry her, I agreed to let her hail a cab, but I made the driver drop us around the corner. What if I did get in and there was someone exiting or entering who also got in and then they'd have seen me and dismissed me as 'taxi boy'? I didn't understand, then, that people of vast wealth were inextricably entwined with all artistic life in Great Britain and always had been. That Jasmine, in her efforts to support my work, wasn't an outlier; that her patronage was possibly the only way for a boy from where I came from to get where he wanted to go.

Someone who's known a lifetime of grand buildings had no qualms about stepping inside Saint Martin's, and she did so as if walking into McDonald's, and

proceeded to request the application form as if order-
ing a Big Mac with fries and a Coke, as if she were
doing them a favour.

She sat in the reception room and read through it.
The receptionist's shoes were surprisingly ugly. When
I told Jasmine this on the way out she said it wasn't a
surprise. Most fashion is, that's why I was different.
Because I championed beauty, just like her.

She asked me if I wanted to hold the application
myself, and I flashed back to my mum letting me hold
my own train ticket. I was not unaware that I may
have been attempting to transition from the arms of
one nurturer by throwing myself into another's. But
it was hard to describe Jasmine as nurturing, exactly.
I'd have hated, for example, to have been her actual
child and found it impossible to imagine her with an
actual child, that it might, in fact, lead to her death
like the coda to *Lolita*. I know about the coda to
Lolita because she read it to me on the Tube. Now we
had the form, we were allowed on the Underground.

But she got an urge and had us leap out at Green
Park, just as the doors were closing. We left the station,
up into the sunlight and went through the park, pausing to sit on a couple of deckchairs and eat ice creams.
She never worried about her figure, at least not out
loud. We never discussed whether there might one day
come a time that she could not devour a 99 Flake
with an extra flake and then take a supplementary
flake from her companion's ice-cream cone.

135

Either struck by inspiration or on a flat-out sugar high, she decided that what we absolutely must do to celebrate our excellent morning was go to a charity shop. Back then, there were no fancy ones. The clothes were all somewhat dingy and sticky, while the shop itself was overlit, a combination that she found energising.

'Look at this!... Now look at this!... Tell me this isn't the best thing you've ever seen!'

'No.'

'What?'

'I've seen better things than that.'

'Hello, can I help you?' asked a volunteer.

'Yes,' said Jasmine. 'Do you have any Murano glass in the shape of tropical fish?'

The volunteer looked at her. 'I don't think we do, love.'

She looked to be deciding whether Jasmine was mocking her. I knew she wasn't. I knew she just expected her heart's desire to always be available. It made up for her dad. You couldn't have the most basic thing a girl deserves, so instead you could have the most complicated and obscure. She was genuinely surprised the charity shop had no glass Murano fish.

This seemed to trigger something in her, some sense of betrayal on the shop's part, because she sprang into action on a scheme.

As we moved between the aisles, from grotty to tatty, lonely to depressing, she kept putting on layers and layers of clothes until she was huge, and she never stopped talking to me while she did it, never tried to hide her crime, wanted me to watch her do it. Every single thing she held up in front of herself to admire she then took off the hanger and placed over her head.

The volunteer was now preoccupied by the world's oldest woman. She had a look on her face like she, too, might be asking for glass Murano fish, as the assistant seemed at her wits' end. When Jasmine could barely move any more, she waddled out of the store, pausing only to engage the shop clerk in a chat as she left.

'Thank you! Have a great day.' Just before the door closed behind us.

'I don't like that, Jasmine.'

'Saying "Have a great day"? I know, it's very LA, isn't it?'

'That's not what I'm talking about and you know it.'

I was furious that she'd included me in the theft.

'It was an anarchic prank. That's what they do at art school, darling. So it was thematic, really.'

'That shop raises money for cancer research. Poor people shop there because they have to. Don't go doing your anarchic pranks on them.'

'You could have stopped me. But you didn't, because you were enjoying it.'

'I didn't stop you because I was appalled.'

'You were scared.'

'Yeah, so what? I was scared. Let me let you in on something in case you haven't noticed yet: I'm always scared. My mum is always scared for me and I picked it up and I internalised it and I'm scared shitless all the time.'

My obsession with Jasmine was a way not to have to feel how scared I am all the time. All obsessive love serves that function.

'Let me meet your mum. I can break through. I can reset your dynamic.'

'No. You're not meeting her.'

'Why not?'

I paused. 'You'll scare her.'

'I am the least frightening person in the world.' She was literally covered in fifteen layers of dead people's clothes. 'That is *not* true. I can't imagine how it is you see me.'

The clothes still smelled of nicotine, bleach, end of life.

'Like a beautiful scary person.'

'Then why are you hanging out with me?'

'For the reasons I just described. You're catnip. You're kryptonite.'

She batted her hand at me and started to cross the street.

'Superman doesn't want to be near kryptonite; you're misunderstanding the world.'

She was nimble, despite her puffed up outer-wear. I rushed to catch up with her, nearly walking right in front of a double-decker bus.

'I want to be near you. Okay?'

She leapt up onto the steps of the same bus I'd just avoided. I raced to make it as she held out her hand to me. I didn't fall and I wasn't crushed beneath the wheels and really it was a triumph in every way, except I thought I was going to have a heart attack.

'I want to be near you, all the time. You're all I think about. When I'm doing the washing and my Walkman isn't working, instead of listening to music, I think about you.'

She was walking up the steps and by the time I met her at the top, she'd already taken a seat.

'Would you ever go straight for me?'

'I haven't decided yet.'

'Whether you'd go straight for me?'

'I adore you. I adore you. I just... haven't decided yet.'

'There's a news flash.'

'I haven't done anything yet. And I feel like an idiot because you've done everything.'

She looked sad. 'It's not like I do those things because I want to especially.'

'Then why?'

She didn't cry as she answered, 'I've started so I have to finish.'

I wanted to shake her by the shoulders and say, 'Just stop! Calm down, take a rest, lie on the sofa watching *Coronation Street* and don't let anybody inside you again until you're really in love!' But the bus shook, and my nerve shook and, like everyone else, I was just happy to be in her company.

She tapped the shoulder of the man seated in front of us, in the 'driving' seat.

'Excuse me? Do you mind if we sit there? I always think that's the best seat on the bus.'

To my astonishment, he nodded his head and switched places with us. That could only ever happen to Jasmine, that if something was better she deserved it, whereas I felt, as a teen, that if something was better it must not be meant for me. Though maybe, in that particular instance, it might not have been because she was lovely, but because she had fifteen layers on and looked mental.

Now we'd been upgraded, she leaned on me and said, 'Some gay men only have romantic love. Not sexual.'

'Which ones?'

'Ancient Greeks.'

'Great. Will you introduce me to them?'

The weeping willows were brushing the roof of the bus, like we were driving through an enchanted car wash.

'Don't be a sad sack,' she admonished me. 'You're always sad for yourself. Not for other people.'

'Who do you help? Do you donate money to charity or only steal from them?'

'Yes. Some money gets donated. But mainly time. I do art with Ilona a few days a week because she hasn't another soul in the world, poor little bird.'

'Who's Ilona?'

'Oh, it's quite hard to explain. I'd rather just introduce you to her.'

We sat in silence for a spell, and then, as we approached Soho, she leapt up, pulled the 'Please Stop' cord and popped down the stairs, like a rather large pixie. I followed her as she picked her way off the bus without tripping over her layers.

'Where are we going?'

'I'm going to introduce you to Ilona.'

They say that toddlers have no sense of time: they can weep inconsolably for their mum who's been gone ten minutes, but if she goes away for a fortnight, on her return, they act as if they've seen her just the hour before. Similarly, Jasmine had no sense of time, which may be why she was so good at making things happen.

Ilona lived in a top-floor flat. I bristled a little when I realised I was not the only poor person in Jasmine's life. I bristled again as it struck me that perhaps she collected us, like layers stolen from a charity shop.

But Ilona was so happy to see her, so careful and loving, all my bad feelings melted. She had the thin, crêpey skin of extreme old age, and the thick Scottish accent of her childhood. Her immaculately kept bedroom and living room were shut in by other buildings. But the view from her kitchen spanned across London, so that's where we congregated.

She insisted on making us tea, and though I very badly wanted to take over because she was too wobbly and too close to the ground, Jasmine insisted I let her finish. Then she gave us digestive biscuits that were so old they could have their past lives read by a psychic. I tried to discreetly spit mine into a paper napkin, but Jasmine insisted I eat it.

'Ilona, you look so beautiful!' And she did, wearing tropical green eyeshadow, as if she'd been expecting us. To wear that every day, when you live alone on the top floor of a tower block whose only good view is from the kitchen, and to be furthermore draped in costume jewellery from travels you would never take again... I could see why Jasmine was moved by her.

Something about the great jewellery triggered Jasmine and she finally removed all her disgusting layers of stolen clothes. She folded them neatly into a black bin bag and it struck me what a good Victorian washerwoman she'd have made if she hadn't been born a twentieth-century heiress.

They got out some gouache and started painting together and pretty soon I asked if I could join in. It wasn't part of what I'd been seeking when I chose to run out of my suburban rut and away with a glamorous It Girl, but it might have been one of my happiest moments with her. It was certainly the calmest. The three of us painted the view and, by and by, we were in rather a trance state.

Eventually Ilona was the one to break the silence, which seemed right, as it was her flat. 'How much longer until they get back, then?'

'Who?'

'Charles and Diana.'

'Oh,' I said, cleaning off my brush on a square of kitchen roll. 'Shall we turn on the TV? There may be a report.'

She smiled and started mottling the high-rise windows with dots of sun glare. 'I don't have a television.'

I thought of the many, endless hours the television was on in our house. How the most extreme behaviours within our four walls were witnessed and nullified by it. The drone, the hum, the constancy against my parents' highs and lows. After I met Ilona, watched her with her paints, I decided never to own a TV once I left home and I stuck to my word.

'Were you always into art?' I asked Ilona.

'I always did it. First it drove my mum mad, then my teachers, then my husband. But he was the one who really loved me for it. He used to sit for me. Have a look in my bedroom.'

On her bed was a pink satin elephant, well loved, and above it, on the wall, a portrait of her husband, just as well loved. He must have sat at a precise angle, looking towards her from three-quarters on, and she had then hung it in a way that they'd be locking gazes as she fell asleep each evening. It was one of those things you come across now and then that makes you feel simultaneously elated and devastated. That's art. That's what it does when it works. It's what I've tried to do with my clothes. It's what she'd managed with the portrait of her long-gone love.

What does someone mean to you, or what did they once mean to you? That's every book, every film, every song that's ever mattered to me. If you can be really precise, if you can concentrate hard enough to record it all exactly as it was in a way strangers can understand, then the love lives on.

Jasmine didn't try and get out of there by a certain time, rather, around five o'clock, Ilona was looking sleepy and she decided we should make our excuses so the older woman could prep for bed.

As we were leaving, Ilona insisted on giving me a chunky Bakelite necklace.

'It's rare to find a Bakelite necklace like this, because it's so easy to break.'

'I'll be careful. I promise.'

'I know you will.'

'I'd love to make you something to wear. I'm just finishing something for Jasmine, then is there anything you'd like me to design?'

'I'd like a snood.'

'A snood?'

I knew exactly what that was. A close-fitting hood worn over the back of the head. 'What pattern?'

'Forget pattern. Let's start with fabric. Velvet.'

'Okay. I could burn patterns into the velvet? That could be nice.'

When we left I said to Jasmine, 'Imagine you being friends with a lady who's lived so long.'

'Why?'

I could see the back of her head in the mirror and she was carrying the bin bag of charity clothes at her side.

'Because you're only nineteen and you're always trying to top yourself!'

She laughed. But as we rode the lift back down to the ground floor, I took her hand.

'You're the best part of her week. You can see how much she waits for it. She'd have really missed you if you'd died.'

She looked genuinely stricken. 'I hadn't thought of that. But I wasn't going to succeed.'

'Well, can you just stop trying now? It's boring.'

'I agree.' She looked at me, absolutely serious. 'I won't do it again.'

Feeling overwhelmed by what I might have just achieved, I called my mum to say I wouldn't be coming home that night. Jasmine's red lips curled upwards like a cellophane fish when she heard me make the call.

'You've won,' I said.

'I always win,' she answered, 'apart from all the ways I lose.'

Chapter 10

It was the first time I'd stayed with Jasmine without asking her or being asked. I stayed because we both assumed I would. She fed the cats, made us Welsh rarebit with extra mustard, poured champagne and turned on the telly.

Diana and Charles had been photographed looking out into the Adriatic Ocean from a yacht. If the idea of ocean breeze and a huge boat in motion would suggest jeans and a white peasant blouse, that wasn't the way she went. He was wearing a suit and tie and she a pearl choker and cream two-piece dotted with blue and orange flowers.

'Is that silk?'

'I hope so. I hope it isn't rayon.'

'I don't think they'd let her, do you?'

'I don't think so, because it would be so likely to stain with sweat out there with all that heat.'

'Is it hot there, now?'

'You'd have to think so.'

We didn't have smartphones or computers to jump online and check and neither of us had seen a newspaper in days.

'She needs one of our hand-painted fans.'

The fact that we'd never got round to making the fans energised her and she started getting excited about the dress I was meant to make.

'Let's do a fitting!'

I think she felt a bit restless and just wanted to take off her clothes in front of me, me being as good as anybody. I got from her wardrobe the dress as it so far existed, which is to say it was two rather sad strips of neglected fabric, and I draped them across her, moving the taffeta this way and that, trying to make it come to life, which can be a challenge with a fabric that heavy. But I got the shape I wanted – punk rock Greek goddess, Diana on her yacht looking out to sea and Debbie in her Rapture – and I put in a few fat stitches to hold my idea together, then carefully peeled it off over her head.

Her breasts were small, her tummy flat, and her bottom and thighs round. She was strong and slim at the same time in a way you more often find with American women. She caught me looking at her and smiled, slicing through that silly opinion with her cut-glass accent.

'Ever been with a girl?'

I put back the dress, attempting to tuck away with it her line of questioning.

'I've never been with anyone.'

'When you find your Knight in Shining Armour, how will you know how to kiss him?'

I blushed. I was still facing away from her but I knew my neck was blushing, too, and that she could see it. The idea that someone might exist who would one day take me away from myself was so over-whelming I could have sunk to my knees. Instead, I went back to the sofa and sat down.

She turned off the TV and knelt before me. 'Let me kiss you, oh please!'

I was so afraid, so longing and so mortified, I looked down at the carpet. Art deco roses, red blooms on black, with a turquoise border. The best carpet I'd ever seen. You often notice something lovely when you're feeling crushed with shame. She put her fingers on my chin and very slowly tilted my face upwards. For a blink of an eye, it looked to me like there were half-moons on her nails.

Then she kissed me, her tongue creeping into my mouth. I kissed her back, trying to copy her tongue.

'Relax it.'

I tried. As we were locked together, I wanted to ask who her friends were, where her friends were? Her real friends. Nobody had visited her in the hospital.

Suddenly she jumped back and leapt triumphantly in the air with one of her pogo movements.

'You're going to be great! Who will it be? Your first kiss?'

'Wasn't it you? Just now? Technically?'

'Oh, I don't count. No, you mustn't count me.'

I felt hurt because I kind of wanted to count her. It wasn't a joke or a trick to me. We'd kissed because we'd been wanting to kiss for a while. That's how it was in my head. I got up and turned off the TV. Poor passionless Diana and her unromantic honeymoon. Cut-glass accents and dry lips.

'Who was your first kiss?' I asked Jasmine.

She scooped up our dishes from dinner and put them in the sink. 'A friend of my father's.'

I didn't know what to say.

'They were having a raucous party. He was handsome. He was old. A Spanish count, I'm pretty sure he was a count. Beautiful penis. Not that I'd know, I'd never seen one before he showed me his. I knew there was no way it would fit inside any part of me and he was so nice about that and we didn't have to, I could just touch it. He was drunk. So was I, obviously. That's why he picked his moment, I suppose.'

'Where was your dad?'

'On the balcony smoking a spliff, probably.' She pointed to the sofa. 'Jagger was sitting there. Right there.'

'Mick or Bianca?'

She looked at me like I was demented. 'Mick. Though you are quite correct to keep a soft spot for her suits. So when do you reckon my dress will be ready, then? Can I have it by next month?'

She didn't say anything else about her first kiss, and I didn't ask.

But something was still on her mind.

'Let's call my dad.'

I hadn't seen him since the time we'd gone to Portobello, and she'd carried on as if it wasn't a big deal. And maybe it hadn't been to her, but it was now. She tried calling but there was no reply. She tried two times, three. She let it ring and ring.

'I can't keep up with all the numbers that man has.'

She tried to stay cool. 'I reckon he'd be in St-Tropez this time of year, maybe Portofino. But that means he'll be stopping through London sooner or later. We have to do a meet-up again.' She said, too cheerfully, 'You'll love him when you get to know him.'

'I already think he's something special.'

Which of course he was. You don't get to behave the way he behaves if you aren't in some way special. People like that, you tut, 'They think they're so special.' And they do. They think it and they are.

As she tried to steer herself back to joyfulness, she began the now recognisable swing into mania: 'I want to revive the personalised cigarette case! Beautiful mother-of-pearl engraving in a twenty-four-carat gold case, with rubies dotted over the "i", if there is an "i" in your lover's name. Wouldn't that be wonderful? Make it a token of love, like it used to be.'

'But now people just think of death, I suppose.'

'But that's so glamorous! When we go to Paris, I'm going to take you to the Père Lachaise cemetery. They say Abelard and Eloise are buried there and you can kiss Oscar Wilde's tomb. It's covered in lipstick prints.'

Though I could tell she was happy to be alive, she was still not out of love with the thought of suicide. I suppose she intended to always have it in her back pocket, to smack down on the card table with a flourish, to know everyone was always going to whip their head round at the sound, always wanting to see which card she had laid down.

'I don't think so. The connotation of cigarette cases isn't just death, it's cancer. Loads of it. I've seen my uncle go through that, it was horrible.' Sometimes I thought I might be too prudish to make it as a great designer or really a great anything.

'Oh, yes, my mother, too, that's why she did what she did.'

'I thought… sorry, I thought she did it because your father left her?'

'Yes, exactly, he left her because she had cancer. Then she did it.'

There was still mania in her voice, which might have registered, incorrectly, to an outsider as excitement.

'Jesus.' I said, without an exclamation at the end because I felt as depressed as I did surprised.

'Anyway, you could have your lover's initials studded into the case with diamonds right there in the store. And coral? You could choose diamonds, coral, turquoise, mix them up, give them something to differentiate themselves from all the other schmos in love.'

'I always like opals.'

'No opal. Never opal. It's bad luck, right through the centuries, didn't you know that?'

I raised my hands in a Woody Allen gesture, which, as the years progressed and I came to dislike him, I would adjust to a Larry David gesture.

'We only need a very small space, cigarette cases are so slim. The store should mimic that, just as you want a jewellery shop to look like a jewel box. Hmmm. We could really do this.'

'Okay.' At this point I was just agreeing with her, in a trance from the story she'd just told.

'I want to talk to my father, have him sign on as a backer.'

'Do we need him?'

'We don't, but I just think he'd be so excited, he'd want to and it is, technically, his money.'

'I could put some money in, too.' Obviously, I was not going to put in any of my money, a) because it was a pipe dream and b) because I had none. But I still smarted when she said, 'Where would you get money?'

She didn't mean it how it sounded. Or maybe she did. She was so generous a soul, her occasional shards of anger or cruelty seemed to catch her as much by surprise as they did me. But the weight of words is like the weight of a fabric: if she'd have said, 'Where would you get the money?' instead of the emphasis on 'you', it would all have hung differently. She seemed to know, and hurried back to the idea itself.

'It's so out of time, that's what I love about it. Don't you feel that way about you and me?'

'I feel that way, sometimes, often, and I can't speak for you but yes, I see it in you.'

'No, I mean us, as a couple.'

'I suppose I don't think of us as a couple.'

'Oh,' she said, and stubbed out her cigarette in the fried egg she'd added to her Welsh rarebit. 'I do.'

I'd have felt sad for her but she speared the egg so brutally through the heart of its yolk, I felt worse for her dinner than for her. I'm not sure if she did ever mention it to her father. We never talked about the couture cigarette-case shop ever again.

'Oh, maybe after you've finished my dress, you could make him something. He's got the funniest body, all sinewy and barrel-chested and all he eats is milk, gallons and gallons of milk.'

'Like David Bowie in his cocaine psychosis era.'

'Exactly!' Then she thought about this and looked sad.

'Do you want the dress I'm making you to be a deep scarlet red?'

'Titian red. Have you ever seen a Titian up close?'

'In books, at the library.'

'Why haven't you been in person?'

'Art galleries are too romantic to walk through alone.'

'But being by yourself is the most romantic! That's what I think. Well. You must see one.'

'Okay.' I didn't mention how often her thoughts on solitude changed.

'No, I mean right now. You can't get the dress right if you don't see the Titian.'

I told her all the galleries were closed. She agreed, but thankfully, she knew someone who actually owned one. A colonel in Belgravia, who seemed pleased to see her and not at all upset about being dropped in on at ten o'clock. He had an empty bottle of cognac on the table, but he offered us some of it anyway.

'He was in the army with my dad!'

'The navy.'

'Oh, you're an admiral?'

'Of course. Why else do you think they call me "Admiral"?'

'I thought it was a nickname.'

The Titian looked down on us, warily, her red hair screaming 'bed head' and 'I would like to be allowed to go to mine, can you fuck off, please?'

'Steven is a genius and he can make you clothes.'

'Hmmm.'

'Give him your admiral's hat, to copy.'

The admiral seemed doubtful.

'It's just to inspire him.'

'But I already gave him a look at my Titian.'

'Go on. Do it.'

And, as soon as she said, 'Do it,' he did, handing the hat to me without moving from his chair, his arm

154

appearing to extend like a novelty fork. I thanked him. The hat smelled, but was beautifully constructed.

Then she hailed a taxi and took us back to hers where she tucked me in for the night in the bed her dad had slept in.

'This room is only for very special people.'

When I woke up she had a mug of tea before her and was wearing the dress-in-process.

'I think you need a dart here, just beneath the bust. Don't you agree?'

I wiped my bleary eyes. She handed me some safety pins and I tried to make sense of the line without sticking her.

As I pinned, she sucked in the air as if standing astride a mountain. 'I think an artist reaches greatness when they start work before breakfast.'

I nodded, not quite seeing or hearing properly as yet. She hovered relentlessly, hassling me to get on with the day. She'd obviously been up for hours, probably watching me sleep and making small noises in the hope that would wake me, without actually shaking me awake. She was wearing a denim all-in-one romper in the style of Farrah Fawcett, but she'd added a feather showgirl plume to her bun. It was a look I'd now call *Charlie's Angels* meets Angela Carter.

I got myself together as best I could and, as the world came into focus, so did my guilt. I knew I was overdue to call Mum. I knew she'd be worried by now.

'Hi, Mum!'

'Oh my God! It's you!'

Her tone spoke of a separation across generations, Odyssean in its stretch. I'd called her before I'd gone to bed, telling her exactly where I was, but in our dynamic I'd allowed her to drift into anxiety. Hers fed mine until I started worrying about where I was and whether or not I was safe. I promised I'd be home by dinner. Jasmine took the phone from me before I'd said my full goodbyes (my goodbyes to my mother taking the back-and-forth shuffle of someone who declares they're leaving a dinner party and then doesn't). I'd have made fun of Mum and my part in this dance, but I knew she was also, somewhere in her worry for my safe return, still the child of Holocaust survivors. That was there, even when it wasn't.

Jasmine got us out of the door and into a cab, and it was only when we were hurtling towards Mayfair that I saw the bag, at her feet, full of all the clothes she'd stolen at the charity shop.

She went from boutique to boutique, placing an item on the racks, between £1,000 jackets and crocodile-skin handbags.

As we left Chanel, I hissed, 'This must be illegal! It's like shoplifting, somehow.'

'No. It's not. We're shop-dropping. I don't see anything wrong with it.'

'Then why are we being so secretive?'

'Because that's what makes it fun. Don't you want to have secrets with me?'

When the bag was empty she was very pleased with herself, a woman who'd put in a hard day's work. The duplicity had made me terrified and her hungry.

'I'm famished!' she said, and guided me towards Claridge's. Flags waved us towards the rotating glass doors, and I felt we were stragglers at the end of a long race. The hotel's flag was draped alongside the flags of the UK and Ireland, as if the hotel were itself a country. Red brick, marble and wrought iron were layered against each other so evocatively they could have been parsley, sage, rosemary and thyme. If you rubbed against them, the cool of the marble, the brick dust, the metallic smell would stay on your skin for days.

'Imagine this building when it's dusted in snow!'

Jasmine waited a beat to be certain I was imagining, and then she led me in, a man in a black top hat watchful as we entered the heavy revolving door. You can't really hold a revolving door for someone, but you can be respectfully present as they navigate it.

Stairs of gilded brass spilled across the black-and-white chequerboard floor, thick wood bannisters burst forth like beloved porn-star erections. Above our heads was the most elaborate plasterwork, which I craned my neck back to study.

'It's called crown moulding, okay?' like she'd caught me staring at her arse and was snapping back.

My eyes were wide at the sight of the hundred-year-old lobby, but she pulled me past the Fumoir, where men were smoking cigars, as if we were just dashing into Tesco's for a sandwich. I thought I recognised Marie Helvin among the cigar smokers, lights proffered from all sides. 'Yes, it's her,' said Jasmine, without my asking.

'How exciting!'

'Oh, that's the least of it. As you know, this is where the West German chancellor negotiated reparations for the Jews, post-Holocaust.'

I didn't know, but I nodded, then started to ask where the toilets were. I am always desperate to see the toilets in a posh place (I still am).

'And where are the… ?'

'Yes, I know what you're asking: room 212 was ceded to Yugoslavia for one day so Crown Prince Alexander could be born on Yugoslav soil while his parents were in exile.'

Sometimes she knew what I wanted. Sometimes not. I held my wee as she marched me towards the tea room.

The great fashion illustrator David Downton was yet to be in residence at Claridge's, but it already felt like the women around us at tea were elegant pencil sketches.

I thought the hostess would be bothered by Jasmine's punk make-up but she cried: 'Jasmine! We've missed you!'

Perhaps the flags waving as we entered the building had been waiting since she last visited, half-mast, for her return.

You can do anything at all if you're rich enough, you can wear anything. You can smell terrible, you can walk in with two different shoes. Oud, that killer ingredient, the most expensive component in the most luxurious perfumes, is made of whale vomit or elephant sperm, maybe fox shit, I forget, but I know it smells terrible yet somehow makes everything around it smell better. Because it's *rich*.

She settled deep into a tufted chair to admire her own childhood through rose spectacles. 'I've been coming here since I was still a little girl.'

I wanted to say, 'You still are a little girl.' Especially after watching the delight with which she greeted the eclairs and Battenburg. She squealed. And then she cut them up and arranged them into a tableau. The she scoffed the lot, offering me every fourth bite. Because of her, I know that beautiful girls can eat whatever they like; they just have to set their minds to it.

She enjoyed pouring the tea, as if wrestling back the status of parent between the two of us, after my scolding her for misbehaving in the boutiques.

'Milk in first?' she admonished me. 'Where were you raised? Bow?' Then she giggled and tried to get me to sit on her knee. When the pencil-sketch ladies turned to stare, she engaged them in conversation.

'I love your brooch!'

'Thank you,' the eldest, white-haired and wicker thin, said, disarmed. Soon enough Jasmine was trying it on and after that the lady had given it to her. I've never forgotten that: how to engage someone who's about to take against you. It's been useful in my career, because it isn't just whether you're skilled or not at your craft, it is how you handle people or, at minimum, find a way not to be around people you know you can't handle.

We finally went to the bathroom to pee and she insisted I come to the ladies' room with her because I had to see the wallpaper. I was delighted. Gold on black, raised deco welts I couldn't help running my fingers over. I'm not going to lie. It was one of the most beautiful things I'd ever seen, London's best toilet, something I'd covet for the rest of my life, and almost worth what happened next.

As we returned from the ladies' room, we heard the shout: 'Everybody get on the floor!'

She tugged me to the floor, landing us right by a table leg. I was very close to tears, thinking that not only would I die, but that my mum had been right to have sounded so worried for my safety. Was it her sixth sense? Or was it that if you worried about everything you would one day be right?

Everyone dug in their bags for their wallets and got out the money they had. The old ladies. The romantic couple. The afternoon drunk. Even the maître d' and the waiters. The robber had chosen the perfect venue at the right time of day to make a mint. He went around the patrons collecting their offerings one by one, like a very rude Underground performer.

'This is so exciting!' mouthed Jasmine.

When the robber got to us, I was quaking in my boots and gave him everything I had. When Jasmine handed him the paltry twenty that was in her wallet, he looked at it, looked at her, double-checked her bag and then handed the cash back. 'Keep it. You need this more than I do.'

'But I'm rich!' she said. 'I'm really rich!'

'She is,' I concurred and he stomped me with his shoe.

It did now seem like I might be about to die. I closed my eyes and thought of the gorgeous wallpaper in the ladies' room. First, I had it fill the screensaver of my mind, and then I imagined myself inside it. I was flying on the back of one of the art deco egrets.

Not wanting to be left out, Jasmine handed him the brooch she'd been gifted fifteen minutes earlier by the pencil-sketch lady. Then, while the man was counting up what he'd made, she reached an arm up onto a tea tray still on the table, and filched a Battenburg slice.

'That's a Battenburg slice,' I whispered, not believing what I was seeing.

'Would you rather the meringue? But I thought it might crunch and alert them to us.'

'Shhh.'

Then they were gone and sirens were ringing.

'How can you be so calm?' I asked her, barely able to stand.

'Oh, I'm always dying. It's nothing to me. I'm well prepped.'

As we left, photographers were already on the scene and she smiled for them as if they were from the society page rather than the crime beat. The woman who'd given us the brooch was sobbing by the now deactivated revolving door, the doorman having removed his hat, the better to comfort her. Jasmine motioned to the photographers, pointed a finger at me and shouted, 'He's a brilliant young designer. Brilliant but troubled.'

They were sensible enough not to ask us for our eyewitness account of the terror.

I was breathing so heavily still, I just managed to say, 'You were so calm. Claridge's might think you were in on it.'

'Only so much as I am aware that we live in a great metropolis and that this sort of thing is bound to happen. It's the price we pay for freedom.'

I think my mum might have spontaneously combusted at that statement, delivered like a cowboy balladeer drawling a love song through a dangling cigarette. I thought I might burst. My body was filled with the rushing sensation that alerted every nerve ending to one thought: I wanted my mother. The red brick, the cool marble, the wrought iron all now looked like weapons.

'I think I ought to go home now. Thank you very much… for everything.'

I wasn't exactly sure what I was thanking her for, it was so expansive and I wasn't sure what, if anything, I would owe her for. I thought she'd give me a big hug after all we'd been through together, so I primed my ribs, still sore from Dad's kicking, when she squeezed me too hard. But she just said '*De rien*' and gave me two air kisses. I knew what *de rien* means and even though I was unnerved by her casualness, I was glad she couldn't intimidate me by the use of French slang. It was just everything else about her that left me in awe.

It took me an age to make it back because the IRA had called in another bomb threat. I tried to call Mum from a payphone to let her know my progress and that I was trying to return to her, but the line was busy. As if psychically connected to Mum, I felt terribly worried, already in trouble for trying her nerves after not having thought of her one bit until this, the very last hour and a half before I'd reach my front door. It felt like not being able to taste any of the chocolates in the box until you get to the absolute last and then the sorrow and terror of the ending just floods you, your senses and your taste buds.

When I finally made it home, she was, of course, in a dreadful state and what really made me ill was that my father was comforting her. 'There there, Mama,' and turning to me, 'see what you put her through? Isn't she good to you?' while she cried into a handkerchief she'd embroidered one weekend when recovering from one of his beatings. Having worked so hard to get home, I wanted to leave immediately.

I was trapped by the places already set with their knives and forks and spoon at the top, by the mushy peas set in front of me, the pie and mash, by the fucking football on the television and my father and brothers cheering and shouting at the screen, interspersed by bananas and custard and me trying not to gag when I got to a lump. My brother saying I was putting it on and me saying, 'No, it really is making me feel queasy. Why would I fake that?'

'To taunt your poor mother,' said Dad, and patted her hand.

I looked him in the eye. I was still bruised and swollen on my face and holding his gaze would force him to see, to see how much I hated him and that I knew what he really was, that as much as he hated himself deep inside, it wasn't enough. But he just looked down at his peas.

During the robbery, I thought I was terrified, but I must have been slightly less afraid than I'd thought, because my brain had wandered, when the robber stomped me, to how horrid to be stomped by a mass-produced shoe.

That night, I took apart the Titian admiral's hat, and then sewed it back together.

CHAPTER 11

They were short-staffed at her shop, so Jasmine was unavailable for a few days. When I couldn't stand home any more, I asked if I could come meet her at work. She gave me the address.

Outside Marble Arch Tube, evangelical Christians were calling through megaphones. 'Sin!' they shouted, like they were hawking it at a discounted summer rate. I wanted to make them an offer. Saudi men in neon shorts were trailed by women in black niqabs. Occasionally, they'd cross paths with a Hassidic man in his glossy curls and fur-covered U.F.O hat (as fabulous as anything Grace Jones would wear), while his wife bore the sadness of her lifeless wig and worn-down loafers. These couples were the purest interpretation of birds in the wild, the males strutting peacocks, the females muted. It bothered me. I wondered if, to balance, the men had grey, sad, underwear and the women's lingerie was pastel fancies.

Jehovah's Witnesses stood silently beside their piles of *Watchtower* magazines. The religious groups were too close to each other, unconnected but touching tendrils. I wanted them separated, like a child with autism separating her peas from her mash from her chicken. Perhaps I was just envious that they had a belief system (the child with autism as much as the religious extremists).

I passed a tatty souvenir shop and then another as I followed the numbers to Jasmine's shop. A pigeon walked alongside me from the first shop to the second, like a decorous suitor.

When I got to the third tourist shop, with its 'My brother went to London and all I got was this lousy T-shirt' T-shirts, toy double-decker buses, miniature replicas of Big Ben, Diana and Charles mugs – I went in to ask for help because, no matter how I tried, I couldn't find her store. There must be, I assumed, a Little Marble Arch or a Marble Arch Place. I'd written it down wrong. When I saw Jasmine behind the till, I assumed she was a mirage. But then she spoke. 'Hi, darling!'

'What are you doing here?'

'I'm at work.'

I tried to orient myself. When I thought I was looking at bad pun T-shirts, was I actually looking at the new Malcolm McLaren/Vivienne Westwood collection and not realising it? But then a German toddler ran over my foot with a motorised Margaret Thatcher, and the pain brought the room into focus.

'This is the shop?'

'Yes. I told you your clothes wouldn't fit in here.'

'And rightly so.'

'And I told you I wasn't a snob. You should have believed me.'

Yes, I nodded, speechless, as she went to help a tourist. (I couldn't describe them as customers. What was the custom? I've bought from souvenir shops since then, in other countries. But in your own country, the idea of in any way interacting with national-themed kitsch, be it as buyer or seller, was something I couldn't wrap my head around.)

The German mother of the toddler bought bobbleheads of the Queen and Queen Mother and then, as she handed her traveller's cheque over the till, Jasmine persuaded her to buy bobbleheads of the Sex Pistols too, all four of them.

'I think no, thank you. I think they frighten my son.'

'But, my God, there's no one more terrifying than the Queen Mother! No, darling, no! You want an authentic British souvenir? Only a Brit could be as turned on by Johnny Rotten as they are by an ancient castle or country garden. It's our greatest strength. It would be the ultimate British purchase. Friends would say, "How was your trip?" and you'd just whip out the bobbleheads, and walk away whistling.'

Then she mimed walking away, whistling as she circled the till, until she was back behind it.

The mother looked dazzled, Jasmine selling her on the bobbleheads like a Selfridges shop girl can sell you on age-delay moisturiser.

After they left, a Saudi man came in. Jasmine hissed under her breath, 'Ugh, he comes in every day. It's like he's stockpiling kitsch for the apocalypse.'

I ate a piece of chocolate-covered shortbread in the shape of Tom Baker. 'There is a lot of End is Nigh around here.'

As the mega-tourist approached her, she turned on a smile so convincing it made me suddenly fearful she might not genuinely like me.

'Oh hello, again!'

He nodded. 'I've come for your number.'

Her voice changed size and shape. 'It's on the front of the store. Where's your wife? How did she like her Eurovision tea towels?'

He repeated again, like a man with one of those End is Nigh sandwich boards: 'I've come for your number.'

'I'm nineteen years old.'

'That's not too old. I've come for your number.'

He stared right into her eyes, which I could have told him was like looking directly into the sun.

'I'm not going to give it to you, you dirty old man.'

He blinked at her as if there had been a malfunction, as if this line usually worked. When she failed to re-boot, he said very quietly, 'Western whore,' and she laughed and said, 'That's my superhero name.'

And this confused him, and he left before she could throw a Bucks Fizz Buck's Fizz shaker at his head.

'Creep,' I sympathised, when he was gone, but I noticed her cheeks had turned bright red.

'I had a Jordanian boyfriend at school, son of the ambassador. He went home to the Middle East right before our A levels. He had depression; his family thought he just needed more sun. I feel, if the Hashemites hadn't lost control of Mecca to the House of Saud in 1924, he might not have been such a terribly sad boy. You carry these tragedies through generations.'

Then she shrugged her shoulders and started to cleanse the shop with sage, waving it in all four corners. The kitsch combined with the smell was a potent and horrible place to be trapped.

'His energy can't have been that powerful.'

'I do this every night before I close the shop.'

As we walked, arm in arm to the Tube, I asked, 'How did you get the job?'

She held her hand to the railing as she walked down the steps of the station. It wasn't like her to hold on.

'It was after the last suicide attempt. Not the one where we met, but the one before that. The psychiatrist said it would be a good idea to take a menial job where I didn't have time to let my brain lose itself in dark corners.'

The Tube map was a tangle of jewelled spaghetti.

'It didn't completely work.'

'There was a full year between attempts. It must have been doing something helpful. So I've kept it.'

When we were in our seats, the Jubilee line making that Tardis sound as it was about to leave the station, I turned to her and said, 'You know a lot about the history of Mecca. And classical Arabic music...'

'That's all from my dad.'

'Don't you think you should do something with all that knowledge? It seems crazy that you're not in university.'

'You know me. I don't make things last.'

I wondered if she wasn't just worried about not being the brightest star there.

'And I don't want to be around all those Hoorays.'

'Poor people make it to university, too. You wouldn't know if you didn't go.'

She started to daydream.

'Edinburgh or Glasgow would have been nice, I suppose. Beautiful architecture. Bath, ancient Roman history.'

She felt strange about being led to consider an alternative way she could be passing her time, and I felt strange about having seen her behind that till. We didn't stay together that night.

My mother, fearing how the summer holidays drag out and knowing my father was on the rampage, had enrolled us in the local youth club. I tried to be stoical. Despite the name-calling I'd likely experience and the inevitable shunning by my brothers, at least I could pilfer art supplies. If I was lucky, there might be a sewing machine.

It felt really weird to be around normal kids my age after my time with Jasmine. The high had been so high that, even though there *was* a sewing machine, this was truly a new low. I'd told myself every day of the term that this was my final year at school, that this daily torment would soon be over. But that nearby relief wasn't soon enough now I was in youth club with the taste still on my tongue of what the world could be.

The walls were dotted with pictures of local junior boxers who'd done well at the nationals. But it didn't matter how well any of our local boxers did; in their thirties they all aged into coaching and fat. Once the physical exercise was over but the Walnut Whips remained, their bodies changed shape in a hostile takeover that haunted both the former boxer and the community. 'Such a shame,' the boys' parents world whisper, while bringing them gifts of cakes to thank them for their coaching.

I would sit out football matches like an Austen heroine yet to meet her true love. Thinking of footballers signing photos of themselves made me return to the notion I had in my head of signing my autograph, over and over, because young people – much lovelier young people than this – had waited in the rain to meet me. They had me sign the soles of the shoes I'd designed (I'd never designed a shoe in any of my drawings but I imagined it would be sensible to franchise).

Some designers lose their name when they take a misstep. Diane von Furstenberg had lost hers so entirely that even my mum wore her wrap dresses that were no longer made by her. My dad had a Pierre Cardin pen that he took out for special occasions even though it was no less pedestrian than any other ballpoint. But it had someone's name on it.

Jews had always been the centre of the rag trade. They'd worked so many generations as tailors that there is a phenomenon called 'tailor's thumb', a genetic quirk where the thumb is a set at an angle frozen from endless hours of sewing. I was sad I didn't have it. But that was the closest I came to seeking ties with my community. I was not going to go to the girdle shop in Bethnal Green. Mum kept saying she bet she could set me up with them and we could put our heads together. I'd avoided this for as long as I could.

After the football I'd skipped (not just because I was bad at it, but because there was a load of coloured crepe paper secreted in my shoe) I pushed my fork around my plate of repulsive food, trying to make sense of what it was meant to be in the first place before I unpeeled its odd corners and dough, its interior flakes of possibly fish. My efforts were interrupted by the arrival of two nasty boys from my class at school, whose names I knew well but one of whom my mind has since then blocked.

'What you doing here, yid? This is a youth club and you're an old man.'

'Don't sell him short. He's not only a yid, he's also a fag.'

'You're Jewish, too!' I said to the second tormentor, an unfortunate boy named Allan Furst, destined always to come larst. 'And you wear spectacles!' I happen to think spectacles are very stylish, but I wasn't telling him that. I could see they were surprised

I was answering back at all. At school I turned on my heel or shrunk into the wall.

'What's got into you?'

'You know you can fight back less now we know what happened at the royal wedding?

'What happened?' I shot back.

'I heard you were so overcome by the glory of her wedding dress that you fainted and had to be taken to hospital in an ambulance.'

'Yeah,' I said. 'That's it. That's exactly what happened. I wish you hadn't found out. I'm really embarrassed now.'

This confused them, more, my copping to the lie and beyond that, confessing an emotional reaction. I wiggled my toes over the secret crepe paper, as if it were one of Jasmine's moon-charged crystals giving me powers. They were so used to me whimpering, 'You won't make me cry,' while I held back any sign of tears.

Then things started to make less sense – to me and my tormentors. To my very great delight and horror, I saw, entering the dining room, Jasmine herself. It made no sense whatsoever and I assumed her to be a mirage induced by the fumes emanating from the dessert that had just been brought out, paper plates of spotted dick. But then she sat down next to me on the bench. She had on her full pile of make-up, with the bat wings that made her whole face take flight.

'Who's this then?' Allan Furst asked.

'I'm just a girl enrolled for the summer in your youth club.'

'No she's not. I'd remember her!'

He was talking to me, refusing to address her directly. That's when I saw her power in action on a kid other than myself. He didn't want to make eye contact.

'Hard to forget that make-up!' he said to his nameless friend.

'Or that arse!' answered no-name.

'No, I don't like being talked to like that,' said Jasmine, sitting up straight.

'Lucky I wasn't talking to you!' But Allan Furst couldn't help himself. 'Who are you?' He was still looking at me when he asked.

'I'm an avenging angel. But I'm his.' She pointed at me. 'I belong to him. So budge up.'

'Oh la-di-da, are we?' scoffed no-name.

'Oh yes, very much, I am quite la-di-da. Will that be all?'

They were so confused that they left us alone and retired to their own table to commence strangulated whispers.

'Oh my God, Jasmine. Why are you here?'

'I suppose you scored the winning goal in soccer?'

I felt like every single eye in the room was on us, and others that had yet even to start attending the club.

'There's some decent art supplies in the cupboard.'

'I know,' I answered. 'That's the only decent thing about this place.' If I told her straight, would she leave? Did I want her to leave?

'Oh, excellent!'

Allan Furst came back to try again.

'You're not from our school. What school are you from?'

She didn't even look up. 'Darling, I'd forgive you barging in, but it's very rude to talk with your mouth full. Chew like a bunny. Here, look.'

And she mimed how a rabbit would chew, circling her mouth like a hula dancer.

'Oh, your mum taught you manners?'

'Darling, she did, but she's dead now.'

'Really?'

'Quite dead. Manners are her greatest legacy to me.'

'Your stupid make-up? Is that good manners?'

'You can't ask me to explain to you. It's like trying to explain what it is to be a member of a society. Do you want to be part of one?'

He looked scared. 'I don't know what you're talking about.'

'Then turn back to your luncheon. Spit-spot!'

'Did you just say "spit-spot"?'

She squeezed my hand. 'Is he still talking?'

I nodded. The clock on the wall moved its arm as incrementally as water in a lake. I knew it must be happening, but it was not visible to the naked eye.

I poked at my spotted dick. She took a big bite. I almost gagged, watching her.

'How can you? Shouldn't we be eating, like, macaroons in sorbet colours?'

'It's macarons. And one can't eat only macarons. One can't have tasted the absolute best of everything by the age of nineteen. What would there be to live for?'

She allowed herself a small smile and I knew she had wandered, accidentally, into talking about herself. She took a big breath and tried to summon her good cheer. I could tell when she was doing it. Her eyes appeared to darken, from pale blue to Indian ink. That's why I use so much of that colour in my patterns. To remind myself how hard she tried, really, really did try to be well and happy.

She took in the faded pictures of the faded junior boxers. 'Oh, it's all so deliciously degraded here! I love it!'

Terry, the youth supervisor, came out of the kitchen and towards us. I could see him clocking her, first that he didn't know her, then that she had terrible make-up, and finally, that she was very beautiful. He tucked that thought away like it was a shirt tail hanging out. His shirt tail was hanging out.

'Can I help you, miss?'

'Ms, if you please. It's been in common usage since 1968 but was used by the *New York Times* in an article only recently. They are the paper of record. If it's

176

good enough for them, it should be good enough for us...' She looked around the room, '... here.'

Terry, who was in his late twenties, looked around as if taking in for the first time ever just how shit our club was. The scales thus fallen from his eyes, he excused himself. He actually said, 'Excuse me,' and she said, 'It was a pleasure,' and she didn't laugh when he left, but made a sad face and said, 'What a tormented soul. He rather reminds me of Kenneth Williams.'

I don't think I knew to feel sorry for the people I perceived as my tormentors until I met Jasmine. You gain so much power when you start to feel sorrier for them than you do for yourself. I felt completely differently about my dad after Jasmine. I could barely look at him any more, but it wasn't from fear now, it was from embarrassment. It felt horrible to see how much ugliness he lived inside. That doesn't mean I forgave him or ever will. There are a few people in life – just a few – whom one ought never to forgive. If it's not hurting you to hold on to your resentment, you can let it be the corners of your moral compass. North, south, east and west. Save yourself four people you don't forgive (you don't have to know them all. I never forgave Thatcher, even when she was dying of dementia).

'Remember the food that we had in the hospital?'

'Shhh,' I said. 'I don't want them to know how we met.'

'Why ever not?'

'Because it makes both of us look pathetic.'

'Well, speak for yourself.' Now her voice got louder. 'Suicide has been the choice of many great thinkers and artists, from Ernest Hemingway to Diane Arbus.'

'It's been the choice of a lot of nutters, too.'

She stood up.

'I'm sorry. Jasmine, I'm sorry. Don't leave me here.'

But she was smiling. 'Come with me.'

I looked at the clock, knowing, by the fact I was eating lunch, that it was only lunch time. 'The day's not done here yet. My mother pre-paid.'

'I've seen all I need to see here. I get it, and so do you. Come along, we need to cleanse our minds, perform some mental hygiene. Ooh, we could just make it into the West End in time to catch a matinee.'

Chapter 12

Oh, to be weightless.

The dancers floated in the air like the trick with lit amaretto wrappers at the end of a boozy dinner party. The men were amaretto wrappers too. The heaviest thing on them was their make-up, and you couldn't even tell that until you saw the photos in the programme.

No wonder every designer of any real significance wants, at some point, to design for a ballet. That moment when you first felt free. People who move exactly as you do in your own dreams, when you look at your friends and family and say, 'I forgot to tell you, when I run and jump, I can hover in the air for many long moments. It just comes naturally to me.' Even with success, nothing beats that moment, and the memory of it is bittersweet. Like amaretto.

I loved the dancers. I loved the dance. I loved the stage and the curtains at the side of the stage. I knew the auditorium was full of people but I couldn't describe any of them now, I was so focused on memorising every detail of the performance.

Le Jeune Homme et la Mort. The Young Man and Death. Why did she take us to see a ballet about suicide? Of anything we could have seen? Because she was still fascinated? Because it made her feel alive? In control? On the edge between worlds? Or because it was on at a time we could make it and it wasn't sold out?

Death was played by a dancer with the longest arms and legs I could imagine working in ballet. She was different from any of the other women we'd seen perform: a tall ballerina. But the poor, tormented suicidee, weakened as he was by sorrow, could still lift her above his head. The world Jasmine had chosen for us today was one where even the weakest had the strength to protect themselves.

'This!' she'd said. 'This is the perfect thing for a Wednesday afternoon!' And it was, because it was beautiful, because it made me cry. The first time I'd cried in front of her. She put a tissue in my hand then used her own hand to move my hand across my cheeks and wipe my tears.

'Beautiful boy,' she whispered. 'That's why I love you.'

I was loved.

In the dark, surrounded by strangers, Jasmine squeezing my hand.

I was loved.

By the first person who wasn't my mother. It was cataclysmic. And as the feeling rushed over me, the boy onstage ascended to the sky, a noose around his neck, his feet kicking, his dance over. The woman playing Death removed the mask from her face and placed it over his. It was sensory overload – to be loved, to be heartbroken, to be astonished by art, to be inspired and devastated by it, to want to end it all, to want to live for ever. It was, I imagined, how Jasmine spent much of her days feeling. All of that. Too much. Of course there'd be times when you felt invincible and others when you just wanted to lie down and sleep and sleep.

Afterwards, Jasmine said she wanted to go backstage to say hello to one of the dancers. Evening had fallen and the audience pulled their expensive coats across their mostly aged shoulders. The young people were beautiful and in love. Like us.

She told the stage manager she was here to see Ekaterina Spiv. 'Who's Ekaterina Spiv?' I asked. I flipped through the programme; a minor dancer in the corps. When the stage manager left to relay the message, Jasmine walked right past him. Seeing that I had not followed, she beckoned me and I took a moment to decide whether to leave her there or follow. I fucking followed.

I Fucking Followed. The name of my memoir, should I ever give in and write one.

She led me up the stairs and into the attic. There were score of costumes, boxed away and hanging out in protective plastic. She ran her fingers along them.

'Don't you want to see them?'

'No. I mean, yes, but. They're not for us to touch. See?'

There was a sign that said 'Do Not Touch'.

'There was also a sign that said "No Entry" and you ignored that.

'I did not ignore it, you made me.'

She was unzipping the dress and trying it on.

'Your breasts are far too large for a dancer, you'll never fit inside.'

I sighed, I couldn't bear to see a costume being yanked about like that.

'Let me help you.'

I ever so gently undid the fastening and told her to turn sideways as she wriggled in. I'd seen it in forties' guides to getting into girdles. Rita Hayworth did it in *Gilda*; Glenn Ford looks like he works in a pet store. That's what I saw when I was reflected at her side. They got that guy because they couldn't get the guy they'd actually wanted for the role.

She sucked in her tummy, then stuck it out again. She looked at herself in the mirror and did a belly dance.

'Jasmine, I feel like we're being disrespectful.'

'To who?'

'To these valuable clothes!'

'I think it's respectful. They've been sitting up here, all alone. We're keeping them company.'

I did notice that the attic room the costumes were stored in looked rather like my attic room, and it made me feel sorry for them. I ran my hand along the leotards.

'Haven't you been waiting a long time to have someone keep you company?'

I nodded, yes, ashamed, but she was on to the next thought.

'Do you think the male dancers are good in bed or rubbish?'

'Oh I don't know.'

'Rhythmic, so that's good. But peacocking for a living, so they might be selfish lovers. I know they all smoke and get hammered.'

She paused, thought about it, looked up at the ceiling.

'Shall we smoke and get hammered?'

But in looking up, she had noticed there was a skylight with a ladder.

'I wonder what's up there?'

'The roof, obviously.'

'The roof of the London Coliseum is a dome; is that still a roof?'

'I mean... yes? It's all semantics.'

'I'd love to see it.'

'So let's go out onto the pavement and look.'

'I mean, I want to see it, from it, get up, right up close.'

I groaned. One of the highlights of her young life, she once told me, had been when she and her father went inside the Statue of Liberty; an experience that warped her both for monuments and for humans.

'You don't have to be up close to everything, not every single thing.'

She made a face. 'Yes I do,' and she reached for my hand. 'When I was a little girl, I'd say to my mother when she put me to bed: "Can you get inside me?" And she was shocked for a moment until she understood I meant, "Can you spoon me?" So she did and that's how I fell asleep.'

She disarmed me by talking about her mother, so warm and loving and gentle, and I felt heartbroken for her and that's the only reason I followed her. Except for that I'd followed her in the first place, so what was one more floor, even if it was a floor that led into the actual sky?

She led me up to the roof exit.

'We really, really can't go there. When you open the door, it's going to set off an alarm.' In truth, I liked the image of half-dressed dancers fleeing out onto the streets of London at Magic Hour.

She pushed gingerly at the door as I pressed my ears with my hands and got ready to run. No alarm.

'You're such a worrier. Are all Jews such worriers?'

'Yes. And we're right to be!'

She took me by the hand and pulled me up the staircase. It felt as treacherous as our friendship. I couldn't deny my life before her was not devoid of drama, in so much as my father had landed me in hospital after a particularly bad beating on the day Diana became the Nation's Sweetheart. But my life also felt very steady and boring laid out in front of me. Just because you get beaten up by your dad doesn't make it interesting – not to me, the beatee.

As she pulled me up I felt myself a freediver moving to the surface of the ocean with my last reserves of oxygen. I burst to the surface and gasped in the London skyline, as far as the eye could see. I have 20/20 vision. I could see far. She scrambled up the tiles around the pregnant belly of the building, and I had no choice but to follow her. Well. I could have turned around but, obviously, I didn't. I'd been so intoxicated by Jasmine these last days, the first thing that had drawn my attention from her was the city itself.

I've moaned and complained my whole life about how much I hate where I'm from. But that evening was when I fell in love with London, as London designers must do in their own way and time, before they make their name. It's usually to do with a view. Our lives feel so small, it's no loss to us to spend our days hunched over a small piece of sewing with the insularity of Talmudic scholars, making our worlds even smaller so that one day they might, from that small square of material, contract so tightly they suddenly expand. There's a reason designers, no matter how posh they end up, tend to emerge from the working class. Bruce Oldfield was a Barnardo's boy; Vivienne came out of punk; Zandra the child of a schoolteacher from Kent... just boring lives. We think staring into the fabric, the pen and ink and design book is our only way out. But it doesn't happen until you combine it with that secret ingredient: a view. It can happen on the top of Primrose Hill. On the top of a double-decker bus. Oh, I may hate everyone I know, but it's fucking wonderful here! If you have a viewpoint and a view, you will become unstoppable.

CHAPTER 13

I hoped the youth club had not called my mother. I knew they probably had.

But I didn't want to let go of my newfound London love, my ability to see the city in certain slivers from special vantage points, so I asked we ride the bus home instead of the taxi.

'Who's your favourite designer?' she asked.

'Zandra Rhodes.'

'Write her a letter.'

'I wrote her a letter, actually, but I never posted it.'

'Oh gosh, I'm the same. I write fan letters all the time and I never get round to posting them.'

When we got home, she showed me a sheaf of them. One to Kate Bush, one to Siouxsie Sioux, one to David Hockney, one to Tony Benn, MP. We spent the rest of the night finding the right addresses, licking and sticking stamps. I rewrote my letter to Zandra from memory, lightly edited to seem less insistent, admiring rather than demented. When we were done, she showed me drawings she'd done when she was a kid. They were vast landscapes, vast, all from aeroplanes.

'They're places my father has been. I painted them as I imagined they were, him looking out of the window. They're not quite right, I know he'd never take the window, he always gives it to the woman he's with, he's very old-fashioned like that, you'll notice he also stands when a woman enters or leaves the room. There's no men like that any more.'

They were lovely, dreamy, sad, endless horizons of different colours with tail wings in the corner of the frame.

'I think they're really good, Jasmine.'

'That's kind, but I have no real talent. I'm just very good at spotting it.'

'Forget about other people's talent. What could you be in the world?'

She put the pictures back in their drawer.

'I am in the world. I couldn't be more in the world.'

She laughed, but I wanted to say, 'You're a helium balloon with nobody to hold the string. You're going to fly away one day.'

'Can you stay the night?' she asked, as if she could hear what I'd kept to myself.

'I skipped youth club. I'm going to be in so much trouble with...'

'With your mum?'

'My mum's going to be upset, but I'm going to be in trouble with my dad. I think.'

'We'll deal with it. We'll deal with it. Just give me a little more time with you to myself then I'll give you back.' It was strange to be described as a possession with a value. I could see why women didn't like that, apart from the times when they did.

I picked up the phone and called my mum, my heart beating in my chest. She did not answer, nor did he, nor did anybody, to my relief and alarm and then relief again, like the bleeding colours of the horizon from an aeroplane. When you pick up a phone today, there's no weight to it, like there's no difference between holding it or not holding it. Then every conversation felt heavier, because the receiver was, and there was a truer beginning and end to it, when you put the phone back in its cradle, a fitful baby soothed back to slumber.

When we woke up the next day, we posted our fan letters. Then we went apartment hunting together in South Kensington.

'I've chosen South Ken so we can be near the V and A. That would be where one or the other of us would walk off steam if we ever got into a fight. I don't ever want to get in a fight with you, but if it happens, we need to have precautions in place.'

It wasn't clear to me whether this flat near the V&A was make-believe or serious, whether it was a fan letter written or a fan letter posted. The guy who took us around was trying to make sense of us. When she saw him looking at her legs, she kissed me and said, 'Oh darling! Don't you think it's perfect for us? We could have a nursery there!' I knew she was pretending, but it also felt like she was practising for an alternate universe.

'Do you want to have children?' I asked her, when we left.

'Of course!' she said, without hesitation. 'Of course I do.'

'Why?'

She shrugged. 'My mother was so good at it, she made it seem easy.' Then she seemed to remember that her mother can't have been 100 per cent mum of the year, her being gone by her own hand and all.

'I'd better take you home now,' she said, sadly, the princess aura having faded from her, and I half expected us to get into a pumpkin carriage, but it was just a regular black cab she flagged, like one my dad drove but a slightly newer model.

We didn't talk all the way back. The rain or her memories had fogged up the windows and she sat in silence, drawing flowers with her finger on the glass. When we got to my street, my dad's cab was in the driveway. Seeing it there, Jasmine perked up. The life drained back into her like watching a syringe being filled. The satisfying pop of air, the excitement and fear of how the liquid would feel in your veins.

'I'm going to come in with you.'

'I'm fine.'

'Why? Are you ashamed of me?'

'No. Why would I be ashamed?'

'Because I'm rich.'

190

'That's ridiculous. Of course you can come in. They won't feel good enough for you, that's all.'

But I looked at her and knew they would not recognise her raggedy glamour for its superiority, they'd just see unbrushed hair, punk make-up and bitten nails. She was right, though. I was embarrassed by her wealth. As embarrassed as often as I was excited by it. For the rest of my life, I have approached the defining characteristic of all my intimates this way. I didn't always want to be around rich people – not at all – but I did frequently hold against lovers what it was that drew me to them in the first place.

I put my key in the lock and walked in, as nervous as I'd ever been, the scene in the film where the American cop has their gun drawn and is peeking around the wall, trying not to breathe too loud, clearing one room at a time. Thankfully, Dad was passed out drunk, there in the very first room.

My mum was so happy to see me.

'Oh. Hello! It's you!'

'It's me,' Jasmine agreed.

'I never expected I'd have you right here in the kitchen.'

She was intimating Jasmine was too good for that. But she wasn't. Jasmine wasn't too good for anything. That's what made her different. And now my mum was seeing it.

She remained aloof for a bit but then, within an hour, they were holding each other's arms and giggling.

When my mum laughs really hard she clutches her huge breasts. I think I don't do a lot of high necklines because they don't flatter big breasts. I want her to feel good about how she looks. I want her to feel good. She deserves it.

'There's something I want to give you,' said my mum. 'I've been waiting for someone to give it to but I had all boys, and I never liked any of their girlfriends. Not so far.'

She left the room and came back with a small leather pouch wrapped in twine.

'What is it?' I asked.

'Let her open it,' said Mum, and Jasmine unwound it with happy little breaths, like someone lovely was kissing the back of her neck. Inside was a small, milky gem.

'Is it a moonstone?' I asked, trying not to be perturbed by this gaffe.

'It's an opal,' sighed Jasmine, holding it to the light.

'Yes. I got it in Australia when I was about your age.'

'Oh I love Melbourne! The best art deco apartments! And the botanic garden in Sydney…'

'It's the one trip I've done abroad,' said Mum. 'I don't think it's worth all that much, but I think it would look so pretty if you set it the right way.'

'Thank you,' she said, squeezing my mum. Mum took a moment and then patted her on the back, a bit embarrassed, embarrassed at the display and perplexed that she'd given it to her.

'It could be a lovely necklace,' I said, trying to get in on it, but Mum interrupted me: 'She'll come up with something great.'

Jasmine said thank you again and squeezed Mum's hand, threading Mum's crescent moons between her own bitten fingers. 'There's a jeweller I love in Paris who'll know exactly how to make it sing.'

After that, we all three of us checked on my dad's breathing. Mum didn't seem to mind, now the ice had been smashed, doing it in front of our guest and it was Jasmine who said, 'Oh yeah, he'll be out for a couple more hours.'

'He's good-looking,' she told my mum, not at all lasciviously, but with sympathy, and my mum received it gratefully.

I opened my bedroom door and it was exactly as I'd left it, as if I were my own missing child. It was the only time Jasmine ever came to my place. We sat and looked through a stack of magazines and she asked my mum to join us, and to my amazement she did.

Jasmine admired my magazines, selecting at random from the pile like she was having her Tarot read. The Fool: Cheryl Tiegs wearing a swimsuit and skin on the cover of American *Vogue*. Death: Gia Carangi on the cover of *Cosmopolitan*. Not just years of *Vogue* and *Elle*, but a Paris *Vogue* I'd procured, my most prized, and a few *Cahiers du cinéma*, which Jasmine was amazed by. Even her dad hadn't brought her back *Cahiers du cinéma*. We looked through the pictures together and we talked about which were our favourites.

'That's a very heavy blush,' said my mum, and, 'I do like this hoop skirt.'

'But Vivienne's a genius.'

'I suppose she is,' said Mum, seeming unconvinced but hopeful of being convinced in the fullness of time. Having Jasmine near my mum – Jasmine, who I'd come to worship like a song on the radio at 2 a.m. when no one understands you – made my mum shine bright to me again. I kept looking at Mum more than I did my new best friend. It was my mum I found utterly beguiling that day.

Jasmine frowned at my room. She tried out different spots: the sofa, leaning out of the window, lying back on the bed, looking up. She held her hand up like a cinematographer. 'Let's stick the magazines over your bed.'

'How?'

'Just cut them up.'

'Cut them up? I've been saving them.'

'Yes, and you get them out to look at on special occasions. I want them over your bed, so they're the first thing you see when you wake up and the last thing you see when you go to sleep, so you're confronted by beauty! It will seep into your subconscious and it will power you to your goal.'

'He wants to be a designer,' said Mum.

'He *is* a designer. I bought his first piece. The first piece ever sold by Steven and I own it.'

'Ruffles,' I said to Mum, by way of explanation.

'How exciting.'

Jasmine had found my fabric scissors and was cutting. She handed me a pair of nail scissors. 'You too, Jean. Do you have any more?'

My mum came back with her gold sewing scissors. Jasmine cocked her head. 'These are lovely. Do you sew?'

'I do embroidery.'

'So that's where he gets his talents from. I'd love to see your work.' When she described what Mum did to distract herself from the prison she'd built for herself as 'her work', I thought Mum might start crying, for everything she'd never cried over since it all went wrong. Instead she just said, 'Well, I'll fetch it,' and she came back in with a square of embroidery in her hand and her cheeks pink.

'Nice nail polish,' Jasmine said. 'I've been meaning to tell you that since we walked in.'

'Thank you. Ladies used to do half-moons during the war, to make the polish last longer. It was just a way of making do with what you had, but it became a proper style.' Now I thought I might cry. I dug into my collage, cutting around Brigitte Bardot, in her original brunette, not blonde (I'm not a savage).

Mum sat down on the floor to cut out her pictures. I'd never seen her cross-legged before, like a little girl. I was so transfixed by the sight, it took me a while to look at the pictures she was choosing. She was cutting out glamorous

195

women and men. Was this what she wanted to be like? Was this the man she should have ended up with?

After we had a good selection, Jasmine oversaw us sticking them to the eaves and she moved one or two. By evening it was a sea of faces looking down on me as I looked up at them. Eye contact, someone who sees you. Jasmine giggled. I started to become aware that my father would soon rise from his drunken slumber, like Dracula posting himself across Europe in a pine-wood coffin; that he would send himself back to us on vaporous fumes and that we would retire early to bed and clutch at ourselves, trying to stay alert even as we drifted off.

'I should finish this up?'

Mum nodded at me. She knew what I was thinking. From *Cahiers du cinéma* she cut out a photograph of Elizabeth Taylor and Montgomery Clift looking into each other's eyes between takes.

'They truly loved each other,' said Jasmine. 'If he could have been straight, he would have done it for her. She pulled his teeth from his throat when he was in his car crash and saved his life. Afterwards, his face was a mess, but she insisted the studios still cast him in her movies, even though his beauty was wrecked.'

Jasmine stuck the picture up. I saw Mum watch her little body stretch out. Mum had had a body as good as Jasmine's and probably better. But she'd been far more tightly coiled; you never could have admired how she moved, because she stayed still. You teach yourself how not to be a moving target. Stay in your teenage bedroom. Stand at the sink doing dishes.

'Monty has been gone for almost twenty years now and Liz is still alive. Strange to keep going when everyone you love is falling at the wayside.'

'I love her, too,' said Mum. 'The only one who didn't have a sad life. Marilyn Monroe.' She tutted sadly. 'And Natalie Wood. And there was that awful business with Lana Turner…'

'Yes,' agreed Jasmine, 'It's tough being a Love Goddess,' and we thought she included herself in that category.

'Do you want some sausage rolls? They're from yesterday, but…'

'Thank you, Mum. I'm starving.'

'No you're not, Steven, you're just very hungry. There's children in Africa starving.'

'I know this awful girl,' replied Jasmine. 'She always says, "Lush, orgasm," when she eats cake.'

My mother's eyes widened.

'As if an orgasm could be compared to a carrot cake!'

I worried from my mother's expression that she might not know from experience.

'I think a woman should have an orgasm daily. How can we, as feminists, find the "courage to be", if we don't do that?'

'Feminists? Courage to be?' Mum looked alarmed, like she was already foreseeing having to get her dustpan and brush and clean up the shattered patriarchy so no one got a sliver of it in their foot.

'It's from *Beyond God the Father*. By Mary Daly?'

We looked blank, so she added, 'The radical lesbian theologian?'

As Mum and I leaned against different walls, Jasmine stood in the centre of the room and quoted, in a mysterious baritone, '"Courage to be is the key to the revelatory power of the feminist revolution."'

Then she tapped my mum on the hand, and smiled. 'The thing about Steven is he can do anything, he is so brilliant. The world is going to quake for him.'

My mum looked amazed. She'd always felt it but would never dared have said it out loud, let alone in such a booming voice. If she felt sad that she wasn't young and beautiful like Jasmine, she let that be superseded by her newfound belief that I was going to get out of here, and I saw on her face the play of heartbreak and hopefulness that I might leave one day. It took me a long time to understand that my mum was still young then, only forty-two; that's nothing today. But her face was so different from the forty-two-year-olds I know now. It was overlaid with every wrong and disappointment, like a layer of tulle that obfuscates the shape underneath.

Jasmine needed to go, and on the way downstairs, we roused my dad, who stood in the doorway. We scuttled to – what? Hide ourselves? Pretend to be asleep? We didn't know what to do with ourselves, so we stayed where we were, except for Jasmine, who strode across to him and said hello, but before she said it, when she was striding, there was a beat where it seemed she might walk right through him. Prove to me that in all these years, I'd only been hating a hologram.

He stood rooted to the spot. It was a hazing of sorts, only he didn't seem to know it. When she was picking up her handbag, he just looked at us and said, 'My God! If she didn't have those pins through her ears, she could be an exotic dancer.'

She was still in the hallway, and she said, 'I don't like being talked to that way, actually.'

'Oh, la-di-da.' But he couldn't think of anything else to say. I could see it was agitating him and that would make things worse for my mum, so I tried to hurry Jasmine out.

'I'll call you soon.' And I whispered, 'Thank you for everything,' because I didn't want Dad to start questioning how much, exactly, I had to thank her for. I didn't want him to start work on how he might spoil it.

After that, I knew I'd be allowed to be with Jasmine whenever I wanted and that I didn't have to worry about my mum worrying.

I'd forgotten about the beating, or at least had put it into a part of my mind where I wouldn't take it out to look at for at least a year. These sad things that happen to us get moved into special photo albums to be looked at when the mood strikes us rather than every single time we open our wallet. I don't think Jasmine had moved anything to any photo album. I think she'd been taking endless photos in her mind of the bad times, so many that they were double exposed and worthless and she both thought about it all the time and not at all.

She'd been good to me. She'd made my heart sing for the first time in years and now she had made my mother happy too. How could I help her?

CHAPTER 14

When I picked Jasmine up from the tourist trap, she was just closing up the shop after performing her ritual sageing.

'Keep Diana safe,' she said, as she circled a stick of Palo Alto over a commemorative wedding mug. When she had finished locking up, she turned to me and said, 'I want us to go to Paris.' From inside the shop, the phone started to ring. She motioned me to ignore it. It was still ringing as we left.

She'd said this almost daily since we met. Only this time she followed through, that same evening. If someone keeps talking about a dream you have to do together, you can almost bet it will stay a dream. She was the exception. She made dreams happen. The only thing was, they had to be her dream and only she knew exactly how the dream in her head went, and if you didn't get it right you were spoiling it.

I objected, a little, just to seem polite, but if someone wants to take you to Paris, you should let them. That's one of my biggest life lessons.

We made it to the airport just in time to catch the last plane of the day, and she paid in cash at the ticket counter. The lady behind the counter looked from the money, to her, to me – I had seen this particular move so many times lately (the estate agent, the youth-club bullies, Terry, my father) it had started to seem like a dance move, a craze we had inspired.

I hated the aeroplane, the takeoff and landing, the turbulence in the middle, I hated it and this would haunt me my whole life, the fear of flying. But she seemed to get off on it, whooping when we hit a pocket of air. She squeezed my hand. 'If we're going to crash there's absolutely nothing we can do about it!'

'Shut up!'

'But it's brilliant! It means that nothing that happens here is our fault.'

It was a strange thing to say. I wondered about the things, down on land, that she might think were her fault. As if I weren't entirely sure, as if I only had an inkling. Teenagers are fearless but they're also cowards. It wasn't until I was much older I could admit to myself that I knew precisely the blame she assigned herself. But there, on the plane, I thought about how often I told her to 'Shut up!' out of fear or embarrassment, occasionally out of crossness, and I resolved to be gentler with her. You couldn't watch Jasmine sleep and not want to be kinder to her. I imagine all the men (and some women) who'd ever woken up beside her had experienced the same compulsion. I imagine it made most of them leave. But for me, I felt more determined than ever to stick around, no matter how hard she tested me in her waking hours.

In the taxi from the airport to the hotel, she reached into her handbag, the same one I'd identified as Bottega when we first met. 'This is our handbag,' she said, and at first I thought she meant that we could share it, but soon understood she saw bags, gloves and hats as favourite songs, playing when particular people or places or events appeared to her. From its inner zip she produced the pouch in which my mother had handed her the opal.

'I've called ahead to Monsieur Pierrot, the jeweller. He knows I'm coming in to have this set.'

'Monsieur Pierrot?'

'Yes,' she acknowledged, 'in Paris, even sad clowns get respect.' She nudged me in the ribs. 'There's hope for you yet.'

I smiled and didn't say how absolutely terrified I was that I was eighteen years old and this trip might be the highlight of my life.

The hotel was either on the left or the right bank, but I remember it had five stars and that I got a disdainful look from the concierge when I leaned against an antique side table. It was much the same look my dad gave me when I stood in front of the TV during *Match of the Day*. I moved off the 1920s side table and into the 1920s elevator.

The bed had a canopy that I drew around us after Jasmine nodded off. As she was drifting away, she held the opal in her hand, rubbing it gently between her thumb and forefinger, as if that's what she always did every night to get to sleep.

I'd never been in a canopy bed before. I'd never slept in a bed with a girl before, either. But the canopy was the part that caught my attention, the way it softened us: our skin, our breath, my thoughts. I started to feel sorry for my dad and then, when I opened the canopy curtains and stepped out for a 3 a.m. wee, I didn't feel bad for him any more.

He was sick, that's true. But beneath their addiction, addicts all have their own personality. And I believed, and still believe, that my father is a person of low character. Not only because he lashed out; it was also the way he blocked us from getting close. That's abusive, too. All those passengers he picked up: I don't think he was listening to any of them. Worse, I don't think he was asking them any questions. If you don't ask questions, you may as well be dead. That hit me so hard after the days I'd spent with Jasmine; everything around us was so fascinating to her, everything worth enquiry. That wasn't because she was rich; it was because she was alive. More alive than anyone else I knew, which was why, every time she tried to kill herself off, she failed.

I looked at her dear face as she slept. How much had they all been a cry for help? How much had she really wanted them to work? We had so many people in our family who'd been killed off. We didn't have any ever attempt suicide, not that I knew of. Maybe my father counted, thought it was just that he was doing it very slowly and hoping to take us all with him.

I listened to her snore, gentle, the little puffs of air a baby makes. She slept diagonally and even though she'd done all this for me, and even though I felt close to her, I didn't feel like I could shove her over onto her side of the bed. That's the downside of letting someone take you to Paris. But it's the only one and though I got little sleep, as soon as I saw the sun rise over the rooftops, I was buzzing.

She kept sleeping past nine, so I put The Specials in her ears and she sat up, happy, the only person I've ever known to always wake up from sleep in a great mood, no matter how it might darken during the day.

'I had a vision! I'm going to get Monsieur Pierrot to turn the opal into an ear cuff. I like the idea of the stone whispering in my ear.'

'Mum would never have thought of that.'

'Yes, she would have. She just doesn't know such a thing exists. If she did, she'd have thought of it.'

'That makes no sense.'

'You're just jealous because you hated sharing your mum, even for a few hours. You were itching to get rid of me.'

But she was still smiling and she threw off the covers, threw them so they landed on the ground at the foot of the bed, where they lay, prostrate like mourners paying homage to a dead dictator.

'I want you to taste the best croissant in Paris,' she said.

If someone wants you to taste the best croissant in Paris, you should let them. I bought a few for my mum, but then I ate them while we walked around Canal Saint-Martin, which looked like a delicate pencil sketch of Camden Lock.

Though I understood little of what they were saying, I enjoyed the ambient sound of French spoken around me, a baby's noise machine switched from 'Waterfall' to 'Gallic Babble'.

Our first stop was Monsieur Pierrot, where a security guard hit the buzzer to let us in when he saw her in the distance. Inside, she spoke immaculate French to a shopkeeper who was closer to Scary Clown than Sad Clown, his teeth mottled with nicotine stains like the pattern on a piece of agate. When she opened the pouch to show him the opal, he shrugged and said in English, 'It's nothing special,' but she stood her ground and told him it had great sentimental value.

'Opals are bad luck.'

'Not to us,' she said. 'We make our own luck.'

She drew him the ear-cuff design and he sighed but promised it would be ready by the time we left town.

'Would it cheer you up if I told you to add a diamond border to the design?'

His agate teeth were revealed in a new shape that I took to indicate good cheer, or as close as he could manage.

'Are we going to see the Louvre?' I asked her, as we waited at the lights. I noticed she obeyed them more stringently than she did in London whereas, in a foreign country, I always feel rules are make believe.

'No.'

'The Arc de Triomphe?'

'Fuck that.'

'We are going to see the Eiffel Tower?'

She pointed. 'Over there.' And she was right, there it was, in the distance.

'But shouldn't we go inside?'

'How dull. You don't want to be a tourist all your life, do you?'

I didn't think I'd even started being a tourist in life yet, I hadn't seen anything of anything, except the streets in which I was raised.

She took my face in her hands. 'I want you to be part of every city you visit.'

We sat in a children's playground, drinking coffee. She read the paper, because she could read French as well as speak it; so well the French treated us with less contempt than I'm sure they'd have preferred. When a child accidentally kicked a football at her feet, it did not occur to her to kick it back. I did (badly) and they didn't say, '*Merci*.'

'I think it's marvellous that they're so rude. Oh they're vile!' she beamed. 'I adore it! It's bracing!'

'It's bracing,' I smiled. Somehow she made not standing up to bad behaviour seem like an act of defiance. Whenever I'd done the same, which is my whole life, I'd just felt like a doormat.

We finished our coffees or, rather, she finished her own and then took mine away. Instead of any of the places I'd asked to visit, she took me to the Greek Quarter, where she bought us two tickets to the Musée de la Vie Romantique. The Museum of the Romantic Life. It contained, within its small frame, several minor masterpieces of nineteenth-century painting.

'But I wanted to show you this,' she said, leading me up the spiral stairs.

There, under glass, was an eighteenth-century pistol, tiny and inlaid with enamel roses. The accompanying text explained it was for a lady to shoot herself with, if her lover were to betray her. Jasmine said she came to look at it every time she was in town. She knew I'd want it too and she was right. You'll see a replica of it in the pattern I designed for my grand finale wedding dress in the 1992 show. I think she thought her suicides had not been as glamorous as they might have been. That it was not glamorous to survive or to end up in a public hospital ward with charcoal on your chin and that it was certainly not glamorous to have no lover to attempt it over, the only time art history truly celebrates the suicidee.

Even the visitors to the museum were romantic, generally individuals from dreamy faraway countries. We followed a Japanese lady in a peach kimono as she moved from painting to painting, like an apricot cloud.

I saw, in a case, a beautiful enamel hand with gold script on the outstretched palm that read '*Tout ou*

Rien'. 'All or nothing,' she murmured, when I pointed it out to her.

'It's wonderful,' I sighed.

'I think so too,' she agreed. 'Let's get it.'

There then followed a back and forth with the museum guard who was, after all, just a museum guard. He was getting increasingly alarmed and turned the gallery director on to us, who immediately fell in love with Jasmine and invited us to tea in the courtyard. He wanted only her there, but she would not let go of my hand (*romantique*). Either he'd ascertained the same as the thugs at school (that I was gay) or he thought I was her boyfriend and didn't give a damn. I hoped the latter, as it felt very French.

Butterflies hovered as we were brought a selection of teabags in a Chinese lacquer box. Honey and milk arrived in delicate silver jugs and, of course, petits fours. When he saw how she gobbled them up, he either went off her or understood she was entirely out of his league. He wandered back into the museum and we went on our way.

She liked to eat meals in reverse, so the sweets had made her hungry for the main course. She knew a Greek taverna, where they scowled at us, which I found upsetting and she found thrilling.

'Don't you want to be liked by people? I do!'

'Yes of course, but people on holiday don't count; they're the exception.'

'On our holidays or their holidays?'

'Either will work.'

I supposed that's why her dad spent so much time on holiday.

Back in our hotel room that night I told her 'all or nothing' was a silly concept. I told her that my ancestors who made it had escaped a Russian pogrom and that had been all or nothing. How they were turned down for citizenship in different cities. Then they got it in Dublin and stayed there a generation. Then they'd made it to London, where they'd opened a corset shop in the East End that was once a great success.

As I described these feats of incredible effort and endurance, she looked at me lazily. 'You should do a collection around that. What they were wearing when they escaped, and end it with how they looked when they arrived in London. In between you have how each city that rejected them influenced their look.'

'That's your response?'

'It is.' She yawned.

'I don't think I'd feel comfortable making clothes that are inspired by someone's pain.'

'Then you'll never be a brilliant artist,' she said as I recoiled. 'If we don't take our suffering and burn it on a pyre, as an offering to the gods, then it's just sad stories. You have to make something out of them. You do! You have to make a collection about our time in hospital, have the models walk through the corridors, tell our story.'

She seemed wistful, as if our friendship were long in the past and she lost in the memory of it.

'Freak 'em out. Confront them. Don't let anyone but the toughest or the most broken want to wear your clothes. You're not going to make froufrou. You're never going to be asked to design a dress for Diana.'

'You don't know that. I might.'

'The best thing you could do is take your idol and have her not want to wear your clothes at all.'

'I'm not Vivienne Westwood.'

'You're right. You're just a teenage boy from Bow. But you'll get older. And you'll get braver. I got braver with age.' She spoke as if she were decades ahead of me, not a few months.

'Well. What do you want to do?'

'In what way?' There was an edge to her voice because we both knew I'd tried to ask this of her before.

'With your life?' I was scared to ask the next part. 'For a job.' I didn't say 'for a living', because I knew she didn't need one.

'This is it.'

'But you have so much to give.'

'And I'm giving it. When you get the reins at your own fashion house, just take me with you.'

I didn't want to fight, not even a little, so I said, 'Okay, Jasmine, I promise.' We put on her Walkman and listened to 'Summer Breeze' by the Isley Brothers. We were quiet apart from both singing along out loud, singing about Jasmine. I've always felt sad not to have a song with my name in it. I used to feel it was why I had no luck in life. She fluffed the pillows under our heads, then adjusted the blanket under my chin just so.

'You're such a good homemaker. For an anarchist.'

She pulled aside the headphones.

'Oh, I don't mind smashing the system. But after I'm finished, I just like to use the broken shards to mosaic a tea box.'

She sounded sleepy and the sleepiness was drugging her just a little bit less guarded, her voice between worlds.

'My mum was the ultimate homemaker. She could cook and garden, and make beauty anywhere and everywhere, catch the corner of your eye with, like, a bleach cupboard whose door she'd upholstered in kimono fabric. She was the opposite of me.'

'She sounds like you.'

'She had been making a papier-mâché cat head with me in half term, and we'd been doing it over days, because you have to let each layer dry. I think Dad was supposed to find her when he rolled in. But I woke up early because I was waiting to see our work. And I got out of bed right before the sun rose to check on it, then I ran to show it to her.'

She rubbed her nose on my cheek for a moment then pulled back to face me again. I looked into her eyes, trying to let her know she could go on.

'I couldn't open her door and I pushed and pushed with all my strength. I was so strong as a kid! She was hanging on the other side. I tried to lift her down but I couldn't. I tried.'

'It would have been too late. She was gone.'

'But I couldn't lift her, it didn't matter how much I...' She looked at me, imploring, as if my hand of friendship might still extend back through time and space to help her. 'I did try.'

I stroked her hair, soft and perfumed with nicotine.

'What did you do next?'

'I put on the papier-mâché head. And I cried. And it melted on me and when my dad came home he saw that first. And he was trying to deal with that, all the glue and newspaper on my face, before he understood what he was really there to deal with.

'I sort of did everything with her, like you and your mum. I was her shadow. But it's hard to shadow someone who lives in the shadows. How do you think a person gets to that place?'

'You got there.'

'I suppose so. But it's really different. To me, it always seems like a reasonable option. Feels like I'm picking a tarot card, one of many choices. She felt she had no other choices.'

She was lying on her back now, looking up at the ceiling without looking. Her eyes were open but all her vision had turned inward.

'And the biggest difference is, I wasn't leaving anybody behind.'

'Your dad?'

'He'd have been okay without me.'

There could have been the most beautiful antique envelope opener or a chandelier made of Murano glass roses, and she wouldn't have noticed. The beauty she searched for had become more addictive, more intense as she felt the increasing pull to the interior. If there had been no more beauty to distract her, if her world were populated only by ugly objects and people, what would have happened? Would her life had become necessarily sorted, her tragedy sifted through, bills all settled, debt-free from trauma?

'But mostly, I'm different from her because I never meant it to work. You know that, right?'

'I suppose so. I didn't know you then.'

'But you know me now. You know what I'm like. Do you believe me?'

'Yes.'

'I was upset. I'm still upset that I don't have that papier-mâché head to remember her by. The last thing we made together. That I broke it.'

'But there's so much you remember her by. And you do it every day, so many times a day, you're keeping her alive.'

'She got it done in one, first time she tried. That last time, when we met? That was it for me. I haven't got the strength to keep doing it.' She laughed. 'I may as well just stay alive.'

'You may as well.'

I fell asleep, trying to think of the appropriate title I'd give her when I got my own fashion house.

When we woke up, she was different. It was very faint at first, like wondering if someone had switched their signature scent from eau de toilette to eau de cologne. You might be right. You could be wrong. But something felt ever so slightly off.

She'd set an alarm for 6 a.m. because she wanted to be at the front of the queue when her favourite bakery opened. My whole life, I've been afraid of street corners in the early morning and dark alley-ways at night, because my mum told me to be afraid.

I've been afraid of walking in the rain because Mum would look out of the window and fret for me, just for me, not my brothers, because she loved me most. But now, because someone loved me most, they were telling me not to be scared, that it was fine to walk in darkness through the rain on strange streets to a shop you could kind of remember where it might be. That there were drunks still going from last night, and men too cheap to pay for prostitutes blowing kisses at Jasmine, and I didn't think, shit, I'm going to need to protect her and myself if something goes awry.

I just assumed everything was all right. Not blinders on to reality. But a faith in the universe, which is strange from a girl who'd been so hurt. Maybe because she'd had the worst card (the suicidal mum, the wandering dad) and the best card (the wealth, the glamour) it gave her comfort that chips just fall where they may. And that it's okay to eat chips off the floor if they've only just landed. Or the food has fallen on the floor in a country you've just landed in.

I knew, despite having met and liked my new friend, Mum would have an anxiety attack at all this. I felt fucking free. I told Jasmine how happy I was until I met her and why, and she sang Joni Mitchell, sang those lines about being free and unfettered, about her future being nobody's to decide. What can be better than singing Joni Mitchell, in the rain, in Paris, with someone you love? It was one of the happiest moments of my life. These moment are easy for me to pinpoint, as easy as telling you the five best dresses I ever made. I know which ones they are. I can show them to you.

All the time we walked, Jasmine was very quiet, like she regretted the night before, telling me what she'd said, and now taking a vow of quiet to redeem herself. I tried to get her chatting, but it didn't work until I picked an apartment as the one I would buy if I had all the money in the world. Then she was chatty again.

It's funny to play that game with someone who really could have any of them. But she could pull the magic trick of making me forget, in her closeness, that she was different from me. Is that the sign of a brilliant illusionist or a hustler? Depends whether you're fighting or not.

There was already a queue when we got to the bakery, even though they were just pulling up the metal gates. Almost everyone there was a local and they looked at us with those pissed-off Parisian faces that just made us hoot with joy. They wore flat caps and carried special bags for their baguette. They had their bikes at their side. Jasmine went to bum a smoke off the cranky old man in front of her. He actually said, '*Non!*' and it couldn't have amused us more. The happier we seemed, the more unhappy he became. That happens a lot in life. I noticed it, early on, with my dad. If he caught Mum being thrilled by a doll's gown I'd made out of a yarmulke, he'd be wretched the whole afternoon.

I'd never seen such a long line of unhappy people buying such a list of beauteous objects. Raspberry tart. Caramel éclair. Green-tea cakes before green tea was a craze.

We got home and towelled off and I put on the kettle while she got into her pyjamas. It thrilled me to see her put her nightwear back on after she'd only taken it off an hour earlier. Coffee came to the boil and she made it with a plunger, pausing me when I tried to press it too soon. I didn't want to tell her I'd never seen a coffee press before, that we'd only ever had instant.

I ploughed through the raspberry tart, caramel éclair and dug into a mysterious lavender triangle dusted in rose petals. Jasmine was smart and saved those for later and just kept gnawing on baguette, crusty and fresh, and swiped in apricot jam like a credit card through a machine. It was the best food I'd ever had in my whole mouth. Then I started, quite quickly, to regret my breakfast choice, as my stomach lilted this way and that.

And then it went wrong.

She helped me to puke, which was nice, and she seemed like she'd done it before so I said, 'Did you used to help your dad puke?' and she laughed and said, 'Yes, how did you guess?' and I said... well, I said, 'Because you've had to parent him. Because your relationship is so dysfunctional.'

She didn't say anything, so I added, 'My dad is terrible, just like yours.'

'What do you mean?' Her voice was hoarse, as if she were the one who had just vomited.

'That they're as shit as each other, in different ways.'

She pulled away from me and started to make the bed. I'd never seen her make a bed before.

'Your dad's a monster. My dad's wonderful. What are you talking about?'

'Jasmine. He let you get sexually abused while he was in the next room with another girl.'

She spun around and I thought she'd slap me and it stung just as badly when she didn't. I heard the unsprung violence in her voice.

'How dare you say that! My dad was there, looking out for me, making sure I was okay.'

'But you weren't okay. The story you told me last night. You needed him more than a girl could ever need their dad.'

'How do you know? Who made you judge and jury? Or cabbie and tailor?'

I whistled through my teeth, which was something my dad did when my mother's blancmange collapsed.

'That's a nasty thing to say.'

'Not as nasty as what you just said to me, after everything I've done for you.'

'You weren't asked to do any of it. Anyway, I thought we were doing this all together.'

'I was the one paying for everything.'

'Have you been keeping a running tab?'

If the conversation had taken place under the canopy bed, would it have been softer?

'I hadn't been but now that I know what you think of me, I want to look back through everything.'

My tummy hurt, as if she'd just punched me. I tried to curl up in a ball, but with my words.

'I think you're wonderful. You've survived unbelievable trauma. I think he should treat you with greater care. You pine for him and he's never there.'

'You're crazy. You're just a sick, crazy boy from a hospital.' She was pacing the room, zigging this way and that. I looked to the door to measure how long it would take to get past her.

'I wasn't the one there by choice. You were.'

'Is this a contest about which of us is more fucked up? In your mind, all this lovely time we've spent together was just about overlapping trauma? Was it?'

'I think that is a part of it. But it isn't all of it. I love you.' I couldn't believe I'd said it. 'Shall we go and pick up the ear cuff?'

'Oh, God, why bother. It isn't even worth the cab fare.'

My face stung.

'You can't just leave it there. My mum gave it to you.'

'Oh right, yes, anything to do with your precious mother, sorry MUM, is worth more than gold. Worth more than geese on flocked wallpaper.'

'It's one of her treasured possessions.'

'Yeah, well, she should get out more.'

She started to cry.

I gathered up my things and started to leave, electing to walk slowly past her instead of making a dash.

'Don't leave!'

'Then don't say these things. That's not how friendship is.'

'How the fuck do you know?'

I opened the door, and she added, again, 'Don't leave!'

I could hear her sobbing as I walked up the street. I had no idea where I was going. I used the last of my cash and, knowing I couldn't afford the flight back, got myself to the ferry before they pushed off.

The sky was grey and the sea a deeper grey and I think it's why I avoid that colour, though it can look lovely in eyes. I've seen it in Dominican people, now I've travelled the world. But the people I went home with were ugly. My fellow passengers were as ugly and lumpen and poor as me. They had terrible children and terrible lives, but I was the one in a terrible mood. I was devastated, quietly devastated, and like a true Brit none of them could tell and if they could tell, like true Brits, they'd have said nothing at all.

I hate stiff upper lips. I hate stiff crinoline. I hate stiff collars. I hate them.

As we rode the slate waves, I listened to 'Because the Night', which Bruce Springsteen had given to Patti Smith and she'd written extra verses while she waited hours for her husband Fred 'Sonic' Smith to call from tour. And how Patti, underground street poet punk priestess, had ended up somewhere she was never supposed to be: at the top of the charts. Amazing. Except she didn't need to be there. She'd still be Patti Smith without the mass adulation. Debbie Harry would not be Debbie Harry without the adulation. Diana wouldn't be Diana without the adulation. She'd be silly and posh and pointless.

It had been an accident, too, my time with Jasmine. What my father had done had been on purpose, but getting inside her, my time with her, that was like creeping into the roof of the London Coliseum when nobody was looking. She didn't mean for me to be up on her roof. Every beautiful memory I have with her wasn't something she planned for me, it's just that she'd been looking the other way, or a gate had been left open. It happened once, at the park, the park keeper had forgotten to lock up at night, and though I wasn't doing much of anything, walking through and stepping onto the children's merry go round, it felt expansive, enlightening, even with the discarded Monster Munch packets at my feet, because I wasn't supposed to be there.

The trip with the ugly people over the ugly waves lasted about two hours and all the way I knew: this is the worst thing that's ever happened to me. I wish I'd never seen the ballet or been on the roof or got let into a Jamaican after-hours club, or tasted a Parisian croissant at dawn so I wouldn't know how boring my memories would be from now on.

I felt ill as I walked through my front door and even sicker when I saw my family. 'Was it wonderful?' Mum asked.

'Yes,' I said.

I went to get her the croissants I'd bought her, then remembered that I'd eaten them. I should have brought her the enamel inlaid gun and I could have turned it on my father. He'd have died with beauty, having lived without it.

My brothers were watching football. I thought how terrible the players' uniforms were, who would play for a team with such colours, and how ugly my brothers looked in their tracksuits. I became obsessed with beautiful tracksuits, designing a tracksuit made from the kimono fabric very close to the one I'd seen on the lady in the museum. Eventually I got to produce it. That was the peril, designing became a way to always have an alternative narrative, a better, more beautiful ending. Experience strained through imagination; my designs have always told, not so much the story of my life, but what I've wished my life could be.

I stayed in my room, lying in my bed, knowing the friendship was irretrievably fucked, that my gate to a beautiful life was gone. How could I have thought that portal would stay open? As soon as she told me about her mum, as soon as I talked her into sharing her worst memory, I'd talked her into leaving me. I looked at the picture she'd stuck up of Elizabeth Taylor and Montgomery Clift. Jasmine hated me, now. If I were to crash my car near her home, she'd let me choke on my teeth. She'd let me lose my screen career when I lost my looks, and say to the powers that be, 'Why would anybody want to look at him?'

She was a spoiled princess marinated in childhood trauma and she felt intoxicating but was clearly toxic. She hated me and I hated her back. I started to cry because I wanted so much to have her near again.

CHAPTER 15

I finally agreed to go with Mum to my aunties' girdle shop in Bethnal Green. 'Get you out of bed.' As we walked, she said, 'I've never seen a face like that on somebody whose just come back from Paris.' I didn't want to tell her what had happened. Now she'd met and come round to Jasmine and was even excited about her, I didn't want to tell her I'd been exiled, like Jews in the Middle Ages, banished from a country in which they'd happily settled. Spain, maybe, because of the heat and architecture, because I thought of Jasmine as such a radiant superstructure. I still fight that survivor's instinct, that people are countries and they'll always expel you in the end.

I daydreamed about Monty and Liz and how they had truly loved each other. Could I have been something else for Jasmine? Married her? Had children? Maybe we'd both have kept lovers, but we could have had a home together and a family. I fantasised about it the whole way there.

When we got there, I stood outside the shop, hoping still not to go in, its façade fading like my will to live. But the aunties saw us from the other side of the glass and came barrelling out, sucking us back towards them like we were bubbles in a milkshake. The Aunties would be a good name for a punk band; Edna and Marsha would not.

'You're here!' they sang, waving their hands in the sky. They could have been waffling around a shtetl with Topol. I was about as depressed as I'd ever been, which was quite depressed.

'How was the journey?' asked Edna.

'It was fine.'

'You're not too tired are you?'

'Too tired for what?'

Answering their questions without looking up, I was being not very nice at all, which hurt, because they were being so sweet.

'We want you to see everything. We know how talented you are and we've wanted to show you the family business for so long.'

They were excited I was there. They were pulling open drawers and getting out samples and they were proud of these clothes, just like I'm proud of my clothes. And I was being an arsehole, an arsehole to old people, and that's the worst kind.

But even as I was being unfriendly, refusing to meet their eyes when they asked me questions, asking them no questions at all in return, I was, under my lashes, taking small peeps at the corsets. I wanted to sit up and start unbuckling them to see how they worked, but I didn't want to stop being sad, or couldn't stop.

I was on the train and I couldn't get off without knocking myself about.

But from under my lashes, I saw what looked like a corset made of wool trimmed with cotton lace, and that was interesting. But then there was a tan cotton twill with dark brown cotton lace and that was very interesting, because who'd have thought to render the erotic in such hey-ho colour combinations, the gentle lace with the sturdy twill? They had. These little old mushroom ladies. Marsha and Edna had thought of it.

'It's a family recipe,' Edna said, 'passed down, like the Italians do with their pasta sauce.'

She stood very close as she spoke, and, since she was an unusual shape, she fit against me despite being low to the ground. I didn't like the idea of Edna as a missing piece of my jigsaw puzzle.

'I want spaghetti for dinner!' said Marsha.

'I wanted spaghetti for dinner yesterday but you said no!'

'Well, now I've changed my mind. I'm allowed to do that? Who says I'm not?'

It was interminable, but if I'd have been in a better mood, I'd have found it very sweet that they still had their defined sibling roles, even though they were in their eighties. And I'd have found it even sweeter, the sight of the low-hanging-titty crew boasting about the uplift factor of whalebone versus metal.

I could see, despite forcing me there, they were getting on my mum's nerves, too, because she said,

'I'll just go and pick up some fish and chips, shall I?' though she might just have easily have said, 'I'll just go and stand over there, away from you.' Her tone wasn't hiding much. The cooler my mother and I became, the warmer the sisters were.

'Yes, and we'll eat them outside so they don't make the merchandise smell.'

'Yes. We can sit there. Or over there.'

From Edna's interest in precisely what angle at which we might sit, I wondered if she had herself harboured dreams at some point of artistic domination. She could have. Neither sister had ever married and, because of the time and place in which they were raised, that meant that they were both virgins. Like Jewish nuns.

I watched my mum clack up the cobbled street and wondered if, by the time she returned, I would have turned into one of them, that when she came back with the chips there'd be three mushroom sisters instead of two.

'Well,' I said, finally looking up, unable to carry on the charade without my mum to bear witness.

'Well, it's wonderful to have you here! You do look like your dad!'

That made my skin crawl. I knew I'd have to become successful, not only because I deserved the acclaim, but so I could afford a nose job that would remove my father from my face. I tested whether or not they knew.

'He's not my favourite person.'

'What?' Edna asked. She poked her sister in her centre, like testing a cake to see if it was baked all the way through. 'What did he say?'

Marsha flicked away her sister's hand. 'Your dad works so hard.'

'Kind of.' Now I was making direct eye contact, but with my other hand I was fondling a corset, tracing the metal hooks with my fingers, a lingerie rosary.

'Yes and he loves you lot so much.'

'Right.' Eight hooks. Eight hooks traced five times, metal notes played on a xylophone.

'And he means so well,' said Marsha, 'Not in his actions so much as—'

Edna jumped in: 'Not in his actions? What else is there? I think he's mean.'

'No!' Marsha said.

'He was mean to us when he was young and he's still mean,' Edna said, surprising me.

I gave her my full attention as I'd seen Jasmine do, to me, to nurses, to people in pubs. 'He beats me up. He sent me to the hospital.'

They looked at each other.

Marsha wavered. 'But it's his spirit.'

'What does that mean?' snapped Edna, 'What a dotty thing to say. Is there anything I can do to help, Steven? Maybe a cup of tea?'

Marsha was relieved to be redirected. 'Oooh, we have a customer.' This seemed a rare event. It didn't have much longer, this business, maybe a year, maybe a few months.

I saw the shadow in the hallway and I should have known. Though I couldn't have imagined her here, among us, I still should have guessed it was Jasmine.

'Are you lost?' Marsha asked.

'No. I'm looking for Steven.'

'He's here!' pointed Edna, like a sniffer dog, even though we were all of us a few feet from the other.

'Hi there!' she said, as cheerful as a skylark.

I gave her the cold shoulder but she kept coming closer.

'How did you find me?'

'Your brothers sent me.'

'I don't really feel like seeing you.'

I wanted to leap into her arms! My heart sang so loud it was like the echo you get on the Tube when you're sitting next to someone wearing cheap headphones.

'What's wrong with you?' she asked.

'What do you think's wrong with me? You dumped me in Paris!'

'No I did not. You walked away. I thought you must need some time to yourself, so I let you go. So you could get your head together and calm down.'

'He seems very calm,' said Marsha. 'He barely speaks above a monotone.'

Jasmine tried to take my arm. 'Shall we go and get some food?'

'Mum's doing it'.

The finished opal ear cuff was on her ear.

'You don't get to say those things to me and then waltz back into my life.'

It was the most I'd ever pushed back against her and she seemed genuinely bewildered. 'Why not?'

Then I thought of her dad waltzing in and out.

'I'm sorry, Steven.'

'You don't sound very sorry,' I answered, though I understood this was just how she'd been cooked.

'I'm not very sorry. But I have to play the game if I want you to come and get lunch with me.'

'You say such shitty things out loud.'

'Ooh, a lovers' quarrel!' said Marsha, a director's DVD commentary on the scene.

'Why would I keep them inside?'

'Because we're English! Keep it in.'

Jasmine took both my hands and looked into my eyes, motioning for me to take deep breaths in and out with her, like I was the spoiled child. 'I'm a moon goddess. Today's a waxing gibbous and that's very good for casting spells. I think we should go to the countryside. You haven't seen the estate yet. Come on. Do you have any wellies?'

'I don't have flippin' wellies.'

'I'll loan you some. I'll give you some! You can have them for ever! Just… don't leave me behind.'

'You left me!' I said, again.

The sisters were fascinated. It was the most fun they'd had in years. Marsha was having so much fun, her whole body was quivering and I was a bit scared she was going to turn from a mushroom into a new being, a fairy perhaps.

'Oh, it was just a lovers' tiff. You took it way too seriously.'

But I remembered her face, how crushed she'd been.

'But—'

'I don't want to talk about it any more.' Jasmine exhaled. 'I think it's very dull.'

She picked up a corset, as if it were a safe word.

I stared at her, daggers, putting aside how deeply I'd longed for her all morning.

'I'm allowed to buy corsets, aren't I?'

Edna stepped in. 'Of course you are, darling. Well. You're very slim, you don't need taking in much.' Between them, the sisters pushed me aside.

'How old are you, Jasmine?'

'Nineteen.'

'Perfect! In my father's day, when he first launched the store, ladies endeavoured to have waists the same size as their age. So let's try you on a tight lacer. Take off your shirt. Don't be shy.' And she pointed at me. 'We're all certain he's a gay.'

'I haven't decided yet!'

Marsha whispered to her sister: 'That's not the right term. They prefer to be called "homo".'

Jasmine shook her head. 'He hasn't decided yet,' and then, taking the corset, added, 'actually, I want to wear it on the outside.'

I had to shake myself out of my crossness to back her up. 'It's a good look. A plain white T-shirt. It's provocative. You could do a whole line like that, Edna, of corsets meant to be worn outside the clothing,' and of course the light bulb went off in my head. It was maybe Jasmine's light bulb that I was using to see my own thoughts with. The thing about a muse is that it can be hard to tell what was your idea and what was theirs.

The sisters buzzed around each other, satellites orbiting. They acted as if they were just offering good service, but I could tell they were competing for Jasmine's attention. Just like anyone who crossed her path. Old ladies with Yiddish accents were no less immune than hot Jamaican nightclub bouncers.

'The flanking bones here, in this one, are whale...' Edna said, trying to take over the sale.

'Are they really from a whale?' Jasmine gasped.

'Of course! Don't look so sad. I bet he had a good life.'

'Until,' said Marsha, 'he was killed by those awful Japanese!'

'I love the Japanese!' screeched Edna.

'No, you don't,' said Marsha.

'No, I don't,' Edna conceded, 'but I do love their fashion. Their lovely art. All them red lips and camellias.'

'You wouldn't like them if they was torturing you.'

232

Edna thought about it. 'No. I wouldn't like that. Did you know that the most popular musical in the history of Japan is *Fiddler on the Roof*?'

'Well, that will be because of "Tradition",' Jasmine said, hooking herself into the corset and the sisters to her.

'That's it exactly. They relate to it.'

'You should come for Shabbat dinner,' said Marsha, turning more mushroom-like with the mention of supper.

I demurred.

'I wasn't asking you, I was inviting her.'

'I'd love to,' Jasmine said.

I shot her a look. 'She's not Jewish.'

'I can tell that,' said Marsha. 'Look at her lovely nose!'

Now I shot her a look. 'It's no better than ours.'

'I think it is.'

'It is,' agreed her sister.

Now I was really annoyed. 'How can you be so self-loathing and yet want to parade around your Shabbat for her?'

'Maybe we want her to parade around our Shabbat, liven it up.'

'It's lively!'

'It's beautiful, you should come.'

'I'd love to come!' she said again. 'Can I bring him?'

I knew our fight was over (even though she'd shown up here to tell me we were golden again) when she asked if she could bring me to the crappy Shabbat, I knew we were back on. I didn't want to go, though.

'If you have to.'

And they each poked me in the ribs, the sisters, then Jasmine joined in and poked my ribs too, forgetting entirely how it was we met and how I'd only recently been clutching them with moaning pain. I couldn't figure out if I was still elated or just annoyed now, but that's all good practice for life. Most of what Jasmine put me through – most of what she took me through – was practice for life.

'You are a handsome boy, though,' said Marsha, at this point so fungal she was practically floating in a soup of carrots and legumes.

'He is!' agreed Jasmine. Clearly she was in the mood to agree with anything they said. 'He looks like Montgomery Clift, don't you think?'

'No, I don't think so,' said Marsha.

'I can see it,' chimed Edna, delighted.

'I can't,' her sister insisted.

'I see it,' said Jasmine, the final word. 'And I'm his Elizabeth Taylor.'

'She converted!' said Edna.

'And she stayed converted!' Marsha added.

'Well, I mean, how would you "unconvert"?' I asked, the voice of pessimism.

'You'd just stop, I suppose. I don't think there's an actual ceremony,' said the cheerful sister.

'I bet there is,' said the mushroom sister.

'Well, she hasn't had it. She's still one of us, up in Beverly Hills in her pink palace.'

I sat down on the floor. The sounds of all their voices was overwhelming. I wished they'd shut up, just a little bit, but my wishes went unanswered. They seemed to grow louder, and as they grew louder they also appeared to grow smaller.

'Are you always doing that?' said Edna, suddenly.

'What?'

'Sitting around on floors?'

'No. I don't just sit around on floors.' My voice sounded like the worst voice. In normal rooms, of people who actually wished me well, I sounded to myself like when you hear your voice distorted by an answerphone.

'On other things? You do a lot of sitting, do you?'

'He's very active, when he's with me,' Jasmine assured them.

'If he's always sitting around on floors, no wonder his dad has such a stinking drinking problem.'

My ears pricked up. In my house we didn't talk about it, we only cleaned up afterwards. And now we'd said out loud twice what we usually kept a secret.

'And he was such a lovely little boy...'

'Me or him?'

'She means you,' said Jasmine.

'I meant his dad. Lovely little thing. Always riding around on a bike, tootling around with his kazoo.'

I tried to imagine my father being small and having a toy, and tootling with it. But when I did, I just wanted to take the kazoo and smash him across the face with it, and push him off his bike. Then he cried, in my imagining, and I comforted him. Funny when your own daydream takes you off-guard. The rest of the day, I tried not to think that he might have been on his bike, cycling as fast as he could from kids who didn't like him. Or that he might have been on the bike, cycling around the neighbourhood just for joy, just because bikes are happy. Were his parents watching him? Or was he on his own? My brain went on a loop about it until it felt like there was a fifty-year-old metal kazoo rusting inside my head.

I wondered what they thought about my mum. Had she scurried away like that when she brought me here because she was worried they knew how bad things were or because she was worried they didn't know? She wanted me to be around them but she was nervy around them herself.

'What's this one?' asked Jasmine, picking up an ivory number from a drawer.

'WHAT'S THIS ONE?' Edna called, even though her sister was standing three feet from her.

Jasmine squeezed my arm in delight. I could see we were very exotic to her, like people you sail on your yacht to see.

'That's cotton twill...' (Marsha)

'Which is called "coutil".' (Edna)

236

'Am I telling or are you telling?' (Marsha)

'You tell.' (Edna) And then she didn't let her tell. 'Those are called "Hercules" clasps and then you got laces up the back. The bones are made of three different gauges of spiral steel. The open sections in each pocket mean you can take them all out and give it a good clean.'

'They don't make 'em like that any more.'

'Well, people don't want to be clean any more.' The sisters nodded at each other.

'I suppose you're right. I suppose when I take a bath, I'm just stewing in my own filth!' Jasmine sounded very, very posh compared to us.

'Like a teabag!' she added, and they cackled and cackled and she folded in with them.

Seeing how easily she won them over, fell in step with their tone and their culture, despite being so different, I was impressed and I suppose, also, secretly, I judged her for it. Why did she need that? Why did she have to fit in? That's what made me wonder why if, in the end, she never pursued her own art. Or work of any kind, really. It wasn't entitlement. It's that she couldn't risk not being liked. And you can't make great work if that's always in your mind. All those years alone in my bedroom, I revelled in having no friends. I felt lonely as hell, I felt victimised, but I also felt proud of the fact that the kids at school disliked me.

'I like to be clean,' I said, not knowing why I'd said it.

'After he washes his face,' added Jasmine, 'he uses toner.'

I could see the sisters try to parse this information (that I use toner, so might definitely be gay? That she had such intimate knowledge of me, so I might not be gay?) I could tell that they weren't sure which to hope for. That it would be wonderful to have another wedding, the high from Diana's having begun to wear off. But that it was quite interesting and glamorous to have a gay nephew, even though I kept insisting I hadn't decided yet.

Most of the time I just wanted to be left alone. Though all I wanted was to escape my teenage bedroom, when I imagined where my talent might take me, my greatest dream was a fabulous room where I could be alone because it was so large, so wonderful, that I would never have to leave it.

I helped Jasmine lace in and this was the closest we got to an apology from me to her for what had gone wrong in Paris. Me touching her while she took deep breaths. Just us, in the dressing room. I could hear the sisters outside, a few feet away, waiting with bated breath that was not very bated because I could hear it. Then Jasmine burst out of the dressing room with a flourish.

'Hello, girls!'

Marsha had a look of 2D horror, her mouth a perfect triangle. 'But it doesn't make sense: everything on the outside that's meant to be on the inside.'

'No, that's it though, that's what I'm trying to say.'
They just looked at me.

'What are you trying to say?'

'That the secret things don't have to be secret? That what makes you beautiful doesn't have to be concealed. If you have a secret weapon, share it with the world.'

'Can't things just be pretty?' Edna looked a little nervous.

Jasmine tried to help her to understand. 'Is it like… is it like how, during Hanukkah, the menorah faces outwards in your living-room window. So that anyone who walks by can be touched by the beauty? That we can be a light, and shine a light?'

The sisters nodded, grasping it with ease, as I looked at Jasmine in amazement.

'Yes,' I nodded. 'Like that.'

I knew what I was trying to say. But she could put it into words. Into the words of a religion to which she had no connection and owed no debt. I took her hand.

She said to them, but really to me, 'The corset is a very beautiful thing because it creates the perfect hourglass figure. And the hourglass connotes the idea of running out of time.'

I could have kissed her, right there, on the lips. But Edna interrupted.

'What do you think was under Diana's dress for the wedding? Do you think she was wearing a corset or do you think it was built into the dress?'

'Built in, I imagine,' answered Marsha.

'That way they could jack up the price!' her sister cackled.

'I'm sure she got it for free,' said Jasmine, further breaking it to them. 'Yes, I'm afraid you get a lot of things for free when you're rich.'

'Well, that's inside out. Like a corset over a T-shirt!' Marsha laughed and her sister laughed and they had a right old cackle together and stopped sniping at each other.

My mum came back with the fish and chips, and when she saw Jasmine there was this look of surprise on her face that soon gave way to… I thought perhaps she might have been embarrassed for the relatives to meet my eccentric friend. It took me a moment, but then I understood it was possessiveness. Mum did not want to share Jasmine.

They hugged like old friends, even though the metal on the corset, worn over Jasmine's T-shirt, poked my mother in her chest. She was happy to be poked by her. Every single person felt validated when Jasmine noticed them.

'I'm sorry they're a bit boring,' Mum whispered to Jasmine. She'd constantly denied that to me, said that they were completely not boring and that I was being totally unfair.

'Oh they're wonderful,' Jasmine whispered back. 'We've been having a ball. And look! Look what I did with the opal!'

'Oh my goodness…'

'Do you like it?'

She touched Jasmine's ear, bending the upper corner like a hamantaschen.

'Yes. I actually do. You are clever.'

'Can you take the fish and chips outside, please? To that table.' (Marsha)

'No, to that one. The light's nicer right now.' (Edna)

She wasn't wrong. I knew my aunt Edna was a frustrated artist, so deeply frustrated she didn't even know about it. That's maybe what had turned her into the shape of a forager's woodland treat.

We sat in the pleasant blue air and ate the fish and chips, which were delicious. Edna sat in the shape of a young girl, one knee hoiked up easily so the foot rested at her crotch. To her horror, Jasmine got a spot of fat on her corset.

'Oh, we should have thought of that. Darn.' The sisters looked genuinely sad.

'But I'm going to buy it.'

'You don't have to,' they said, as one. I could see they expected her to.

'I wanted to. I was going to buy it anyway. Not just this one. I want the one with the removeable whalebone.'

Now they looked at each other. I wondered what they saw. Were they still young in each other's eyes or were they horrified by the way the other had started (and continued) ageing? It's not that some people stay youthful, so much as some faces were more committed to ageing than others. Ridges and creeks, hollows, like fabric. If I could make an eyelet as textured as Harry Dean Stanton, I'd be happy. And I'd call it the Harry. I feared young people and I enjoyed old faces. Jasmine was my favourite young person of all time and again, I fought the urge to kiss her in front of all my living female relatives.

'Are you sure? It's pricey,' warned Edna.

My mum nudged her, attempting to explain through one knee-shove that Jasmine was so rich we shouldn't even be talking about money in front of her.

When she went to the loo my mum told the sisters, 'She could buy the whole shop.'

They looked a bit alarmed. 'Has she come to buy us out?'

'No,' I reassured them. 'She buys from everywhere. She just likes your stuff. She thinks it's well made.'

'It is well made.'

'I know.'

'Then why didn't you come and see us before?'

'Well, now I know. Now I wish I'd come to see you before. That was my mistake.'

'We forgive you.' And they showered me with kisses, or at least they tried to but they were too near to the ground, so they blew kisses upwards and I grabbed at them, giddy and light-hearted, because Jasmine and I had repaired things and my embarrassing family had somehow impressed her.

'This is the one you want. Since you've come all this way,' Marsha said, handing her a corset from a floor-level drawer. It was cream with pale blue ribbon at the front and hooks at the back. It was cut at a rounded 'W' beneath the breasts. She seemed so sure that I suddenly wanted it, too.

'This, you see, you cannot get into unless you have a friend to lace you in.'

'Does it have to be a friend?' Jasmine asked, 'What if you want to be alone?'

'If you're feeling isolationist...' Marsha looked pointedly at me. 'That's okay.'

She shovelled Jasmine out of the one she had on and into this new one. 'Once you've had help being laced in, it remains in place. After that, you can just do it by yourself with the front hooks.'

'So you only need help the once, from one person?'

'Exactly.'

'Then that's a very special job. I'd better pick the right person.'

She smiled at me. Everything was back to normal, or to abnormal. Everything was... hopeful again.

'Ouch,' she said, pulling at her ribs.

'You'll get used to it,' insisted Marsha.

Edna cackled. 'And at least, if it's on the outside, everybody will know why you're squirming. It's good advertising for us, this whole over-your-T-shirt malarkey. You will wear it with a nice T-shirt? No offensive slogans or anything?'

243

'I promise,' she said, and I was already thinking of offensive slogans I thought might work well. She took it off and packed it in her bag with her other one, and three pairs of orthopaedic stockings that she said she would use in one of her arts and crafts projects. She was planning on making an erotic puppet of Ronald Reagan but I didn't tell the sisters that (they wouldn't have approved of the satire or the misuse of medical undergarments.)

I felt very sad when we left. We all walked together, eventually parting ways when Mum and I went home and Jasmine went back to Notting Hill.

'Will I see you tomorrow?' Jasmine asked, her voice warm as a scented milk bath.

I looked at Mum, who answered for me. 'Go on, you'll see him tomorrow. I'll send some cakes along with him.'

'Have you ever ridden the Underground before?' My mum wasn't being bitchy, as you know, that wasn't her.

But I snapped at her, 'Mum! She rides the Underground all the time. She takes it more than we do!'

'Even if I had a limo, which we haven't had in some years, I want all the modes of transportation. Because each one sparks a different kind of thought. Walking, or the bus, or the Tube, or a taxi or plane, or if you're very lucky, the train, they all make me think in a different way, and when they're all in rotation, that's when I get my best ideas.'

I made note of this and practise it to this day, and I advise every one of you to do the same. I've added to it: different times of day. Different thoughts come on a bus at night than early in the morning. What I think she was saying is: you don't ever get your best ideas sitting at your desk. That's just where you jot down what came to you while you were moving.

Mum also really looked sad to see Jasmine go. I watched as she followed her into the crowd with her eyes, Piccadilly Circus separating them, my mum's attention returning to me.

I wondered if she was fretting about what or who we might be going home to. Just the boys. Or Dad. And Dad in what state? I felt her whole body tense. But maybe I felt the tense-ness of everyone, all worrying about what they were walking in on when they crossed their own thresholds in half an hour's time.

Mum put her arm through mine, as if I were a proper gentleman or as if she wanted one more shot today at being treated like a proper gentlewoman.

Our footsteps echoed up the underpass and I realised I was less worried than I used to be that we would be horribly attacked before we reached the other end. My nerves were less frayed, certainly than they had been earlier in the day. But I noticed, in general, I had started to feel braver. Maybe there is not light at the end of the tunnel, and if that were the case, maybe you are the light.

The sky was elegant when we got back into the world, a beautiful dove grey, with a quarter moon. I wondered what spell and which crystal was appropriate for a quarter moon.

As soon as I got home, I called Jasmine to ask, dodging around my father who, thank G-d, was slumped in front of the TV.

'Now is a time for sloughing off dead past,' she said. 'The snake.'

'The what?'

'The snake is the animal that sheds its skin instead of growing with it.'

I felt sad, wondering whether the sisters knew that their corset shop would soon be over. And whether they knew that reason it was coming to an end was because women wanted to be free now. And I felt sad, very sad, for Diana, wearing a boned dress up the aisle for a wedding she was contracted to.

I wished she could be happy. Like I was.

CHAPTER 16

Fashion is a manipulation, if you're doing it right. The cut of the dress is so skilful that people just assume your waist is really that tiny. The cowl neck directs people to look into your face, framing it, like it's worth a great deal, even when you're no oil painting. Since I started going to galleries with Jasmine, I realised 'He's no oil painting' is a strange saying, since oil paint has been used to create the most confrontational art. Perhaps they mean 'She's no watercolour'?

But I watched how she moved in the world and I took what she did to people – how she flattered them, lied to them ever so skilfully and without malice, the way she veiled things, her touchability – and I applied it to clothes. You stay loyal to a particular designer's particular point of view because you not only accept the manipulation, you enjoy it. The subtle trickery is a form of relaxation, both for the wearer and the maker. It was the same as I watched Jasmine and the people with whom she interacted, myself included. Both sides felt soothed, even if only one side had achieved something. The day she came over to my mum's and admired her embroidery and got her to help us with the cutting and pasting, that was pure manipulation.

Its success meant I was freer to travel with Jasmine, me to go and her to take me. But, in the course of the manipulation, they also had a good time.

When she went to my aunties' corset shop and made such a fuss of their wares, she could have lived her life without buying from them; she didn't need what she walked away with (she never did make the erotic Ronald Reagan puppet). But both sides had a good time and my aunties even made money, and got some hope that the shop would take off again.

I couldn't tell them it was just one outlier girl, one liar outlier with great intentions and no ability whatsoever to see things through. All the great paintings, the great ideas, the possible novels, the film scripts in her head, make-up range, satirical puppet shows, literary salons, tea salons, Pilates/karate hybrid, moon-cycle workshop: they were with all good intentions and no solid base. There was nowhere in her or around her from which these things could be sustained.

And now she kept banging on and on about the country estate. 'It's a train ride!' she said, as if that were the answer to any doubts about anything.

'But I need to finish my Saint Martin's application.'

'We'll do it on the way. It's just a train ride!'

I agreed, without asking how long the bloody train ride was. But she got me through the four hours with the attention and ingenuity of a party hostess, a synchronicity of old-world literary hostess and thrower of a toddler's birthday party. She'd packed extra things I'd never seen in secret compartments of her handbag and she'd pull them out when she thought I was getting grumpy. I imagined her doing the same for her father. I imagined she'd have been a good mother. In her way.

'Look. Here's a cigarette compact that Laurence Olivier gave to Vivien Leigh when they were both still married to other people!'

I held it in my hand. 'It does feel scandalous. But refined.'

'He was mainly queer, you know?'

'He never decided, I heard.'

'Of course, yes. Just like you.'

'Why do you keep swinging back to it? You're like a demented driver going in circles.'

'Am I making you feel sick?'

'No. It's just quite rude.'

'Oh no!'

As if I were the first person to point out how rude she could be. Maybe I was the first person.

'I just want you to be happy,' she said, 'and it helps to be happy if one has clarity.'

'David Bowie is bisexual.'

'That's true. But he's quite a good deal more beautiful than you, so he does have greater options. I'm just being honest!'

'Thank you.'

'Look. Here's a fan my father got me in Barcelona.'

'Why doesn't it say "Duty Free" on it?'

'Let's not go there again.'

'You're right.' I looked in my bag. 'This is my letter to Saint Martin's. It's a work in progress. Will you read it?'

'Oh, brilliant! That's my favourite thing! Let's have a gander!' It always amused me when she used Cockney slang, though she was the only posh person who could do it, otherwise it made me feel violent.

'Dear Saint Martin's, I want to be inside you. Love Steven.'

I looked at her. 'I'm joking!' she said.

'I am aware. I did write it.'

'You are quite a miserable sort, aren't you?'

'Yes. I am. Thanks for noticing. Will you read it, or shall I?'

She went in a side pocket and put on reading glasses I'd never seen before nor heard tell of.

'Do you need glasses?'

'Obviously.' She shrugged. 'You don't know everything about me.'

'I haven't even known you very long.'

'And you've done very well. Better than anyone who's come before you.'

She sat in my lap and started reading as people walked past, looking askance or tender, depending how their own hearts were feeling or which class they were sat in. I maintained the expression of someone who always travels first class, as she read aloud:

'To whom it may concern. I have been sketching and designing since I was a little boy. I didn't know it was something you could do for a living for many years. The common thread, when I found out, was that the artists I admire went to your school. I used to be embarrassed by my family but embarrassment is silly and not very useful for design purposes. My family are big-hearted and annoying, and big-hearted and annoying are things I think a designer can work with.

'There's people in my family I hate and when I see them in front of me, I see how much they want to fade into the background with their clothes, but how, in seeking that, they still draw attention with their anger, the bland uniforms exacerbating their emotional incontinence. From growing up with the main male figure in my life, I want the clothes to be the only thing about me that's angry, so it's all there, and I am free to be more relaxed than what I'm wearing. That's why I'm focusing my collection on corsets.'

She looked up at me. 'You fucking genius.' There were actual tears in her eyes. It's always so much better in a movie when a great actor almost cries but doesn't, instead of watching an actor weep openly. She went back to the letter, telling me to read the rest. I took a deep breath through my nose and exhaled my incantation:

'There's other people in my family who want to be so like everyone else that they dress as close to their friends as they can. But the way it comes across to me is the safety of the crowd and the cruelty of the crowd. The things you can get away with when you look like everybody else. I think it's harder to be unkind when you dress eccentrically. You can always get picked out in a crowd, so it inclines one towards better behaviour. I've never heard an unkind word about Quentin Crisp or Adam Ant. I'd be shocked if Kate Bush were a bully.'

By the end, I felt like I was performing onstage at school in front of an audience and, as I looked up to see Jasmine's response, I saw that the train had gathered to listen in.

'I don't quite understand it,' said a man with a briefcase, 'but I think it's wonderful!'

The man pushing the food cart said: 'Add in the princess to your list of great dressers.'

'Which one?'

'Which one? The princess!' I thought he might have meant Grace of Monaco but actually I didn't I knew who he meant and I wrote down 'Diana'.

'She's not a very good dresser, not at all,' I whispered.

He looked crushed, so I adapted, 'But you feel her kindness and her vulnerability, like she could strangle herself with all those pussy bows.'

'Thatcher wears the same thing!' said the man with the briefcase.

'Yeah, but she'd be strangling you.'

Having taken offence on behalf of both their princess and their prime minister, they went back to their previous positions. If they could have rescinded their round of applause, they would have.

'I like it,' said Jasmine. 'It doesn't suck up too much. You're a good manipulator like that.'

'Hey!'

'But then I am too. Don't lose it. It's a good life skill.'

She put on her make-up from the same bag she'd had in the hospital bed. I watched her closely.

'What?'

'Just… it seems an age ago you were doing that in the hospital.'

'For ever ago.'

'But it's hardly any time at all.'

'I feel completely different, don't you?'

'I feel different,' I agreed.

'Well, that's it, we're on a path. We're both going to make it this year. Isn't it wonderful to be alive? I don't always say that after I make it. Usually I'm furious to still be here. But now, I just feel we have so much we're going to do together in the world.'

I kissed her gently on the lips, no tongue, the kiss of someone who hasn't decided yet, but who wanted to express that if they had decided, it would be her, just her, only ever her.

When we pulled apart, she blushed and put away her make-up, saying, 'That's Dolly Parton's foundation.

I had it tracked down and sent all the way from Nashville.'

I loved her too much to ask: 'Do you mean that's the same brand she uses or is it literally hers, passed on to you?' Or, 'Isn't anything just yours? Does it not hold any value if there isn't some crazy story or auction behind it? Not just, "I went down the shop and bought myself some foundation. They were charging two for one at Superdrug so I bought two"?'

As if hearing my thoughts (or not hearing them) she pulled out a pack of Tarot cards and said, 'These were hand-painted by artisans in Mexico.' The kiss had kicked in her fight or flight and her version of flight was to babble. 'My dad brought them back from a wild fishing trip he had with Keith Richards. Neither of them remember much of what happened, only that they had the most incredible fortune read. She laid out everything, to a T, about every month of their lives to come.'

'What did she say?'

'They don't remember that part.' She gave it not another thought. 'Now cut this in half in the middle, shuffle it, draw five cards, lay them face down. Don't show me! And lay another five horizontal across them. Yes, I know it's tough asking a Jew to make a crucifix, but the whole thing is occult, so you're buggered anyway.'

The passengers looked round. I wasn't sure if it was for the Judaism or the Satanism, but either way,

I suddenly understood why my family never talked religion, most certainly not in public. You just didn't know who was listening or what they held in their hearts. People are crazy. Speaking of…

'OH MY GOD!'

I leapt in my seat.

'This is the most wonderful card!'

'It's the death card. How is that wonderful?'

'Because it means new beginnings. You're about to have a huge change. In my readings, you're always the Knight of Cups.'

'What do you mean always? In your readings?'

'Oh, I've been reading your Tarot since the day I met you. You just weren't there for it. But it's how I knew we'd come back together after our fight.'

'Didn't take me very long. Your powers of prediction were confirmed pretty bloody fast.'

'They usually are.' She looked sad. 'Anyhoo, I'm the Princess of Pentacles and my father is the Lover.'

'That's weird.'

'Maybe, but it's just how it is. I don't get to choose; the card chooses you.'

She even read Tarot for the family sitting across the way. They were laughing about it until they got sucked into the read. I was annoyed that she invited them to sit, but she did and they took their turn, one by one.

We got to our stop and she packed away the Olivier–Leigh cigarette case, Barcelona fan, deck of hand-drawn Tarot cards. We took a taxi from the train station. The back of the driver's head looked like my dad's. She didn't tip him enough and, looking him in the eyes, I tipped him more as she walked ahead.

CHAPTER 17

You could see, from the outside, that her house was actually a House, with a capital 'H'. Its exterior was what marked it as a true country estate. You could see, from the fifteenth-century stone, the turrets and the blanket of creeping vines, that we were entering, if not a time capsule, then certainly an ecosystem.

I ogled her bath first, because I think it's the best place to start when you're trying to get inside someone's soul. What are they looking at when they're naked and vulnerable but not sexual? What's the view from the window? Is there even a window? A skylight, so you can feel the stars witnessing your sorrows as you soak them off. The floor had gold leaf and a mosaic of woodland animals: hares and foxes and other English creatures. The tub had claw feet and was painted dusty pink.

Jasmine had her childhood bedroom intact. It had, neatly lined on the bed, teddy bears from all around the world. A koala bear in a Sydney T-shirt. A Dublin bear with four-leaf clovers in one paw and a beer in his other hand. A King Kong bear clutching the Empire State Building. They spread out onto the bookshelves, a party out of control. She had a lifetime supply of duty free, but to her it was irrefutable proof that he always remembered her, that she was always on his mind. Children are loyal to their parents and children are even more loyal to damaged parents.

As I brushed my teeth, the moon pressed down through the skylight as if it longed for me. As if, like Jasmine, I was incandescently beautiful. She came in to brush her teeth alongside me and talked at me as if we were already in bed.

'You've got to try having an orgasm on a full moon. It's the absolute best. It might not work because you're a man. But then it might work because you're gay!'

'I haven't decided yet!'

'You keep saying that.'

'Who would I possibly have sex with, anyway?'

'Yourself! I mean, if you really want to enjoy it? If you want to feel powerful instead of subjugated, really best to have sex with yourself. I can be in the next room from you, so you're not alone.'

'I don't like that idea. At all.'

'No, but you'd love it, I promise. We'd feel each other's energy. We'd hear each other.'

'I'm scared.'

'That's good! That's going to create extra-powerful waves of pleasure.'

I moved away from her.

'When you feel that you're close, say, "Now is the time and I am the one." Over and over: "Now is the time and I am the one." And whoever you're thinking about when you come, make sure those words are a mantra in your head when it happens. Then anything and everything you want will be yours, even things you don't know you want yet. It's a very powerful spell.'

I quite visibly blanched, whiting out any magic in the air.

'Listen. I'm helping you out here. Trust me. If you don't take control of this now, your first years of sex will make you feel so powerless, you'll hover outside your body looking down on this numb person being moved into different positions. I don't do anything I don't want any more. I don't go with anyone I don't want.'

She paused.

'I'd sleep with you if you could be persuaded...'

'I haven't decided yet...'

'But it would be taking advantage. Yes, you've said that. I'll wait for you to come to me. But for the meantime. In the next room. Don't forget your candle. Oh, you'll need some carnelian. Do you have some on you?'

'No, I don't have some carnelian on me!'

'I have some spare rose quartz. It's not quite right but it's better than nothing. You have to be careful with these things. I once put some lapis lazuli up my bum and I had the most fearful nightmares.'

'Well, you would.'

'But you can put rose quartz in your arse, that's fine.'

'I'd rather not.'

'You have to.'

'I don't have to do everything you say.'

'My gosh, no. You don't have to do anything I say. You're a young person of entirely free will and all your decisions thus far have led you to the rich and fulfilling life you so enjoyed before I met you.'

I sighed and put my hand out. 'Give me the quartz.'

CHAPTER 18

I consider it my first sexual experience, even though there wasn't anyone else involved. There was no one in the room, but there *was* something up my arse. And she was next door. I knew she could hear me when I came. I could hear her. She walked in, her cheeks flush, the skin across her throat and chest blooming.

'Who were you thinking about?'

There was some Swedish pop, with a bit of Farley Granger in *Strangers on a Train*, and Jasmine had been there too. It felt simplest to say, 'ABBA.'

'Which?'

'All of them.'

'Oh, brilliant! Was that Benny or was that Bjorn? Who can say? I love to be confused by an orgasm. Did you remember to set your intention?'

'It was difficult with them there.'

'The beards, yes. Oh, well. Next time.'

'Who were you thinking about?'

'I was thinking about sun on my skin in St-Tropez. I was on a yacht and I opened my legs very slowly and felt the heat.'

'And that did the job?'

'My goodness, yes. I set my intention very deeply. I'd be astonished if this spell didn't come true.'

'What was it?'

'I can't tell you or it won't work.'

Even though I'd known her such a short time, it upset me that she would keep something from me, even if it were a spell, even if saying it out loud would defeat its purpose.

'Let's dress for dinner.'

She showed me a wardrobe. Well, it wasn't a wardrobe, it was a room. 'These are eighty years old. They have to stay in a dark, cool room to keep them at their best. Dracula dresses, gowns coming alive at night to suck your blood. Did you know the Dracula myth was rooted in anti-Semitism?'

I shook my head.

'Yes. In Victorian England, the story became very popular at a time when there was a fear of the Eastern European coming and sucking the lifeblood out of the economy. And the whole blood ritual thing, drinking the blood of Christian children. No offence.'

'None taken.' I tried to imagine what it must be like to say constantly offensive things and no one minds because you're just so charming. I suppose that's what it is to be upper class. I'd been taught to mock posh people, that they sneered at us, but I was transfixed by her and she'd shown me more kindness than I'd ever had in my life.

'The vampire also...'

'Can we stop talking about vampires?'

Night was falling and even though I adored her, I was still a bit scared of her, like she was Kate Bush and Siouxsie Sioux put together.

'The vampire also puts you in a trance...'

It didn't bother me when she ignored me. It wasn't like being ignored by my family or the kids at school.

'Dracula says, "If you'd only love me, as much as I love you, then I could show you my true monstrous self, which I've never had the courage to show anybody."'

She moved closer to me, holding a candelabra, fixing her eyes intently on my throat. Right when she was inches from my neck she said, 'That reminds me. I need to buy tampons.'

'Doesn't your mum have any?'

I wanted to kick myself.

'She did leave some behind, but I've gone through them. I vacillated a long time before using the final one. But I was bleeding onto the tiles, so I used it. It's always necessity that puts an end to my romantic sorrows.'

I examined the dress before me at the front of the wardrobe. 'Clothes have a lifespan, and I don't mean that they go out of fashion.'

'You mean like a wine?'

'I don't know about wine, but I suppose so. If you don't wear this soon it will just disintegrate. It's silk; it's decaying.'

'How would you wear it?' she asked as she tried to style the straps.

'I'd cut it at the thigh.'

'You'd cut an eighty-year-old dress?!'

'I would, yeah.'

'You and I are so similar, we really are. We could be the same person.'

People who bond through trauma often think that. It's rarely true.

She got a Turkish ceremonial knife and I picked exactly the spot and then she hacked it.

'What should I wear?'

She led me to her dad's tuxes.

'I feel weird.'

'Don't be. You'll give them good energy. Your energy is radiant and beautiful and powerful. Just like mine.'

I'd never met someone before whose self-esteem problem was that it was too high.

Dinner was disgusting but I loved being there and I guess I was used to being served because my mum always did it for us. Suddenly I missed her terribly and wanted her to be there with us, though I don't know what we'd have discussed. I just wanted her to be waited on and I resolved to do that when I got home. I just didn't plan to be home any time very soon. When the blancmange arrived, Jasmine, speaking through its pregnant curves, announced, 'I signed the lease on Onslow Gardens.'

'What?'

Her face rose above the pudding. 'It's perfect for us. You can walk to the V and A when you have costume research to do. I submitted your application to Saint Martin's.'

'WHAT?'

'Yes, when I was posting a letter of encouragement to Esther Rantzen. So I wouldn't have to walk to the post office twice.'

'You did that without asking me?'

'Why should I?'

'It's my life.'

'It's my life too!'

'But you have to ask someone before you place them, literally, directly, in your life, in the same space as them.'

She looked around her dining room. 'Well, what are we doing now?'

I felt like an idiot. And I felt doubly an idiot because she had my heart. 'I'm not some toy.'

'How on earth,' she asked, eating her dessert, 'would you take my signing a lease for us as anything less than a sign of my commitment?'

We had a big fight. Well. Not that big. Nothing after Paris was a big fight, because, after Paris, we knew we could get past them.

I sat in the claw-foot tub, stewing over her entitlement, when she got into the bath with me. Responding to my facial attempt to maintain the squabble, she just started running more hot water and said, 'Here's my official title: Jasmine, the Honourable Lady of Wessex.'

'That's not bad,' I answered, because it wasn't, and because she was so deep in my space, she wouldn't even let me bathe alone, except that it wasn't my bath, it was hers she was invading.

The phone rang and she pointed to me to pick it up.

'I've never answered the phone in a bath before.'

'You've never done a lot of things.' She dunked her head underwater.

I answered. 'Hello, Jasmine's phone.'

The man on the other end sounded disconnected and urgent and the crackly distance made what he was saying sound like an actor in a radio play. 'I'm trying to get hold of Jasmine Mellor. Is the right number? We've been trying to reach her for days.'

Jasmine was now standing up, shaving her pubic hair with a razor.

'She's right here. Who may I say is calling?'

When I told her it was the hospital, she handed me the bearded razor and took the receiver.

'Yes? This is Jasmine.'

I could hear the sound of the woman's voice but not the shape of her words. Whatever she was saying, Jasmine rolled her eyes.

'Well, I mean, my God, I've been busy.' Now she tapped the side of the tub with her long nails. 'No, I can't actually. I'm not in London. I'll call you when I get back to the city.'

And she hung up.

'They want me to come back for tests. I mean, really, that part of my life is over. I don't need to be dragged back into it. We've been having such a good time. Who wants to think about the horrible hospital? Everything's so beautiful now.'

'I don't want you ever to go back there.'

'No, neither do I. Enough, okay? It was a phase. It's done. To life. *L'chaim*!' she said as she clinked a shampoo bottle against a conditioner. I laughed and she climbed onto me, wrapped her legs around my waist, kissed me on the mouth with her tongue. She put my hand on her breast, moved a little on my lap. Then she pulled away.

'Nope. Nothing.'

'Nothing,' I agreed, blushing.

'Well. Worth a try. It would be so convenient if we could be together that way, together together, but it isn't to be and that's that.' And she hopped out to dry off, holding her hand out to me to follow.

'We're still together,' I said, as I let her untangle my damp hair.

I wanted to add, 'I can still protect you without needing to be inside you. I can look after you without sex.'

Sex was the Velcro – to her it stuck her safely to the other, to me it was just an unfortunate fabric. I wouldn't always feel that way. But it was how I felt then, still disgusted by the sounds and smells, the invasiveness, the ungainly rudeness of inserting your body into a body.

She put a wooden comb to my curls, whispering, 'Only ever comb your hair when it's wet. My mother taught me that.'

The next morning, we picked our way through a meadow. My curls had separated perfectly. On the path were pansies, and when we got off the path, honeysuckle; all these things my mum loved to embroider, that she took at the height of prettiness, and she was right. I stopped at the honeysuckle but Jasmine pushed me on, prodding me in the back. I wondered if that's how she was with lovers, prodding them to indicate where they should go and how deep. The thought made me a bit queasy.

'Oh my goodness, you're flaming, anyone can see that. But it's nice to be kissed. And to be close. Isn't it?'

Now we were in a forest with weeping willows and oak trees, trees that stood beside each other, aware that they complimented each other's good looks by dressing so differently. There were other, less well-dressed trees, which seemed to have expressions: you expected them to start talking to you and for elves to emerge from the hollows. There were butterflies and frogs. All the things I'd seen embroidered on my mum's pillows, but never actually seen in real life. Why not? I could have taken a bus; I just never thought of it. I never thought of a lot of things until Jasmine led me to them.

There were a cluster of leaves of different colours and I couldn't understand how they'd coordinated that if they were all subject to the same light and soil.

We lay down and looked up at the sky, the tall trees hugging us. We were holding hands but we put distance between us. Perhaps because our faces were not turned towards each other, she began to talk, with no preamble. He appeared from nowhere in her head, as he did in her life.

'When he's decent to me, the way a normal dad should be, it is unbearable. That's when I go to my room and cry. The sadness is so endless when he's here and he tries. I know he can't do it. But he doesn't know. He still thinks he can. It's awful for a girl to know more than her father.'

I knew she was crying, not the snuffling ugly kind, but the tears that roll in twos as a sacrificial offering. She didn't wipe them away and when I looked they were sitting, perfectly still on her cheek like the Man Ray photo. The whole forest was still with them. 'When he returns, it's like the start of a new relationship, every time, that period when things are wonderful and can only go right. But it can't stay that way if he sticks around.' She paused. And then: 'Let's sing!' she said.

'What do you want to sing?' I was shy even when there was no one but her to hear me do it.

'"October" by U2.'

'I don't know it.'

'It's only one verse. How about something from *Turandot*, or do you not speak Italian?'

'I don't know it.'

'Okay, I'll sing you both.' And she did. Her voice was broken from crying, but lovely, and the more it cracked the more it somehow swooped.

'It's all the echo, it's not me. It's wonderful to sing in the forest. You're really missing out.'

Adam Ant had two hits that summer. I sang her 'Stand and Deliver' and I acted it out and she joined in and let me pretend to rob her carriage.

'You are such a good Dandy Highwayman.'

'I missed my calling.'

'I'd sleep with him,' she sighed. 'Would you?'

I blushed. 'Yes.' I looked up as she laughed. 'I'm human and my heart isn't stone.'

'Oh, darling, obviously. All those wonderful fine bones in his face. He looks like the painting by Charles le Brun of Cato, who committed suicide. Do you know that one?'

'No. You know I don't.'

We began to walk back to the house.

'Cato was a Roman politician who could not be bought. Like you, my love. I mean, you'll sell, you'll make it, I know that, but you'll do it exactly the way you intend to, with all the integrity that first drew me to you.'

'And will I die at the end?'

Instead of answering, she stopped and pointed at the ground. 'There. There they are.'

'There what are?'

'That's what I took. To do it. That's how we met. I'd had it with Valium, aspirin; I'd done all that. This last time I ate a bunch of poisonous toadstools. Just like these ones. My mum was such a good gardener. She'd made absolutely sure I knew which plants I must never touch.'

I felt a violence towards the toadstools, and before I knew it, I was jumping and squashing them and stamping on them, until there were none left.

'I heard Montgomery Clift used to do that at Gucci with all the sweaters.'

'Yes,' she agreed, 'I heard that, too. But it was in his later years. You've still many, many decades before I'd permit you to lose the plot.'

Everything about her called out 'Damsel in Distress', but when she felt you trying to save her, she was disgusted. We were very quiet on our way home. She didn't sing. I did once, trying to remember the words to 'October' but she didn't sing back, so I went quiet. I followed her footsteps until we were back at the honeysuckle and then at the pansies.

When we got back to the house, the fire was roaring, stoked by a man called Bertie who she introduced as an old friend, but who was clearly the groundskeeper.

'There's a party tonight at the next village over,' he mentioned, and her eyes lit up.

We took a tractor there. She drove the tractor and I just looked amazed that she was driving the tractor.

'I've never seen farm equipment up close before, let alone used it as a mode of transportation.'

She pulled a lever. 'You'd have been a fat lot of use back in the shetl.'

She was wearing a 1930s gown and Doc Marten boots. There was a half-bottle of priceless whisky at her feet. She had on a tiara of daisies and a real tiara of diamonds sitting just behind it so both could be admired. One of them got lost during the party but she couldn't remember which.

'Just the daisies,' she said when we got home. And we sighed with relief.

Then she double-checked, 'Oh no, it was the diamonds,' she said as she held up the daisy crown.

I told her I'd rather she didn't wear the dress – with its frayed edges – until I had finished making it, but she said she wanted to give it a test run, as a work in progress.

'This is its dress rehearsal,' she said, and I hoped it would make it through the night without collapsing, spotlight trained on it, bad side magnified, audience asking for a refund.

We pulled up at a pub with the kind of exposed beams I, decades later, saw expensively recreated in a banker's Manhattan apartment. The village was happy to see her, chatting as easily with her as she did them. A baby in a crochet shawl was being passed

272

around for admiration – it turned out they were cele-
brating a baptism. Wide-eyed and round cheeked, the
baby looked like a Mabel Lucie Atwell illustration I'd
once clipped from a library copy of *The Water-Babies*.
Jasmine held her well, cradling her head and keeping
her close to her heart. A parallel life of what might
have been.

But no domesticated woman wears a half-hemmed
dress missing its interior bodice and straps. She needs
all her willpower to hold it up. There's no mental
energy left over for a kid.

After downing a glass of amber liquid, the uncle of
the baby sidled up, his wife looking anxious from a
corner. Late thirties, almost handsome but then, at the
last minute, ugly, he had a shaved head and overflow-
ing hands, touching both her and me on the arms, the
elbow, even the stomach as he talked.

'Where've you been, then? We've missed you
around here.'

'What were you drinking?' she asked, ignoring
the question as I tried to piece together the history
between them. I don't like pubs because I don't like
aimless conversation with strangers. I prefer any
conversation in which I take part to be remembered.
As they orbited around each other I pictured Soviet
satellites, redrawn boundaries.

He brought her a drink and, taking it with one
hand, she pulled me close with the other. I couldn't tell
if I was being used to ward him off or, as their flirting

elevated, being drawn into an unsavoury threesome (the actual third, the wife, so far distant as to be in Siberia).

'This is Steven. He's from the city. He's Jewish – bet you've never met one of them before.' I felt like an object being moved around a chessboard – not even a chess piece, a free toy from a cereal packet, an object that did not belong anywhere near the game.

'I haven't,' grinned the uncle. 'Are you allowed to be here? I mean, it's okay by me, but is it okay by him?' He nodded at the ceiling.

'We'll see. We'll see if I turn to ash.'

Now when he touched her, she held his hand on the pretext of moving it away from her, but actually I could see she was enjoying squeezing him, that she regained her power. It was hard to tell which of them was more predatory, entwined like spaghetti cooked too long.

She prodded my good arm. 'Nope. Still flesh.' She ruffled my hair. 'But the night is young.'

In the distance I saw that the wife was very pretty. And that she was crying. Very, very quietly so no one else could tell. But my vision is perfect and always has been: I can unpick a stitch, untangle a necklace and tell when someone is silently crying.

I tried to steer Jasmine away, but she wouldn't be moved until she'd had another glass of liquid amber. Then she held the baby too jauntily, less maternally, and the mother politely took her away. She followed the baby with her eyes a moment, but then it was lost to the well-wishers and her eyes had grown cloudy.

When a pub band set up their equipment, she hustled us out, of her own volition. She drove the tractor onto a road that turned left and after twenty minutes became a bumpy path. The sky was turning from blue to black, a bruise too closely watched.

'How did you know that guy?'

'Which one?'

Spinning her half-lie, she hoisted the strap of her unfinished dress.

'The baby's uncle?'

'Oh, I don't really know him, only to say hello to.' She winked at me. 'And only when I'm in town.' She fussed with the lever and we slowed down, pausing then crushing each dent in the path like it was a pimple to be popped.

She shivered in her silk.

'Shall we find someone for you tonight? Country boys go both ways, you know. They just never talk about it.'

'I'm fine,' I said.

'You're so funny about physical affection. Are all Jews like that? I know it's not a working-class thing because the people in the village get sloppier than I do!'

I gritted my teeth. 'It's just me.'

She laughed and squashed my knee with hers.

'Please will you have a drink? Just one. Please? For me.'

If I was going to spend the evening being part of her anthropological study of class and ethnicity, I knew I'd need a drink. I fumbled for it in the darkness, twisting the bottle cap and holding the glass to my lips. We hit a bump.

'Shit!'

'Oh shit! You've cut your lip!' She licked it off and spat it into the road. 'Now rub some alcohol on it.'

'No!'

She took a swig and spat it at my face.

'Hey!'

'What?'

'Don't treat me like an object!'

'But you are an object to me.'

The discontent that had been percolating in my heart was about to boil over. I was about to shout, 'Pull this tractor over, right now!'

But then she added, 'The best, most beautiful, valuable, life-enhancing, sparkling, rarefied object, discovered at a flea market, taken home and restored to its proper glory...'

I was smiling now, smiling broadly despite the blood pooling at my gum.

'I'm honoured to have you by my side.'

I pressed my leg against hers. We were silent for a while. Then she whispered, 'You know Liz Taylor saved Monty Clift's life? She was first to the scene of his car wreck and she pulled his teeth from his throat so he wouldn't choke to death.'

She liked telling this story. I liked hearing it.

'That's love.'

'And that's not all. After he healed and his looks were spoiled, she insisted he be cast with her in *Suddenly Last Summer*. That's love! Fighting for the protection of a friend who's lost their looks.'

'It's not a crime to lose your looks.'

'It's different when you've been a very great beauty. My mother was that way. She was ten times prettier than I am. In the old pictures. Then it changes. You can see it happening, like a flipbook that you flick with your thumb and the stick figure moves. In the years before the end, her whole face changed. In the months before, she was like herself in a photo negative. But I remember. I remember what she was. The cornflower blue of her eyes. The feel of her hair when she'd bend down to tuck me in at night.'

I squeezed her hand and suddenly she laughed, shattering our intimacy and then tucking it under a rug to deal with later.

She wouldn't tell me where we were going, but I heard it before I saw it, the thump thump thump like a bad dream in neon: an all-night rave deep in the forest. It was before we had the term 'rave', but we did have city kids coming in to get wasted and dance until dawn in front of a country bonfire. We parked and disembarked. We were the only ones who'd made it there that way. The revellers had no cars I could see. If you'd told me their mode of transportation was shape-shifting, I'd have believed it.

'I love your dress,' said a girl in dungarees as she handed Jasmine a drink.

'He made it!'

'Wow.'

'He can make you anything, any kind of gown for any event.'

'Wow,' the girl said again, the metal hooks of her dungarees glowing beside the bonfire. She squinted her eyes at me and then back to her.

'Are you the girl from the castle?'

'It's not a castle, it's a landmarked former carriage house. But yes.'

'And who's he?'

I waited for her to say I was a Jew or a striving son of a cab driver. But she just said, 'This is Steven. He's my best friend.' And she handed me the drink she'd been handed. And I drank it, identifying it as cider, as full and fruity as my heart felt, no sour notes.

We danced, cheek to cheek, to a song without words, just a beat. When there are no lyrics to cling to, I don't know what, in life, to cling to, so I clung to her. She held me close, strong, the silk of her dress too cool to stop her nipples hardening against me. I wondered, I wondered, if I could kiss her there? Kiss her like a heterosexual, out of gratitude for pulling my teeth from my throat? As thanks for getting me hired after I'd lost my beautiful looks?

Embers from the bonfire rose up, revolutionary sparks, gliding towards the stars, the same shape and glow, just destined for a shorter lifespan. I leaned my head against her shoulder and we slow-danced while everyone around us was pogoing. When I looked up, the uncle from the pub was walking towards us, his work boots crunching the leaves. She had told him where to find us. Cider-slutty, she ran towards him and leapt into his arms, wrapping her legs around his waist, my half-finished dress hiked up. The open air had set her free to act out; no walls, no witnesses except trees, except me.

I backed away, but when she led him by the hand into the woods, I took another glass of cider from the girl in dungarees. But then her dungarees made me too sad – I told myself that what was making me sad – and I followed Jasmine down the path, walking softly so as not to alert them. They wouldn't have noticed me, anyway.

They were leaning against an oak as big as my dad in one of his rages. I knelt down behind a rock, as I'd seen my mother do, getting as low as possible. I watched as the uncle took off Jasmine's dress – my dress. It laid there in a crumpled heap, as crumpled as I felt. I waited, like a handmaiden, to retrieve it, and silently help her back into it when she was finished. He walked away first. She didn't seem to mind or feel self-conscious as she saw me approach.

'There you are,' she said. 'Have you been having a good time?'

She leaned heavily on me. She wiped between her legs with her discarded underwear and then absent-mindedly handed it to me. I put it in my pocket, cycling desperately to go with the flow, doing elaborate mental gymnastics so I didn't scream: 'This is wrong! This is dirty and gross and sick and the point you are proving, the groove you are stuck in, is untenable.'

All the baths I'd taken in her presence and it culminated in a feeling of such derelict mental hygiene. It was the first clear moment I thought, 'This is sickness and it could infect me.'

The sun was stirring as we edged towards home. Pausing at a farm at the foot of her estate, she wanted to stop to brush their horses. She said it was her favourite thing to do with her mum when she was a little girl. She was walking in heavy, unbalanced footsteps like a mummy, the least terrifying monster, the one I'd always felt most pity for. I watched as she pulled her hairbrush out of her bag and tried to reach through the gaps in the fence. But she couldn't reach the horses, so, as drunk as I'd ever seen her, she tried to brush the cows. That was difficult, too. She settled, in the end, for brushing pigs.

Before we passed out, I washed her underwear, turning my head to the side so I didn't have to see what I was doing as I scrubbed with the nail brush. Then I hung them in the window.

When we woke up later that day, she said she didn't feel well.

CHAPTER 19

She lay in bed a long time, turning down the tea I brought her.

'Of course you don't feel well,' I said, 'you've got the worst hangover in the county.'

I didn't mention the man or what I'd seen. She agreed I was probably right, and I bundled her into a taxi and then the train. She leaned against my shoulder and moaned, wordless but for that sound, which got deeper and softer. The volume on her skin was turning down, too. And by the time we reached London she was having trouble breathing.

Jasmine looked at the doctor and the doctor looked at her and I was looking at a *Vogue* from five years ago but when I noticed the tone change, I put it aside.

'We asked you not to check out.'

'I know, but—'

'We left you a lot of messages,' he said.

'Did you ever remember to call the hospital back?' she croaked at me.

As pathetic as she was, I wanted to slap her.

'It's your liver. It's shutting down. We need to keep you in.'

'I drank too much? Ha! I finally drank too much?'

'The alcohol certainly didn't help,' said the doctor, 'but that isn't what's shutting your liver down.'

'Shutting it down? How long am I staying on this drip? How long will this take to fix? We have a concert we want to go to tonight. Ian Dury is playing at the Astoria.'

'There isn't a fix.'

My head was banging from the night before. I wanted a cup of PG Tips and bed, my own bed.

'If there isn't a fix, then how do you fix it?'

'You don't.'

She looked over at me, as if I might translate for her. I started to feel the adrenalin coursing through my body, mine shocking itself awake as hers was winding down.

The doctor took her hand and she looked at his fingers like he was a stranger on the Underground. 'This is related to what brought you in to us two weeks ago.'

'But I was fine. I survived. I made it through. Like I always do.'

'Not this time. The toadstools you ate are an exceptionally dangerous kind called *Amanita phalloides*.' The death cap.

'I know that. My mother told me never to touch them.'

'She may have mentioned there can be a delayed effect of up to a week before the effects kick in.'

'No. She didn't say that.'

'She should have.'

'But it's been over two weeks!'

He held her wrist. I flashed on the uncle holding her against the oak tree.

'I suppose you're very strong.'

She flicked his hand away. 'We have a concert tonight.'

'We need to keep you here.'

'What's the prognosis?' I asked. I wished I'd asked him alone, and so did he.

He looked at me properly for the first time. 'It isn't good.'

I didn't know what to say. So I said, regretting it, as the words emerged, bleary eyed into the harsh hospital lighting, 'Who'd have thought, so much damage from such a little mushroom?'

It hit her. 'This one is the closest it's come to working. I'd better tell my dad.'

I squeezed her hand as she told me, though she'd just told me a day earlier: 'I gathered it from the estate in the country, brought it down in a leather pouch, as if I were a character in a Grimms' Fairy Tale.'

'You are.'

'I know because you're in there with me! We're in the same story.'

But I felt our stories diverging, and I couldn't stop that, no matter how I tried.

'You have to get well.'

284

'Of course I do. But what if I can't? You heard them.'
I shook my head, which annoyed her:
'You have to trust in medical wisdom. It's the hall-mark of civilisation. Have you ever read Maimonides?'
I could see she was really afraid. She was an out-of-control girl because she chose to be an out-of-control girl. But these events were not her choice; in fact, in the last week, she'd chosen the opposite.
'No, I haven't fucking read Maimonides!' I was crying now. She ignored my tears, like someone with good taste.
'Oh, but you must,' her voice was trembling. 'He's one of the very best minds your people have to offer, and that's saying something.'
'How do you know everything you know? About art and medicine and fashion and the moon and herb gardens and...'
Now her voice calmed down. 'Because it's all worth knowing. Can you imagine a life where we just look at pictures of ourselves? It would be unbearable.'
She lay back on her pillow.
I couldn't face staying at the hospital. I went home to my mum. She climbed out of bed with my father and came up and got in bed with me and held me.
'She's really, really sick, Mum.'
'You got a letter.' It was a padded envelope full to brimming with swatches of fabric and trimmings in it. A note inside said, 'Keep designing and follow your dreams, Love Zandra!'

I held them against my mother's skin and laughed out loud.

'She answered my fan letter!'

Mum smiled. 'There's such kind people in the world.' Her half-moon nails were just visible in the dark. I wanted to tell her: 'There's a power in your crescent fingers, you can be a good witch, cast magick and have the things you deserve.' I could imagine her as a sexual being, her red nails on the chest of a man she wanted and who wanted her back.

I wanted to tell her everything. But we were quiet together and because of the darkness, it was only as I was falling asleep that I saw she had a black eye. She knew I'd spotted it, and she apologised.

'I'm not a strong woman like she is.'

CHAPTER 20

This time Jasmine was put on the adult ward.

She was passed out asleep when I got back, but when I took her hand in mine, her eyes opened and she asked, 'Is my father here?'

'No.' She looked like she was holding back tears. 'But I think he's coming.'

I couldn't stand the silence, the whir of the machine in the background, a mouth breather on a Tube train stuck in a tunnel.

'I got swatches of fabric in the mail from Zandra Rhodes.'

I showed them to her, but she couldn't see properly, her vision was going. I rubbed them gently on her skin.

'See, you were right,' I said. 'It's worth writing a fan letter. It's worth going to hospital. You might make a friend.'

'It's worth going to hospital so you can get out and start afresh.' Her skin was peeling off her nose and cheeks and a patch of her neck. Her breath smelled of blood and metal.

'Steven? You know the Onslow Gardens flat has been paid up for a year? I don't think you should let it lie vacant.'

'I'm not going to stay there without you. I'll wait for you. I'll wait!'

'No. Move in and get it ready for me. Your name is on the lease, too.'

Her dad didn't come that night, nor the next morning. She was disintegrating, like a vintage slip stored carelessly. We waited through the afternoon and I tried to distract her by finishing up her dress, sewing the halter strap around the shoulders with sequins on brown leather.

'You're going to get well. Because otherwise I've done all this work for nothing.'

'I wore it in the countryside.'

'It wasn't ready yet.'

'It worked fine.'

'Then why did you take it off so soon?'

I meant to rib her, but the question hung in the air, smoke from a votive candle that was lit as a blessing. I prayed the smoke would dissipate before it set off an alarm.

She motioned to the other patients. 'They're worse off than me. I've had a life. A big one.' She smiled, brave. And then it all crumbled, granules of courage sloughing off, along with her flesh, and she trembled and whispered, imploring, 'Where is he?'

She passed out again. I called all the numbers for her dad I could find. Finally, the girlfriend answered.

'Please. I don't know if she's going to…' I choked up and couldn't speak.

She said, 'I'll get him there.'

I felt faint, truly, like I might hit the tiled floor. I steadied myself against the wall and tried to edge back from terror: a pencil skirt the earthy yellow of turmeric but with powder-pink lining. That would be a good combination. I closed my eyes and tried to visualise it.

It was past 10 p.m. and I was edging the hem of the dress with sequins, but on the underneath, so they'd just appear in flashes. That's when the girlfriend walked onto the ward with him. I heard the clacking of her heels. Stilettos have a different clack from steel-cap boots, which are different from the clunky heels on square-toed Mary Janes. When she had deposited Jasmine's dad at the entryway, she walked away. He stood there, blinking, wearing a satin cowboy shirt that made no sense. Not the happy nonsense invoked by the idea of a dry-clean-only fabric at a rodeo, but because it was smattered with band badges that had ruined the smooth fibres. I felt sorry for him for wrecking it, sorry for him for wearing it still, sorry for him that he didn't care it was wrecked.

I didn't know if it was because of the situation or because he was confused or annoyed to see me there that he stood there blinking. Just in case, I reminded him of my name, but he only drawled, 'Where is she?'

'Just…' I took a breath and tried to think of a way to put it in language he might understand, '… make her feel fine.'

My request at pretence triggered an alarm bell for him, pretence being the milieu of the wealthy and not what he expected from someone he'd believed to be 'salt of the earth'.

'Okay, sure.' He was still bravado, wearing a sheen of it, like sweat staining his satin shirt.

'Make her think everything's all right.'

He nodded and started to light a cigarette, and he looked so handsome that I got angry. How dare he get to keep his looks when the world was falling apart?

He walked towards her.

I think she told me more than she'd told others. I don't think she was sorry she told me. I believe, as soon as she spied me, across from her on the hospital bed, all beat up and useless, she knew I was the right church confessional, even if I was Jewish.

Her dad pulled up a chair and sat next to her, taking her hand in his. I moved to the corner of the room.

'There's my baby girl. Look at you, my sleepy angel. You look like your beautiful mama in this light.' His voice sounded like gourmet honey, tucked away in a pantry and forgotten. I was so sad, I wanted someone to make love to me, maybe him, someone to make me feel like I was disappearing instead of her.

She opened her eyes. 'Papa?'

'Yes, baby girl. I told you: I always come back. Papa's here. Papa's always here.'

It was so untrue I wanted to stamp on him like the toadstools in the forest. But she looked so happy, her face finally untwisted from the pain. I could never give her the words she wanted to hear, or be the right scent or the right weight of hand in hers. That was him.

'What did you bring me?'

He hung his head in mock shame. 'I didn't bring you anything.' He didn't say, 'I was pulled out of a nightclub by my young girlfriend after Steven tracked her down.'

He patted her hair off her forehead. As he touched her skin, something seemed to move through his own. 'I think you have enough stuffed bears. You have more than enough toys from duty free.'

'Make-up. I'm a grown-up.'

'You're not a grown-up. You're my little girl. Rest, now. Dad's here.'

I could see how much he was enjoying comforting her, how good it felt, how right. I also knew that if he'd had to keep doing it, even with the best will in the world, it would not be something that he could sustain.

'Do you want to listen to some music?'

She nodded. Her eyes were starting to lose focus. He pulled out a ghetto blaster, put on Blondie, fast-forwarded the tape to 'Rapture', got up off the chair and danced for her, moving his pointing fingers in and out, an unlit cigarette in each, his elbows at his chest.

'Face to face, sadly solitude.'

Then he danced on the chair, free, devoted, fearless, rather than a middle-aged upper-class man riven with anxiety about his uselessness in the world.

'You go out at night and eat up bars where the people meet.'

He was a blur in front of her and even with the nausea, she was so enjoying the outline of him. It was a such a silly dance from one who'd wreaked such destruction.

'Rapture! Be pure!'

When he sat back down, she tried to clap, but she was too weak. A male nurse walked in, took her vitals.

'Gentle, please,' said her dad, as if he'd never been anything but her best and most present guardian. The nurse knew what was happening, that he'd walked in on an atonement, and he beat his retreat, looking sadly behind him.

As soon as he was gone, Jasmine opened her eyes wide and whispered to her dad, 'I don't want to die.'

She wasn't whispering because her voice was shot. It was still there. She was whispering because she didn't want others to overhear and think her weak or pathetic, even here, even now.

'You're not going to,' he lied again, just as I'd told him. I don't think he had any idea he was lying. He thought he'd got there in time to makes things right. Because he always had before. But he'd seen it in her eyes, and smelled it on her breath, how close this call was.

'Barely breathing, almost comatose.'

I was watching, always watching. I leaned against the window and looked at the moon, saying 'Please save her, please save her.'

'Hang each night in rapture.'

He came up to me and said, 'She's happy her papa's here. She'll feel a lot more comfortable now.'

As he started to move past me, I shocked myself by spitting, 'I can only guess how many times Jasmine must have done this for you. "It's okay that your friend made out with me; I'm still laughing, I'm still dancing." So you could keep dancing. All the times she reached you long distance and didn't tell you how long she'd been trying to get you, how many different numbers she'd tried.

'That you'd used the cover of a bad phone line on the yacht so you couldn't tell that her voice was cracking and she was all alone, a young girl by herself on the top floor of a Notting Hill mansion, looking out across a massive city, with not a single person by her side.'

I sounded gay. Even though I didn't know for sure yet I was gay, I knew I sounded it. I'd never sounded as lilting as I did in his presence. Years later I wondered if, on a deeper level, I sensed that this public schoolboy may have had more gay experiences than most men I'd yet met. He was just watching me, his only response the inhale and exhale of his Marlboro. I was furious, and loud now, as well as gay.

'No boundaries. No safety. No father holding her hand, just a dad waving to her in Polaroids that he had girlfriends take because he loved his daughter so much, but that he only sometimes remembered to post. The ones that did get sent were treasure like love letters, in a lacquered box, with her most special things. The waving Polaroid that made it across the ocean could have been displayed in the Musée de la Vie Romantique alongside the enamel floral pistol that you shoot yourself with when your lover betrays you. *Tout ou rien.* You did feel *tout.* You just gave her *rien*!'

He was absolutely quiet and then he said, 'Sit down.'

'What?'

Now he hissed, 'Sit down!'

I was used to an angry father who takes it out physically. I had no prep for gentle rage, a blade that doesn't cut your skin as it shaves your face, but is still a blade.

'My friend did not touch her at a party.'

'Yes he did. She told me—'

'She didn't tell you the whole story. It was at her mother's wake.'

I searched his face to decide if he was telling the truth, but it was soft lit by smoke, instead of a lens smeared in Vaseline to make an ageing star look younger.

'We'd come back from the funeral and I went to the balcony to smoke a joint.' He put out the cigarette. 'But I couldn't roll it because I was crying. That's the first time since I was twelve years old that I've failed in my attempt to roll a joint.' He looked to me to see if I'd laugh with him, but when I didn't, his face turned to slate like London sky in February. 'I sprinkled the wasted hash over Notting Hill like we'd just sprinkled her wasted mother.'

I couldn't look him in the eye. Because it sounded a lot like the truth.

'When I came back in, she wasn't on the sofa where I'd left her. She wasn't in the kitchen, which was always her comfort place with her mother. I found them together in the upstairs bathroom.' The beautiful de Gournay wallpaper. The metallic birds hovering as a halo around her youth. 'I put him in the hospital. I was trying to reclaim something for her. That's what I'd meant it to be. But as soon as I punched him, I knew it was for me, not her.'

He looked to where she lay. 'It was all too much. I left her with a nanny and I went on the road.'

I didn't know what to say. 'Her mother wasn't wasted. Her mother made beautiful things all the time.'

'She did,' he agreed. 'I saved some of my favourites. I used to look at them every day. Now I look at them sometimes, on special days.'

I kept waiting for him to cry but he didn't. He looked like he was waiting for himself to cry, surprised as the pain flowed but the tap stayed closed, his mouth gaping, an expensive shirt with a missing button to which your eye keeps being drawn.

'Just because I couldn't do it doesn't mean I didn't love her. She was my heart.'

I saw, as he said it, the degree of difficulty it took to be him. To face himself every day. To face out, instead, towards incredible vacations, sunrises, sunsets, tropical vegetation, mountains climbing out of crystal oceans, was safer. Robin's-egg blue with an aubergine lining would be a good combination. How, alone in his childhood library, he'd occupied himself with, 'Burundi tribal drumming with William Blake is a good combination.' I softened. I had to. I took his hand in mine.

'Which one of them was your heart?'

He looked down at my hand, his fingers so huge over mine, squeezed it in something I surmised to be gratitude, and then let go.

'Both of them.'

When she slept again, her father moved from the chair, quiet as a cat, and slunk to the back of the ward. There, he leaned against the payphone and started making calls to experts on the continent. When the doctor approached him, he waved him away, as if they, who had been trying to make contact for days, had no useful knowledge to share of this illness.

It was all too much. I took my canvas bag with my notepad and wallet and started walking. First up the hall, then into the empty lift. I must have pressed the button, but I don't remember doing it. I just remember the sensation of descent.

Brown might look good with powder pink.

With baby pink.

With bubble-gum pink.

With dusty rose.

No. It wouldn't look good with them at all.

Outside the hospital, London was very much alive, a strong heartbeat that pulsed with each step I took. An echo chamber of record-breaking temperature rising off bodies, couples' kisses heating and expanding.

It was my least favourite English weather: when it's hot but the sky is still grey. I moved towards the West End, like a pilgrim towards Mecca, unable to lose myself in religious devotion because the sky was the wrong colour grey. Not dove. Not powdery. It was slate, as only London sky can be. And it's never a blank slate. It's full. There's no space for any new ideas. Not mine. Not hers. If I thought that weather would never change, I would want to die too. Except she wanted to be alive, that's what she'd decided. Rip that fucking sky apart and find the sun. Now she was too weak to do it.

The soul-numbing sky was matched by a dull ache in my heels, as if I had been walking upside down through the city, my feet absorbing the grey. I pinched my hand to try and slap at the melancholy, as if sorrow were a bug that could be caught. I dug a fingernail into my wrist until my eyes watered. All the while, I never stopped moving. And I understood, as I dug my nails in, what Jasmine had been angling for through all those attempts: pain, in small bursts, that can be described in place of pain that is indescribable.

When I got to Oxford Street, I saw that Selfridges was still open, beckoning summer, Friday, late-evening shoppers, the flags outside waving 'Shabbat Shalom' at congregants. I paused, for the first time since I'd exited the hospital. I stood still and looked in the windows. Ordinarily, I'd have been in awe of the full-length gowns, swathes of satin set at an angle across long, lifeless limbs so you could see the diamante heels. Selfridges had stood at that spot since 1909. It had passed from its youth to its teens and then twenties. It had become old enough to require a facelift. It had made people happy.

But that night the clothes in the window just made me feel exhausted. I didn't want anything rich. Not rich face cream or leather-bound diaries, or pricey food-hall delicacies.

All the other shops were closed, the reasonable middle-class bastions: Marks & Spencer, Phase Eight, Monsoon. The places still open were only the tatty souvenir shops. The diametric opposites – extravagance and discount shop – were the ones most closely in sync, the ones with a shared nocturnal rhythm. My feet now blistered – a true pilgrim – I walked all the way to Marble Arch until I was standing outside Jasmine's shop.

I went inside. It was evening and people wanted to buy things. If this was all they could buy – Brighton rock and novelty bobbleheads of the Queen – it would do. Shop hours are all wrong, since shopping can fill the same insatiable hole as late-night eating. The internet was many years away. For now, no midnight shoes online from Farfetch, couriered from Turin or Tokyo, to plaster the fear that your husband was cheating or your children would leave for university and never come back.

Fat Americans picked out miniature flags. Slender Swedes bought caseloads of Scottish shortbread. The boy behind the counter was a boy like me. Useless. Ugly. But, as I waited for the buyers to move on, he looked at me like I was beautiful. Like I was special. Like she looked at me. He looked at me like I didn't belong in there. His hair was the kind of electric red that looks dazzling on women, but that renders many males merely stricken by it. He was one.

'Can I help you?' he asked. I was going to say 'I don't think so' and then tell him where I'd come from and who was waiting there, between worlds. Instead, I chose a lighter with the Union Jack on it and took it up to the till.

'Do you want your receipt?'

'Sure.' Like I would change my mind about the lighter or find it not up to scratch.

'Do you know Jasmine?'

'Yes,' he said, 'I'm her manager. I was. But she hasn't shown up for work all week. So she's been let go.'

'Does she know?'

'She will when she comes back to work.'

How I wanted to think that she'd go back to work and get fired. It would mean she'd been able to get out of bed.

'I'm her friend. I'll tell her for you if you'd like.'

He shrugged. He couldn't have been older than her. He'd have been there, not as a psychiatrist's experiment to occupy his mind so as not to let it wander to darkness, but because this was his best job option. His skin was ridged so badly with acne that it looked tender, both to the touch and the heart. I smiled.

'What's your name?'

It took a minute for him to remember.

'I'm not hitting on you,' I said, and he blushed, because he hadn't decided yet. But he knew. He knew.

I put the lighter in my pocket and went outside and something made me turn off Oxford Street and go round to the side of the shop. The wall was cracked, despite having been plastered over several times. I took a biro from my bag and then dug for my notebook but found, as I did, my fingers brushing what I thought was a leaflet. When I pulled it out, I saw I was holding a piece of Adam Ant stationery. His face on the letterhead in place of the monogram I'd one day have. The Highwayman's hat. The stripe across his nose. I knelt on the pavement and wrote on it:

'Save her.'

I folded it up and wrote her name on the front. I hoped her dad was talking softly to her. I hoped he had hung up and was at her side. If I couldn't get to the Wailing Wall, then I could slip prayers between the cracks of the wall outside the tat shop. I tucked the folded receipt into one of the cracks.

'Please,' I said, looking at the flag of Diana kissing Charles, her neck long. 'Please let her live. Please.'

Then, before I left, I took out another piece of the paper, folded it and wrote her father's name on the back. Inside I wrote:

'Forgive him.'

I tucked it into the wall.

Forgiveness is different from redemption. The blushing boy caught sight of me through the glass. He saw I was crying. He put his hand on his heart. I walked away.

When I walked back onto the ward, a doctor was waiting, a nurse at his side. 'Can you get her father to talk to us?' the nurse asked me.

Despite the circumstances, I was flattered that they had registered my place in her life and that they imagined I might have some influence over him and his reckless, unredeemable beauty.

Thus emboldened, I walked towards him to bend his ear, trying to mimic his cat steps, that he might think me one of them instead of one of *them*. I'd spent enough time with her to understand that her class pick it up in the most minuscule signals. Not who you have become, but how you were raised, in your every movement, in the way you breathe. I think my family – my whole neighbourhood – walked with such heavy steps for fear no one would ever notice us.

When I got to his side, he looked up at me, cupping the telephone receiver with one hand. The hand was huge, which made me hard, and it was manicured, which made me sad for him and therefore even harder. I'd carry that sexual quirk for ever.

'I know a surgeon in Switzerland,' he whispered. 'I met him on a boat in Monaco,' as if the meeting place and the mode of transport by which it had been reached were themselves a part of the lifesaving surgery he'd map out.

'They want to talk to you.'

'What do they have to say? They let this happen!'

So he knew. He knew it was over.

'They tried to stop it.'

'What utter rot.'

'They tried. I think you should talk to them.'

'So they can tell me how hopeless it is? Anyone would feel hopeless in here.'

And he motioned around this room where, landing there, battered and bruised, I had felt the first spark of real hope I'd felt in perhaps my whole young life.

I put my hand on his arm. 'They want to make her as comfortable as possible.' Beneath my palm, his bicep rippled in disgust.

'Well, don't! Wake her up! Get her dressed! Get her uncomfortable and get her the fuck out of here. She can pull through. She can be just fine. I have the best medical contacts in the world.'

'Well, where are they? In discos? On yachts? On twin-engine planes? They're here...' I pointed at the nurses, 'Five grand a year. They've been really good to her, like they were good to me and they'll get maybe five or six hours' sleep by the time they get home. And then they'll be back. Because they give a fuck. And they know what they're doing. Talk to them.'

He nodded. He looked, if not shamefaced, then as if he was having two thoughts in opposition and was being pulled to the one that was the harder work, an action at which he was unpractised. But now a switch had been flicked. He nodded again and went to hang up. Just before the receiver made it back to the cradle, a voice murmured on the line...

Her father jerked the receiver back to his ear.

'Pierre!' her father exclaimed. 'Thank goodness! I'm sorry to wake you, but my daughter's in a bit of a pickle and we rather need to pull a favour. Well, they're saying she's had an overdose. Which of us hasn't? Ha ha, just a good night on the town. But they don't know what they're doing here. She's ended up in some ghastly NHS hospital and I'd rather get her perused by you. Excellent. Yes, of course. Price no problem.'

Then he hung up and started dialling again, making calls to his accountant so a plane ticket could be booked for the continental surgeon. As he made his arrangements, I took his place beside her, rolling her hand in mine. There was a chip in the varnish on three nails and so I busied myself fixing them, as I did on a regular Sunday night with my mum.

I blew the first coat on each nail before starting the second.

One leg crossed over the other, Jasmine sat bolt upright, admired my handiwork and cooed, 'You've got bloody good eyesight.' Except she didn't say anything, just slept, a gurgling audible from her lungs like a visible stitch. I'd got to her little finger when she passed away, just after midnight, with a sigh. In her father's re-telling, he said it was just a sigh. But that wasn't true. I was right beside her and I heard a word: 'Mama.'

Her father stayed there a long time, even when the doctors and nurses he'd declined to talk to came in.

'We're so sorry,' said the doctor, and I crumpled into the ledge, weeping.

When I came back up to draw breath, her dad still hadn't moved.

I heard the clippy-clop of his young girlfriend's stilettos as she came back into the room, but she saw my face, she saw his position on the bed, she saw, last of all, Jasmine, her skin turning grey, and she walked out and didn't come back. I didn't blame her. She was too young for this. I was too young for this. I needed my mum.

Her dad came up and hugged me and I hugged him back and, despite my resentment, I didn't care; it felt right. We held each other.

'I did the best I could,' he said.

I knew that part was not a lie, not to me, not to him. He really had just done the best that he could do. That was his best.

I walked around the hospital in a daze, buying a can of Coke I wouldn't drink. I pressed it against my temple. I passed the maternity ward, all those new babies with their wrinkled red faces and wrist tags, tiny VIP passes for a club that was way too loud for their just-hatched ears. They wriggled and screamed that they were in the wrong place, that this was all a terrible mistake, that they were meant to be back in the womb.

The next day's papers arrived at reception. They said Diana was back from her honeymoon. Now her life would begin.

Chapter 21

All the days I stayed in bed, my mum sat by my side, working on an embroidery.

I was mourning Jasmine, of course. But, rippled through that, I was also in shock that I wasn't going to get to leave my family after all. Jasmine had been Joan of Arc, hearing voices and born with a silver sword in her hand, and I was going to follow her into battle. She was so charismatic and her sword, held above our heads, caught all the light. I could see myself in it and I looked beautiful. But it doesn't matter how impressive she was, Joan was doomed. Now there was no more saint and no more war. I avoided my reflection.

'Why don't you get out of bed?' Mum asked.

I felt for the edge of the duvet, rubbing my thumb and forefinger on the well-worn cotton. It was the softest thing in the house.

'I am so entwined with you. I don't know how to get us both out, and I can't leave you here.' I tried very hard to keep talking. 'I felt like I finally had somebody reaching out their hand and guiding me through the smoky corridors to safe air.'

'It's safe here!' she said.

'It's not, Mum.' Now I started to cry. 'Don't say that to me. And don't say that to yourself.' I was so angry at her. 'I don't know why you chose him.'

The needle paused and for a moment I thought she was going to sew it through her own hand. But she put it aside and sat on the edge of my bed.

'Because I wanted to get away from my parents. They'd been through so much. I couldn't figure out how to separate from them. He asked me to marry him. And that was my way to leave. I couldn't think of any other.'

I took her hand in mine. Her nails were bare.

'What are you making?'

She squeezed her eyes shut and when she opened them again, they were glossy with every bad decision she'd ever made, because she thought she'd been doing it for her children.

'It's for Jasmine,' she said. She handed it to me. When I saw the words she'd written on it, between the roses and the flower pots, I got out from under the duvet and took her face in my hands.

'I'm going to get you out of here. I'm going to look after you for the rest of your life. I promise you. I'm going to make it. I'm going to make clothes that make women feel good about themselves. Even if they're having a terrible time.' I looked her in the eye. 'Leave him. Let's both just go. We can't stay here any more.'

The Onslow Gardens flat – paid up for a full year – was empty and it would stay empty, unless…

Diana probably only did end up where she was because she was a bit directionless. She was great-looking and looked beautiful in clothes – so what? She had a big heart, that's all. She had a big heart and she was a bit fucked up. That's a powerful combination: beauty, heart, unhappiness. She gave a lot of people their direction.

CHAPTER 22

The coffin was carved from rose quartz, the stone you carry with you to give and receive love. Someone can carve you a coffin from crystal in only a week if you have the money.

Jews, like Muslims, have to be buried within twenty-four hours. We have to take what we can get in our mad dash to the afterlife which, for us, is cyclical. There's no before and after. Which is hard for me because I feel as Semitic as anyone in England, but my life is a panoply of 'Befores' and 'Afters'.

She was wearing the dress I made her, her commission complete, too late, but just in time. Her father was there with his girlfriend. The pain he had not been able to transmute into tears was now flowing out of him like water through a colander. He looked as though he was crying for everything that had ever happened to him and everything he had ever felt ashamed for. I wouldn't see that in an Englishman again until Diana died, when the streets were lined with men like him. The girlfriend stepped away and he cried alone.

My mum came with me. When the opportunity arose, she walked up to the casket. She took her embroidery from her pocket and laid it in the coffin. I went up next and looked inside. The rose quartz was beautiful for Jasmine's skin. The dress lay not quite right because she wasn't standing, and would not stand to let me check where the hem fell now the sequins weighed on it, no matter if I implored her. She'd lay like this, spread on her back, aged nineteen, for the rest of time. My eye travelled down her perfect body, soon to be imperfect, one day to be gone completely, and I saw my mother's embroidery. In intricate stitching it said: 'Courage To Be Is The Key.'

I was so proud of Mum my heart could have burst. I was so sad there was no heart to burst.

When I walked back, I touched her dad's arm, nodded at the rose-quartz coffin. 'She'd have loved that. She'd have known you really understood her.' And I didn't say, 'Even though you don't know yourself.' But it was there. Looking at his broken face, I knew he'd not be much longer for this world. Or that he'd live to 105, haunted, too decrepit to keep running away to different boats and parties and concerts. Finally alone with himself. All those years of picking up stuffed bears, duty free, a life of parenting duty free, fatherhood with no tax. The pain was being held in escrow for him. It would hit one day and I couldn't say whether that made me happy or sad.

At the wake, I found him outside the bathroom with the de Gournay wallpaper. He was trying to smoke, but he couldn't draw it to his lips, his hand was shaking so badly.

I kissed him on the lips and he was so grateful, and kissed me back. Then I pulled away.

'Can I see you again?' he asked.

I knew he was asking because he was desperate, because he didn't know what else to ask or of whom, and that I was in front of him, like an ocean-front view.

'No,' I said, 'I don't think so.' As I walked back downstairs, I heard his lighter finally spark and catch fire.

I find I often say of someone, 'Well, they got what they deserved.' But I rarely know if that pleases me or not. Sometimes it does and half an hour later I find myself crying. I take a hot bath. I light a candle. I think of her, jumping into my bath with me. If I look into the candle long enough, sometimes she's no longer nineteen when she gets in. She's in her thirties and her body has changed from childbirth, is softer. She brings a baby in with her. She's late forties and she's let her hair go grey and of course it looks smashing. Like David Hockney got to have with Celia Birtwell. The beauty of watching your dearest friend age alongside you. Then she gets out, to dry herself and she says she's going to get me a towel. But she never comes back.

What is the Top 40 pop song that you know you're wrong to love as much as you do? A song by an artist for whom you have no particular respect or interest, who you'd never in a million years pay to see in concert. If you were at their concert you'd resent and judge the concert-goers around you and know you had nothing in common.

Except loving that song.

Except you only love it in an ironic way, hiding it behind something equally well regarded in your well-regarded collection, like a *Playboy* behind a copy of the *Guardian*. I'll start:

'Drops of Jupiter' by Train.

'Pure Shores' by All Saints.

'Summer Breeze' by Seals and Crofts.

You can see yourself doing karaoke to it, and it's the greatest karaoke performance ever given, plus you're singing in a voice you never even knew you had. It breaks hearts and it heals hearts (the people who need to be broken open have instinctively gathered together in a section across from the people who need to finally have closure). It's a performance that rights wrongs. It brings together Heads of State who had for decades broken off relations.

Which is incredible because, as you have accepted for years, the song is not even a good song. It is quite surprising that people should be healed like this by 'Pure Shores' by All Saints but then, finally, we understand why they are Sainted.

Except, when you finish your performance there's nobody in the room except you. Which makes it all the more magick; that this was the most healing moment of your life and nobody else was around to witness it.

They're all one-hit wonders, or, maybe, at a stretch, two-hit wonders, because it couldn't last. It's become popular in recent years for a serious artist to do an acoustic reworking of a song that is a camp classic. It works because that's how we live inside our heads, right? Turning something silly into a piece of profoundness. It's pop cultural alchemy and it lives in every one of our hearts, if we could only sing.

That's Jasmine.

You were never wrong to love it as much as you do. You were wrong to question yourself for loving it. And anyone who tells you otherwise can go straight to hell.

It's weird how this one-hit wonder makes the hair on your arms stand on end. It's really weird how it makes you cry, by yourself, at your desk, on your jog, in the toilet cubicle, holding your breath best you can when you hear someone enter. That you find you once request it, by yourself, to a late-night phone-in radio show on a Saturday, as night becomes early morning. You dedicate it to yourself, though you pretend you're talking about a friend. You're kind of making it up, but not really.

After all, you are your own friend.

In the end the death card she pulled from her Tarot deck meant huge change, but it also did just mean death. Both the esoteric and the realistic can be true at once. You can be earthed and floating above the atmosphere. That's what I reach for with my designs. But then that's a very 'he's floating above the atmosphere' thing to say. Maybe my clothes are nothing more than me trying to make you happy, as I tried with her; only with the clothes, when I don't succeed, I know there's always a season to come.

Because the line has done so well, my mother has her own floor of the house, with a claw-foot tub on which I painted red half-moon claws. She has a rail of velour tracksuits with her name on the back. I told her she could have a beautiful wardrobe made, but she wanted the tracksuits out there on the rail to look at as she falls asleep to the sound of Radio 2. You'd suspect it was daft for anyone but a pro boxer to have leisure wear with their name emblazoned on it. But women who've been beaten or gaslit or both can do with the visual reminder that they were once their own person and that they can be again. She embroiders them for other wives and girlfriends now. She sponsors a shelter in north London, and it's the first thing the women receive when they make it there.

'If he were dying,' she told me recently, 'if I knew he were really at the end, I would go to his bedside, and I would sit next to him and I would hold his hand and be gentle with him. And I'd do it so he could see that I'm back to who I was when he met me, not who he made me become.'

CHAPTER 23

I don't talk in public about how often I've thought about going the way she went. How every few years I think hard about it. All people do, not just artists. But I stitch the clothes as a suicide note, with everything of worth and beauty I can think of. Then, when I'm done, the feeling has passed. I never get fatally overwhelmed because, so far, my work makes me feel 'whelmed'. I know I am one of the lucky ones.

After Mum and I moved to Onslow Gardens, I saw my father once, because I hailed a cab and he was driving. I thought about letting it go, not getting in. But I found myself, as if propelled by an outside force, opening the door, sitting in the seat, buckling my seat belt, and telling him the address. We didn't say anything to each other the whole way from Shepherd's Bush. But when I looked at his face in the rear-view mirror, I saw that he was crying. I paid my fare through the slot in the cab, so he didn't have to turn his head. He let me out at my house, and my life.

My aunties' corset shop did close down a few months after Jasmine died, as if in solidarity with her passing. As soon as I could afford to, I had the sisters come to work for me, using their secret sauce recipe that had been handed down through the generations. As you know, the corset is the hallmark of my work, and my aunts, who I'd avoided all my childhood, were a part of launching me on the international stage. They stayed with me until not long before they died, just a few weeks apart. It's all right to die of old age, so long as you don't get left alone for too long, without the people you've loved most.

As I segued into adulthood, as nineteen got further and further in the rear-view mirror, I kept a running list of all the silly things Jasmine never got to see. That U2 became global superstars in 1983. That would have infuriated her, I think. To have to share them. To have to share them with Americans! Michelle Obama's toned arms and shift dresses, oh she'd have loved that. Trump. The Spice Girls. Certain dance crazes. The Macarena. The true birth of hip-hop. Amy Winehouse's life. Amy Winehouse's death. So much death you have to see, if you stay alive long enough.

Kate Bush's comeback gigs at the Hammersmith Apollo, even though it's not called the Hammersmith Apollo any more. That you can be feted and loved in old age by young people just as young and beautiful as you ever were and they love you for still being there, they love you for existing, no matter how much weight you've gained.

Jasmine's in all my clothes, things that aren't able to last (they are supposed to last, they just are not able to, like the silk she had to wear because fabrics have a lifespan, before they decay). If you know things are going to end soon enough, you can cut valuable dresses off at the hem with a big pair of scissors because that's what makes them look best.

I remember how, after the wake, I went back home to the estate and lay on my bed and looked at the collage ceiling she'd made for me. Each night it was the last thing I saw before I fell asleep. Each morning it was the first thing I saw when I woke up.

How, one day, my mum said, 'There's a letter.'

That it was from Saint Martin's, telling me I'd got in.

I remember looking out my bedroom window at the ugly grey buildings and ugly grey sky. And how, the morning the letter arrived, the pigeons on the phone wire were gone. They'd been replaced by two brightly coloured parakeets.

ACKNOWLEDGEMENTS

At Bloomsbury, I'd like to particularly thank Alexa von Hirschberg, Marigold Atkey, Allegra Le Fanu, Alexandra Pringle, David Mann, Sara Helen Binney and Philippa Cotton. I'm grateful to Justine Taylor, who was lovely and her edits thoughtful.

Thank you to my agents: Felicity Rubinstein, Kim Witherspoon and Elinor Burns.

This was the last I got to write before I left California after a decade living there. I want to especially thank The Chain of Los Angeles women who hiked with me, had my daughter and me to stay, watched her so I could snatch a few hours work on a Sunday, passed me books that made my month, sent me unexpected letters or flowers:

Annie Segal, Natalie Portman, Marieme Djigo, Lindsey Garrett, Lucy Fisher, Noor Haydar, Debra Diez, Bella Heathcote, Shaye Nelson, Tiffany Kimball, Autumn Durald, Jemima Kirke, Elishia Holmes, Sia Furler, Lola Kirke, Marnie Alton, Christina Stone, Minnie Driver, Kim Roth, Rosanna Arquette, Sarah Bennett, Jennifer Grey. Gratitude eternal to Una Leiba – no childcare, no novel.

I landed in London to the kindnesses of Susie Ember, Eliza Mishcon, Barbara Ellen and Indira Varma. I am endlessly supported by my sister, Lisa Forrest and my sisterwife, Leah Wright.

I want to thank my parents, Judy and Jeffrey, for turning me on to Sister Corita, for providing the particulars of the family lingerie business and for buying me Adam Ant stationary when I was little.

Thank you dear Gaetano, who shall remain surname-less but who has helped so many of us.

And last but not least, Rowena Arguelles – my favourite reader *alive*.

A NOTE ON THE AUTHOR

EMMA FORREST has published three novels, an essay collection and the memoir *Your Voice In My Head*. An Anglo-American currently based in London, she recently wrote and directed her feature debut, *Untogether*.

A NOTE ON THE TYPE

The text of this book is set in Linotype Sabon, a typeface named after the type founder, Jacques Sabon. It
was designed by Jan Tschichold and jointly developed
by Linotype, Monotype and Stempel in response to a
need for a typeface to be available in identical form for
mechanical hot metal composition and hand composition using foundry type.

Tschichold based his design for Sabon roman on a font
engraved by Garamond, and Sabon italic on a font by
Granjon. It was first used in 1966 and has proved an
enduring modern classic.